"Great book."

—Rosie O'Donnell, actor/author

"A tautly written, complex, and emotionally charged love story that takes the reader on an unforgettable, unexpected, and deeply moving journey."

—*USA Today*

"A breathtakingly beautiful and deeply moving story. *When Ashes Fall* owned my emotions to the very last word."

—Jodi Ellen Malpas, #1 *New York Times* bestselling author

"Sucked in completely and jealous of such a clever story! You won't put this one down. Marni will have readers desperate for every soul-gripping page . . ."

—Rachel Van Dyken, #1 *New York Times* bestselling author

"If you're reading a book by Marni Mann, I'm warning you now: grab a glass of cold water because her spicy stories are going to set you on fire!"

—Monica Murphy, *New York Times* bestselling author

"Marni Mann is my spice queen! She delivers every single time. With smoldering chemistry and impeccable writing, her books are utterly addicting."

—Devney Perry, *Wall Street Journal* bestselling author

"This book is perfection, and that's not even a good enough word! Chef's kisses!"

—Natasha Madison, *USA Today* bestselling author

"If you're looking for your next wickedly hot read, look no further. Marni Mann will have you fanning yourself all the way through."

—Laurelin Paige, *New York Times* bestselling author

"Sierra-approved sexiness on every page."

—Sierra Simone, *USA Today* bestselling author

Mr.
Hook-up

ALSO BY MARNI MANN

The Hooked Series—Contemporary Romance

Mr. Hook-up

Stand-Alone Novels

Lover (erotic romance)
The Better Version of Me (psychological thriller)
Before You (contemporary romance)
Even If It Hurts (contemporary romance)

The Spade Hotel Series—Erotic Romance

The Playboy

The Dalton Family Series—Erotic Romance

The Lawyer
The Billionaire
The Single Dad
The Intern
The Bachelor

The Agency Series—Erotic Romance

Signed

Endorsed

Contracted

Negotiated

Dominated

The Bearded Savages Series—Erotic Romance

The Unblocked Collection

Wild Aces

The Moments in Boston Series—Contemporary Romance

When Ashes Fall

When We Met

When Darkness Ends

The Prisoned Series—Dark Erotic Thriller

Prisoned

Animal

Monster

Mr. Hook-up

MARNI MANN

 Montlake

Published by Montlake, Seattle

www.apub.com

Amazon, the Amazon logo, and Montlake are trademarks of Amazon.com, Inc., or its affiliates.

ISBN-13: 9781662515521 (paperback)
ISBN-13: 9781662515538 (digital)

Cover design by Caroline Teagle Johnson
Cover images: © G-Stock Studio / Shutterstock; © K.Yas / Shutterstock

Printed in the United States of America

To Nina.
I promised you I'd be there in fifteen minutes. It might have taken me just a little bit longer to get dressed and rush downstairs, but I made it.
Because of you . . . so much of this is because of you.
And the rest is history.

PLAYLIST

"Sex for Breakfast"—LoFi Waiter, mood., Shiloh Dynasty
"Go Fuck Yourself"—Two Feet
"living room flow (Bonus)"—Jhené Aiko
"Love Is a Bitch"—Two Feet
"Lovers"—Anna of the North
"Day by Day"—Frank Walker, Two Feet
"Chills (Dark Version)"—Mickey Valen, Joey Myron
"Be Your Love"—Bishop Briggs
"I Feel Like I'm Drowning"—Two Feet
"Where Are You Now"—Lost Frequencies, Calum Scott
"Power Over Me"—Dermot Kennedy
"Tell Me the Truth"—Two Feet
"Haunted"—Beyoncé
"Not Enough"—Elvis Drew, Avivian

PART ONE

They say time stops at nothing.

I say time stopped when I met her.

CHAPTER ONE

A 100 percent match.

That was what the screen showed as I stared at it, silently, my mouth so wide, my jaws hurt.

How in the hell had I achieved that percentage?

As one of the founders of Hooked, a hook-up app my best friends and I had launched just today, I knew that number was nearly impossible. While we were in beta testing, we'd run every possible scenario through Harvard's database, trying to configure an average percentage among our future users. We'd learned 100 percent was statistically equivalent to the odds of winning the lottery.

The average would be in the eighties. An overly impressive number would be in the low nineties.

But 100 percent?

Shit, that almost couldn't exist.

But it did.

With me.

And I was gazing at that number as it flashed in the center of my phone in twenty-eight-point green Garamond font—a font, size, and color my best friends and I had debated over for weeks—and underneath was the user I'd matched with.

SaarasLove.

All right, Love, who are you? And are you going to rock my whole world?

That was the reason we'd developed this app in the first place.

To be rocked.

And rocked hard.

With my friends and I nearing the end of our final semester of grad school at Harvard, we lacked two very important things—time and money. We didn't want to spend hours at the bar every night, fishing for women, buying drinks, when we were after only one thing.

Hooking up.

After a late-night session of the three of us bitching about how tired we were of the relentless pattern of time, money, and courting, Hooked was born.

But never did any of us anticipate a perfect match.

If I logged on to the mainframe and checked the users who had already signed up, I was positive there wouldn't be another with a number so high.

Unless . . .

My heart began to pound, my throat tightening as I pushed myself off my bed and peeked out into what used to be our living room and was now our makeshift office. My best friends, who also happened to be my roommates, were on the couch. Grayson had his laptop resting on his legs, a beer in one hand, his phone in the other.

"Easton, you look like you just swallowed a fucking goat," he said. "You all right, buddy?" His backward hat gave just enough slack that he could furrow his brows.

"Is there a glitch in the system?" I nodded toward his lap. "Check right now and make sure couples are matching at all different percentages."

He dropped his phone and began to type one-handed. "We're all good." He took his hat off and ran his hand through his dark, untamed mop. "Jesus, you just scared the shit out of me."

Holden was in the same position, but double-fisting two mugs with a set of headphones stretched across his head, cupping both ears. As though he could sense my fear, he glanced up from his screen, using his shoulder to free his ear. "What'd I miss?"

"Just Easton taking ten years off my life, that's all," Grayson barked. He held the bottle to his lips, guzzling until it was gone. "He thought there was a glitch."

Holden shot up straight, setting both mugs down and knocking the other headphone off his ear, the headband crashing to the couch as he began to type. "Was there?"

"No," I told him.

Satisfied with my answer, Holden lifted both drinks off the table, taking a sip from one and then the other.

"What do you have there?" I asked. "Two different kinds of coffee?"

"Coffee in this one"—he held up his right hand—"and water over here"—he held up his left hand. "You see, I've got to chase the caffeine with something neutral or I'll be climbing the walls soon."

It wasn't even ten in the morning. One was already drinking beer, and the other had enough energy to run the Boston Marathon.

And we all had class in an hour.

Holden placed one of the mugs down and rubbed his dark-blue eyes. "What made you think there was a glitch?"

I took a seat on the chair next to the couch. "I matched with someone at a hundred percent."

Grayson reached into the six-pack sitting on the floor and took out a full beer. "Impossible." He twisted off the cap and tossed it toward the kitchen, missing by several feet. "I don't believe you."

I held the phone out so both could see the screen.

"I still don't believe it." Grayson used his free hand to type, pecking the keys much harder than he needed to. "I'm reaching out to David and Brennon to make sure something else isn't going wrong, or maybe there's some weird shit with your account."

David and Brennon were our coders and good friends who were finishing up their master's degrees at MIT and had developed our entire app. It was amazing what an unlimited supply of weed and beer had bought us, an arrangement we wouldn't have gotten from anyone but them.

"Well, I believe it," Holden said as he crossed his legs over the coffee table. "Think of how perfect you and this girl will be if you're already this compatible."

"He's not looking for perfect, he's just looking to get his dick wet," Grayson replied.

Holden wiped off the creamer that had stuck to his golden-brown mustache. "Regardless, it'll still be pretty wild if you're hooking up with someone you have that much in common with."

"Shit." Grayson slowly looked up from his laptop. "David said nothing is wrong. You really are the fucking unicorn of this app, my friend."

"I can't believe it." I shook my head. "We know the chances of this happening. How did it happen to me?"

Grayson turned his tall frame, positioning himself into the corner of the couch, and crossed his long legs. "I'm just glad it didn't happen to me. I have zero interest in anything perfect, permanent, or pouty—all potential possibilities when you match at one hundred percent."

Grayson, the forever antiromance spokesman, would rather be castrated than settle down.

Holden laughed. "Well, I think it's phenomenal"—he winked at our grumpy friend—"and maybe this was the whole reason why you came up with the concept of Hooked: fate matched you with the One."

Even though I didn't agree, Holden had an interesting take on it, which didn't surprise me given that he was the romantic of our trio.

Hooked, initially, was my idea. I'd been the one to lead the bitching session.

But this couldn't be why.

I was sure of that.

Grayson rolled his eyes. "It's a good thing we have Mr. Romance over here, creating happily ever afters for us."

"What's her username?" Holden asked me, ignoring Grayson. "You know, so I know what to call your future wife."

I waved away that thought, but still replied, "SaarasLove."

Grayson snorted. "She better not turn into your wife. I need a side-kick while I continue sleeping my way through this city, and we know this dude"—he pointed his thumb at Holden—"is getting hitched the first opportunity he gets."

"Have you matched yet?" I asked Grayson.

"Eighty-one percent," he replied.

"Who would have thought there were women in Boston who would have anything in common with you," Holden said to him.

"Miracles happen," Grayson shot back.

"What did you end up scoring?" I asked Holden.

He flipped on ESPN, waiting to hear the score of last night's Sox game, before he replied, "Eighty-nine percent." His smile was so polished and white and straight, he could score himself a toothpaste commercial. "I'm seeing her tonight."

Grayson took another long drink of his beer. "This motherfucker will show up with roses and wine, I'll bet my dinner on it."

"So?" Holden scratched his two-week-old beard. "I consider that kind of stuff foreplay, and there's nothing wrong with it."

"Except the app wasn't created for that reason," Grayson said. "Why don't you save the money you don't have and just focus on pus—"

"I'm going to let you two hash out whatever this is," I chimed in, interrupting Grayson. "I have to go message Love."

"Love," Grayson roared as I got up from the chair. "Good luck with that."

I flipped him off and returned to my bedroom, adjusting the pillows behind my back as I loaded the app, pulling up SaarasLove's profile. What set our app apart from our competitors' was that instead of using first or last names along with photos of the user's face, we allowed only usernames and body shots or icons to protect everyone's identities. Within the private chat feature, users could exchange whatever information they wanted—pictures, names, phone numbers—but that was at their discretion.

What I could gather from SaarasLove's profile was that she lived within a sixty-mile radius of the zip code I'd provided—a distance she couldn't exceed, or we wouldn't have matched—and her picture was a long-range, out-of-focus shot of her sitting on a rocky beach, fully clothed.

I needed to know more about her.

I opened the chat feature under my BostonLifer account, a name that had come to me when we'd gotten closer to launch, and typed out a message.

Me: Hey you, my 100% match. I've got to say, that's an impressive number. I'm pretty sure it means we're supposed to meet up.

SaarasLove: Hiii! Honestly, that number kinda shocked me too. So, who are you, Mr. Boston? Tell me everything, don't leave out a single detail. ☺

Me: Getting right to the point, I like it. I'm in my last year of grad school, I just started a business with my best friends, I'm an avid Pats and Red Sox fan, I'm pretty athletic myself, and I'm into all things outdoors. Your turn.

SaarasLove: Just finishing up my undergrad and working, like you, but for someone else, not myself. I wouldn't call myself athletic, but I love to walk. If I could turn traveling into a career, that would be my ultimate dream job—which I do a lot anyway for my employer. I love bad reality TV and ice cream, the chocolate-ier, the better. In fact, if frozen Hershey syrup becomes a thing, I'll be their top customer.

Me: And it looks like you enjoy the beach, according to your pic.

SaarasLove: I do. I love it.

SaarasLove: Is that scotch in your pic? Whiskey? Are those the same—forgive me, I'm a simple drinker and just stick with wine.

Me: Scotch, yes. When I feel like indulging, that's my drink of choice.

SaarasLove: Except you're on a college budget, like me, and drowning in student loans, so you wait until the pub has $2 drafts, amiright?

Me: Lol. You're definitely not wrong about that.

Me: What are your plans for this weekend?

SaarasLove: I'm actually headed home. I've got some things to tie up there.

Me: Is home far?

SaarasLove: It'll feel like a totally different world from here.

Me: I was going to ask you if you wanted to meet up.

SaarasLove: Mr. Boston, what I love about this new app is that not every student I go to school with knows I'm on it since they can't see my name or my pic. What I hate about this app is that I have no idea what you look like. Show me something, anything, just so I can have a feel of you to know if there's any chemistry.

I laughed as I read her message.

If she only knew she was speaking to a co-owner, something I wouldn't tell her.

The guys and I had decided not to tell anyone until we absolutely had to. We just didn't know how that would go over when we were meeting up with women we'd matched with.

I certainly wasn't going to ask one of my roommates to come in and snap a picture of me. The amount of shit I'd get for it, especially from Grayson, would be endless. So I slipped off my T-shirt and moved in front of my full-length mirror, aiming the camera at my chest and abs, areas I worked hard at when I was at the gym, and I turned my face to make sure it wasn't included when I took the shot.

Pleased with the result, I attached the photo to the message and sent it.

Me: Love, your wish is my command.

SaarasLove: Hold a sec. I need to process THAT. And maybe wipe the drool from my lip.

Me: Lol.

SaarasLove: Mr. Boston, wow. WOW. Wow.

Me: I'm glad you like what you see.

SaarasLove: You're freaking chiseled. Like, no. Love, yes.

Several seconds later, a picture of her came through. It looked like she was at the same beach as in her profile shot, but in this one, she was in a bikini. Her knees were bent, and she was holding them against her chest with her arms wrapped around them. She was looking away from the camera, the angle showing her long dark hair and toned arms, her thin frame, the tiny ball her body was tucked into.

Me: Love, you're gorgeous . . . and that body, damn.

SaarasLove: Thank you. ☺ But it's not exactly a close-up shot like yours, so you're not seeing everything, ya know?

Me: I've seen enough to know you're beautiful.

Me: How about that date when you get back from home?

SaarasLove: I'd really love that.

CHAPTER TWO

I sat on the armless chair in my room, gazing at the woman I'd been dreaming about for days, as she stood in front of me, a leg on either side of mine.

Naked.

I tucked a chunk of her dark hair behind her ear. "Can I call you Love?"

"I love that name, so yes, of course."

There was nothing sexier in this world, nothing more beautiful than her.

Love.

A woman I couldn't stop thinking about.

Her eyes took me in as though she wanted this as badly as I did.

Her body had looked perfect in the picture she'd sent, but it didn't compare to this—a petite waist that I wrapped my hands around, the curve of her small tits that I leaned forward and kissed, skin that smelled so sweet. And while I took my time traveling to each spot, feeling them out, listening to her breathing change, I eventually made my way to her heart-shaped ass. "You're exquisite. In every way that I had imagined, but so much more."

She lifted her hands from my bare shoulders and ran them through my short hair. "You're not so bad yourself, Mr. Boston." Her palms spread across my chest and down my abs. "And these, my God."

I couldn't recall taking off her thin, flimsy, black lace thong, matching bra, and sky-high red heels, but as I looked past her, they were all sitting on my bed.

"Love"—I reached up and held her chin—"you have me here, hard as hell, what are you going to do to me?"

She lowered her body until she was sitting on my lap, pressing herself against my erection. She ground over me in a circle, then swiped my full length.

"More." I held her tighter. "I need more of you. All of you."

She licked her bottom lip, the dim lighting in the room making her gloss glow, giving her a heavy pout. "You're going to get more. Let's see how patient you can be."

Patience, I had. But when it came to her, I made no promises.

To urge her on, I circled her nipple with my tongue, rocking her ass forward to aim her against my tip. "How many orgasms do you think you're going to have tonight?"

Her head leaned back, a long, deep, echoing sigh coming from her lips. "One."

"Wrong."

She faced me again, holding my cheeks, pointing my mouth to hers. "Two?" She paused. "Impossible."

"But it's not."

She rose just enough to place me at her entrance, allowing me in only an inch. And it was that amount—that inch—that she bounced over.

A taste.

A tease.

Enough to make me want to explode.

"Ahhh," she exhaled, her breath warming my face before her movements stopped. "What is it going to feel like when I have all of you?"

"It's going to make you scream."

She smiled, a sight that showed me all white and nothing else. "And wake your roommates?"

"They won't mind, I assure you."

In fact, in the morning, Holden would ask if I'd scheduled date number two with my soon-to-be wife. Grayson would high-five me if I made her moan loud enough to keep him up.

"How are you going to do that?" she asked.

I pinched the same nipple I had licked, rolling it between my fingers. "Easy. I'm going to make you feel better than you ever have."

"You're that confident?"

"Yes, Love, when it comes to this, I'm extremely confident."

She slid her hips forward and back, without my prompting, bringing my crown with her. "Oh God, yes."

"You need to know something." I held her back, pressing our chests together, and when I was satisfied with that placement, I wrapped her hair around my wrist. "When you finally let me in, I'm not going to be gentle."

Her laugh filled my ears, a sound I surprisingly couldn't get enough of. "No?"

"No."

"Do you know how I'm going to make you feel?" She moved her mouth to my ear. "And what I'm going to do to you?"

I couldn't wait to hear this.

But I didn't answer her immediately because I wanted this moment to last as long as possible.

A place where I could still feel her wetness.

Her tightness.

Both taunting me, causing me to ache in the best way.

I grazed our lips together, inhaling the warmth from her skin. "Tell me, Love. What are you going to do to me?"

Her lips returned to my ear, where she breathed across the shell, several long, extended exhales, before she said, "I'm going to tell you to wake up."

Her words didn't make any sense. "Wake up?"

"Yes, Mr. Boston." She kissed my cheek. "Wake up."

My eyes burst open, the sunlight so strong as it came through my blinds, I could do only a quick scan of the other side of my bed and the chair in front of my tiny desk before I covered my face with the blanket and groaned, "It was a fucking dream."

This was the fourth morning in a row that I'd woken like this, poking at Love's entrance, her nakedness positioned around me in some way, before I was forced awake.

And just like all the previous mornings, I rose with a raging case of morning wood.

Goddamn it.

At least there was the scent of bacon in the air, what Holden, our designated chef, had apparently chosen to make us all for breakfast. A scent that was strong enough to pull me from bed.

I shoved my cell into my pocket and opened my bedroom door, expecting to find the guys parked in our makeshift office.

There were guys, all right, just not the ones I was anticipating.

"Where's Holden and Grayson?" I said to our coders, who were stationed on the floor, using each end of our coffee table as their desk, fingers pounding their laptops so hard, it sounded like they were jackhammering cement.

"Class, I think," Brennon replied. With his back to me, all I could see was his thick, wavy hair, looking like it hadn't been washed in days. The same dark fuzz covered his back and arms—his hairiness was a constant joke in our group. "Our landlord is dealing with our mice problem, so we're here until that's handled. Lucky you. Those little fuckers ate a hole right through my bedroom wall."

"City living," David groaned. "Anyway, Holden made about two pounds of bacon before he left. We helped ourselves." He finally looked up from his computer, and the second our eyes connected, he immediately shielded his. "Jesus, Easton, put that fucking thing away."

What fucking thing?

I looked down my body and saw the tent inside my mesh shorts. "Shit, sorry." I tucked my erection under the elastic waistband. "I can't stop dreaming about this girl I met on Hooked. This is what those dreams do to me."

"You and almost a million other users as of this morning." David's glasses had fallen down his nose, and he pushed them to the top, the frames so small they looked like they were made for a doll.

I froze halfway between the living room and kitchen, realizing I hadn't logged on to the database when I'd woken up, a ritual I'd been doing every morning since launch. "You're kidding. We're at . . . a million?"

Brennon went over to the window, cracking it open a few inches before he took out his one-hitter and lit the end. "Not kidding." He coughed as he blew out the smoke. "And because of that wild-ass number, we're at hour twenty-nine, I believe."

"What's twenty-nine hours?"

"That's how long it's been since I've seen my bed." His bushy eyebrows pushed together as he exhaled another hit. "Which means I need more of this"—he held up the small device, which looked like a cigarette—"and a fat raise."

"Yeah, yeah," I replied.

Since we were offering a free one-month trial to all users, we wouldn't be generating any membership revenue for another three weeks. That was assuming any of the million-plus users would want to continue using Hooked. With our projections much higher than we forecasted, another source of income would be ad dollars, and we'd soon be meeting with an agency that would help achieve that potential.

But I didn't want to talk specific numbers with the coders until I had more substantial data. What we knew for sure was that we had to pay them a lot more than they were earning now.

And we would.

I continued to the kitchen and poured myself some coffee. "Do either of you want a cup?"

David raised his energy drink off the floor. "Unless it can lift me to the moon like this shit, I'm good." He returned the drink to the floor and put his long, slick strands into a ponytail.

"You?" I asked Brennon.

He blew out a cloud and said, "I prefer bud," and he closed the window.

I placed some bacon on a napkin and carried my breakfast into the living room, taking a seat on the couch. "What are you working on this morning, fellas?" I popped one of the greasy strips into my mouth.

Brennon sat on the floor in front of his laptop. "We're making sure the app doesn't crash, that it can continue handling the traffic that's been coming in."

I stopped midchew. "Did it crash while I was sleeping?"

"Close," David admitted. "We had several areas not working correctly, but we got it under control."

"Was that last night when it happened? Or this morning?" Brennon scratched his arm, the sound almost like the sticking and peeling of Velcro. "I don't even know what day it is."

"Honestly, I'm as overtired and lost as you two. I think I got about two hours of sleep last night, and I don't know if that made me feel worse or better." My phone vibrated and I took it out of my pocket, seeing multiple notifications that had come in during my nap; the most recent was from Hooked. "Messages are working great. I just got one."

"That's a relief," David said.

Brennon shook his head. "They *should* be working. Shit, I've been writing code for them all morning."

Although there were several new matches and messages, the most important one was from Love, so that was the one I opened.

SaarasLove: Hiii! I'm back, whoop!

Me: Did you have a good time at home?

SaarasLove: Home was . . . home. This trip was sad. Emotionally draining. I'm much happier to be back in the city.

Me: Sounds like you should have just stayed here and gone out on a date with me.

SaarasLove: Normally, I'd totally agree, but this trip was unfortunately very necessary.

SaarasLove: I recently lost a close family member—nothing we need to talk about, I'm just putting it out into the universe, so you get where my head is at.

Me: I won't make you talk about it, but I do want to cheer you up.

SaarasLove: Tell me something funny, then.

I glanced around the living room and kitchen, trying to think of something, and then the obvious hit me.

Me: I had a dream about you last night. A pretty detailed one that involved us naked. Your face wasn't really shown that much, just your incredible body that I saw in the bikini shot you sent. I woke up and went straight into the living room. The guys called me out—let's just say, I had to adjust myself, the view in my pants wasn't exactly appropriate.

SaarasLove: Oh my God!

Me: Yeah . . . I've clearly got you on my mind, Love. Looks like I already can't get enough of you.

SaarasLove: Mr. Boston, stop flattering me. ☺

I wedged my coffee out from in between my thighs and took a drink.

The tempo of the guys' typing was a constant tap, like the beak of a woodpecker against a tree, and it hadn't lightened up at all. If anything, their speed had increased.

"Have you guys joined the app?" I asked.

That question seemed to garner their attention, both pausing to look up at the same time.

17

"Joined the app?" Brennon huffed, his eyes red and hazy in the middle of long lashes. "Who the hell has time to date? Don't tell me you do?"

Instead of answering, I addressed his partner. "How about you, David?"

David shook his head, several pieces of hair falling out of the elastic. "I'm on a wicked dry streak. Haven't brought a girl home in, what, a couple months, I think." He rubbed his cheek against his shoulder, unbalancing his glasses, which he didn't fix.

"That's why you need to join," I told him. "You could be on a date by tonight."

"Except tonight I have class," David told me. "And I've got to figure out a way to make rent, so that means I might have to pick up some freelance in between homework and coding for Hooked." He tucked the loose strands behind his ear. "Think I can fit a date in there somewhere?" He laughed.

For the three of us founders, our stress wasn't any different. Our class load was identical to theirs. Where they had pressure to ensure the app was working properly, ours was to make sure new users continued to sign up, maintain our social media accounts, and plan a massive kickoff party, attempting to spread the word not just in Boston but all over the country.

"I get it, man. This is a lot to take on in addition to everything else." I finished off another piece of bacon. "You know we're feeling it too."

"Except when this becomes the top dating app in the country, David and I are going to be floating in dinghies. The three of you partners will be in yachts."

I finished the rest of the coffee, setting the napkin of bacon on the couch. "Don't say that—you know we'll take care of you guys. Besides, if that day ever happens, we'll be buying all of us yachts." I checked the time on my phone, seeing I had less than an hour before I had to head to class, and there was a new message from Love waiting in my notifications.

"I know that," David said, his hands already back on his keyboard. "I'm not worried."

I finished the last few pieces of bacon and went into the kitchen, yawning as I set the empty mug in the sink. "I'm going to hop in the shower and get ready for class. You guys make yourselves at home."

"Already did," Brennon said.

I went into the bathroom and turned on the water, and while I waited for it to warm, I pulled up Love's chat.

SaarasLove: That was a funny story—at least for me, maybe not so much for your friends.

Me: They'll forgive me. Hopefully. At the very least, I pray I didn't scar them for life.

Me: Are you taking the day off to drown yourself in wine?

SaarasLove: That does sound like fun, I'm not going to lie, but no. I'm a multitasking queen at the moment, sitting in class, typing notes, talking to you, answering work emails, trying to semi pay attention to the professor since he's going over our upcoming exam.

SaarasLove: In other words, SEND ALL THE WINE.

Me: I hear that. I'm headed to school in a few where I'm going to be doing the same.

SaarasLove: Then, multitasking king, have yourself a good day.

Me: You too, Love.

CHAPTER THREE

Me: Homework? Class? Work? Are these solid guesses or you're doing something else that's a lot more fun?

SaarasLove: You know the kind of moment when you should be doing all three? But you're not, you're doing something so far outside the box?

Me: I like where this is going . . . yes.

SaarasLove: I love tiny tattoos. Like loooove them. I always wanted one, so I'm finally making it happen. My bestie and I are at a tattoo shop right now.

Me: Love, that's badass. What are you getting and where?

SaarasLove: Initials on the inside of my wrist.

SaarasLove: Do you have any tattoos?

Me: You're going to laugh, I have a tiny tattoo.

SaarasLove: YOU DO?

Me: I got it with my best friends a couple of months ago.

SaarasLove: Of what? And where?

Me: A fishing hook on the inside of my bicep. I know that doesn't make much sense, but it means a lot to the three of us.

SaarasLove: I love that so much.

Me: I'm assuming you're getting the initials of the person you lost?

SaarasLove: Yep.

Me: This way, they're never gone. They'll be there forever.

Me: You guys have fun. Text me later.

SaarasLove: ☺

SaarasLove: I want to know something about you, Mr. Boston. Are you the kind of guy who likes to chase women, or do you prefer a woman who falls at your feet?

Me: Interesting question.

SaarasLove: Because you've never been asked it before?

Me: No, I haven't. But it's also interesting because I don't know if I've ever really thought about that question. What do you think my answer would be?

SaarasLove: Well, I don't know much about you, but I sense that you're a pretty sexual guy—and not just because you're on a hook-up app. It's just a feeling I get. Am I right?

Me: Definitely right.

SaarasLove: Then, a part of me thinks you'd prefer the view of me on my knees. But a much stronger part of me thinks you'd rather have the view of my butt. ☺

Me: Shit . . . that's a hard one.

Me: I'm going to go with your ass.

SaarasLove: I thought so.

Me: What other questions do you have for me? I like where this conversation is going.

SaarasLove: I just think you like me, Mr. Boston.

Me: I can't deny that.

SaarasLove: Which is what I find sooo interesting since this app isn't about liking. It's all about sex. Feelings aren't allowed to be involved . . . or are they?

Me: If feelings come up, I'm certainly not going to push them away.

Me: Another interesting bit of info. I haven't been much of a feelings guy in the past. I've been more on the side where I just want to keep things fun.

SaarasLove: Is that how you feel about me?

Me: What I can say is that, so far, things have been very different with you.

SaarasLove: Ditto.

◆ ◆ ◆

Me: I have two very distinct images in my head right now.

SaarasLove: Oh boy, let me guess, me on my knees? And you chasing my butt?

Me: Fuck, you're good.

SaarasLove: Lol!

Me: What are you up to? How's the tattoo healing?

SaarasLove: A little sore, but perfect. I'm so obsessed with the way it came out. I still can't believe you have one too. I don't know, I just find that awesome.

SaarasLove: And bestie and I are on the couch, watching The Town. Have you seen it?

Me: Seen it, that's a Boston classic. I'm just surprised you're watching it.

SaarasLove: I think I've watched it a hundred times.

Me: What do you like about it?

SaarasLove: One: Boston. Two: Ben Affleck. Three: Ben Affleck hahaha.

SaarasLove: Surprised I love a good thriller over a romance?

Me: For sure. I pegged you for more of The Notebook kinda girl.

SaarasLove: Nope. The Notebook isn't for me. Neither is horror. Surprise me, yes. Scare me, hard no.

Me: You're saying I shouldn't take you to a Stephen King movie for our first date?

SaarasLove: Unless you want to watch it alone, no. 😉

Me: That first date needs to happen soon.

SaarasLove: Yes, it does.

Me: Do me a favor . . . keep Saturday night free.

SaarasLove: I think I can make that happen.

SaarasLove: PS: thanks for making me smile today.

Me: About Saturday night, I have an idea.

SaarasLove: Hiiii! Oh, I can't wait to hear it.

SaarasLove: And, btw, a few of my friends and bestie have joined Hooked and none of them have matched at 100%. I'm dying to see what this connection is going to feel like when I finally get to meet you. I wonder . . . am I going to become addicted to you, Mr. Boston?

Me: We're going to find out.

SaarasLove: Tell me all the details about Saturday.

Me: Not sure if you've heard but Hooked is throwing a massive party that night. I just read about it on their IG page. I guess they rented out a whole ballroom at a hotel and it's masquerade themed. Let's meet there.

SaarasLove: Now that sounds like fun.

Me: Fun . . . because you want to see the rest of me naked?

SaarasLove: Ha! Well, yes, there's THAT.

Me: Love, I can't stop thinking about you.

SaarasLove: Same. So much of the same.

SaarasLove: See you soon. I'll be the one in all red . . .

23

CHAPTER FOUR

"Tell me you're nervous because of the party and not because you're finally meeting Love," Grayson said. He stood next to me at the mouth of the ballroom, Holden on my other side, the massive space now completely filled with Hooked users. "If you're acting all fidgety because you're about to meet Love, I'm going to think you're getting soft on me."

"He's allowed to be nervous about Love," Holden announced before I had a chance to respond. "He's about to meet his perfect match. Shit, that's huge."

"But since he started talking to her, our dude's been acting different."

I adjusted my mask, making sure it was secure. "I haven't been acting different, asshole." The murmurs from our guests, the warm lighting, the decor—it was all finally settling in and giving me a buzz. "I'm just trying to balance things. We've got a lot going on, more than we anticipated. Love is only adding to that, and yeah, I like her. Sue me."

"And she's making you soft as fuck," Grayson countered. "You've never let a woman affect you since I've known you."

I tore my stare away from the party and looked at my best friend. "You're right."

"I know."

"Now, can you take a look around and actually appreciate what we've done here? Or are you so focused on me, you're going to waste the whole night obsessed with my softness?"

Grayson's hand went to my shoulder. "We have put together one hell of a party, I'm not going to deny that."

"You can say that again," Holden said. "I mean, things only kicked off about half an hour ago and everyone seems to already be having a blast."

We'd instructed the party planner to go with a luxury-meets-fantasy theme. She had outfitted the entire room in black and red, draping the walls in velvet and the ceiling in feathers, with spotlights shining through from above, creating this rich, dark lighting that was a mood of its own. And when you added in the costumes and masks and our guests' anonymity, that only gave it a more mysterious, enticing, and extremely sexy vibe.

Our hope was that after tonight, the videos and pictures of the party would go viral, creating even more awareness for our brand. Now that I saw the way everything had turned out, I had no doubt that would happen.

But aside from what this event would do for Hooked, tonight was also about Love.

Every time I thought about her and what I was going to do to her body, my hands clenched, and my dick got hard as fuck. I didn't know what it was about her, but a feeling of excitement grew each time we texted, when I learned something new about her—a connection that was endlessly taunting me.

I wanted her.

And, fortunately, I didn't have to wait any longer to have her because I'd already spotted her on the other side of the bar. Since guests were given name tags with their usernames when they checked in at the door, I'd already verified that it was her when I'd walked by a few minutes ago, during my final loop of checking out the ballroom.

The details I'd picked up on in her photo, even the ones I'd seen in all my dreams, were confirmed now that I was in her presence. Each one made me more breathless, something I hadn't expected to happen tonight, but as I took her in, as my gaze traveled the length of her gorgeous body, I couldn't help it. What the picture hadn't shown was that Love was petite, the perfect height to lean down and kiss. Her thin frame still had plenty of curves, the dress hugging each one, showing tits that were just a handful and a narrow waist that begged to be grabbed. Her dark hair hung long and curled, a length that I could easily wrap around my wrist and tug.

Aside from being skintight, the dress was a crimson that reminded me of lipstick, made fully of lace, and the same material covered her face, with cutouts for her eyes and pouty lips. She held her drink with one hand, the other arm resting across the top of the bar while she spoke to two women I assumed were her friends.

While I moved closer, slowly scanning her body, I felt a weakness. Another sensation I wasn't expecting, but it made me clutch my vodka on the rocks; it made me suck in the deepest breath; and it made me tame the thoughts feeding my hard-on.

I stopped in front of the trio, looking at her name tag one more time before I said, "Love," and held out my hand.

I just wanted to touch her, even if that meant only her fingers.

"Mr. Boston," she said back, her lips pulling into a smile. A sight I couldn't get enough of. "Finally."

"Have you been waiting long?"

"Maybe not a long time, but it's felt like an eternity."

The mask made it impossible to see anything besides her gaze and grin.

But I felt them.

All over my fucking body.

Our hands stayed linked for several seconds, the warmth of her skin moving through me at a speed I couldn't control. "Well, I'm here now, and I'll make up for lost time." I looked at her friends, introducing myself, hearing their responses, but not absorbing a single word. "Can I buy you ladies a drink?"

Love dangled her glass in the air. "Just got one—we all did."

I needed her full attention.

I needed her alone.

"Then I'm stealing you away." I reclasped our hands and said to her friends, "I'll return her later. Safely, I promise."

Well fucked, but in one piece, I thought.

With our fingers locked, I brought her to the edge of the ballroom, where the music wasn't as loud and the crowd wasn't as thick. "It's quieter over here. Makes it easier for us to talk."

She let out a small, soft laugh. "You're so tall and broad and"—she wiggled her fingers out of mine and touched the whiskers on my chin and jaw—"I see so much handsomeness even though you're only showing very little of your face."

I reached around and grazed the small of her back. "Do you want to know what I think of you?"

"I can feel it. When you were approaching us at the bar, a heat moved through my body, and when you stood there with my friends, it happened again. And now, I can feel it once more. There's nothing simple or secretive about your stare, Mr. Boston. I don't know if just any girl could feel it, but I certainly can."

I gazed at her glossy lips—their roundness, fullness—and pulled away a piece of hair stuck to them.

"Am I right when I say you can't stop thinking about devouring me?"

A sound came out of me that was half growl, half chuckle. "Yes."

"Well, you have me here. What are you going to do with me?"

I took a step back, shaking my head. "I'm going to spend as much time as I can admiring you because one, I can't believe you're finally in my presence, and two, you look even more incredible than you did in that photo—something I didn't think was possible." When I stepped toward her again, my hand dived into her hair, holding it, squeezing the locks into my palm. That was when my dick started to fucking throb. "And sexy. Love, you're so goddamn sexy."

"I'm blushing. The lace is just hiding it."

My hand moved to her face, palming her cheek, tilting it up toward me. "You know, since we Hooked, there's something that's been eating at me."

"Yeah?"

"I think I mentioned—or maybe I didn't—that it's almost statistically impossible to match at one hundred percent." Was that a conversation we'd had through text or one that had taken place only in my head? I couldn't remember—she was making everything fuzzy and impossible to recall. "That means we're perfectly compatible, and I'd wondered what that would feel like when I finally met you."

Her hand landed on my chest, dropping as low as the center of my abs. "How does it feel?"

"It's hard to describe."

I saw the whiteness of her teeth, the nipping of her bottom lip. "How about I take a stab at it?" She paused. "There's this tingling in your chest that's moving low, low, low, but it doesn't disappear. It restarts like a constant loop. And this flutter, like the feathers from the ceiling are tickling every inch of your skin." Her chest rose and fell, visible only because the top of her dress was so fitted. "And there's this constant urge to touch me."

"Yes." I nodded. "All of that. Every bit."

"Mr. Boston, do you know what I find interesting?"

Her voice was like this mesmerizing song, one I could listen to forever. "Tell me."

"This app was created for hook-ups, one-night stands, where you get what you want and move on. So, technically, after tonight, there's a chance I'll never see you again. Never talk to you again. We'll share something so wild and passionate . . . and then be done."

Hearing her define a night of sex, using *wild* and *passionate*, was so fucking hot.

And before Love, that was all I had wanted.

One night.

But the need to see her again, touch her again, before I even had her, was overwhelming.

As those thoughts resonated, they shocked my system.

I'd developed Hooked for the opposite reason—the reason Love had just described. Why was I suddenly making this so complicated?

Why was I craving more?

She was the answer to all those questions.

The feeling in my body, the tightening in my chest. Two things that would have happened even if we hadn't matched so high.

"Love, there are no rules. We can do anything we want, even if that means seeing each other after tonight."

She drained what was left in her glass. "I like that." She glanced at the watch on her wrist. "But before we decide anything, let's see how good we are together. Mr. Boston, you have exactly fifteen minutes. What are you going to do with me?"

"Fifteen minutes? Now that's not a lot of time."

"Time, unfortunately, just isn't something I have much of tonight."

Why was I disappointed with that answer?

Why did it hit so hard when I realized that once those minutes passed, she would be gone? Out of my hands. When, in my mind, I'd planned to spend the whole night with her, and that was a thought I liked much more.

Or maybe it was just the thought that I'd be able to have sex all night long. That it had nothing to do with her at all.

Shit, I didn't know.

I was so far outside my usual territory, everything felt jumbled and confusing.

"But fifteen minutes . . ." I laughed. "That's barely even enough to get me started."

"It's something." She shifted her hair from one shoulder to the other. "And it's all you're getting, so how are you going to spend those minutes? How will you make me never forget you? Or, I guess in this case, want to reach out to you again?"

My hands clutched the air, closing into fists, then releasing. "Can I use my mouth?"

"You can use anything you want." She traced a finger down my chest.

"Anything?"

She nodded.

"And I can take you anywhere?"

She looked at her watch again. "You're down to fourteen minutes. Ticktock."

I had a room upstairs in the hotel, but it would take a few minutes to get us to the elevator and onto the high floor, and that was time I didn't want to waste.

But fourteen minutes? Hell, I'd planned to spend at least that and more just going down on her.

I took the glass out of her hand and placed it, along with mine, on a nearby table, and said, "The first thing I'm doing is getting you out of here."

I led her out of the ballroom and into a stairwell.

I wouldn't have known this spot even existed had I not been here earlier, when the decorator and her staff were setting up the ballroom. This was the entrance they had used to bring everything in from the parking lot. When I'd passed through several hours ago, I'd noticed the small alcove under the staircase. Now that I was getting us closer to it, I noticed the space was just high enough that I could stand. Wide enough that I could hold her back against the wall. And hidden just enough that if someone were to walk in, they would have to really look for us.

Once I had her in position, she took a look around the tiny area. "Creative." Her eyes landed back on mine. "But the question remains: What are you going to do with me now that you have me here?"

"It's not what I'm going to do *with* you." I lowered my face, my lips landing on her neck. "It's what I'm going to do *to* you."

I didn't need to ask for permission—she'd already given that to me.

What I needed was a taste before I could go any further.

My hands went to the wall on both sides of her and I dived toward her mouth. Even though I was in a rush, I didn't immediately kiss her. I hovered over her lips, waiting, breathing.

Fantasizing.

Taking in her scent, which was a mix of a tropical breeze and a piña colada and a coconut macaroon.

And what began to form between us was a build.

I could smell it in the air, and I was letting it peak.

"Are you wet?" I asked.

"Why don't you go see for yourself."

Of course, I could do that.

But words were as sexy as foreplay, and that was where I decided to start.

"I asked you a question, Love. Tell me, are you wet?"

Her exhale breezed across my face, sending me more of that island flavor. "Dripping."

"Because you know what I'm about to do to you?"

"What I hope you're going to do to me . . ."

My hand left the wall to circle her neck, squeezing just enough that her eyes widened before I lowered to her chest. Now that I was really touching her, I noted that the red material was a mix of something other than lace, so in some places, it was more forgiving than others. Her tits were one of those spots, and since she wasn't wearing a bra, I could tug her nipples through the dress. Flick them with the tips of my fingers. Bite as I drew one into my mouth.

"Ahhh," she moaned.

And while my teeth stayed occupied, my hand traveled over her hips and across her ass.

Gripping.

Binding those cheeks with my palm.

"Shit," she gasped. "That feels—"

"You've felt nothing yet."

After tonight, I wanted to know her body.

I wanted the images in my head to measure up to the ones I was feeling now. And even though time wasn't something I had much of, I didn't rush the tour my hands were taking. The way my palms drew up and down her sides, measuring, inhaling. They circled her navel and dipped to her hips and down the outsides of her thighs. While they stayed busy, my mouth was just as occupied. I focused on her breast, the curve that led to the center, the softness in between her cleavage, the way the other side rounded until I met her nipple.

"Oh yes," she cried.

Her movements, the way she gripped my arm and held the back of my head, told me she wanted more. She wanted friction between her legs. She wanted pressure. She wanted an orgasm that would consume every part of her.

She would get that.

All of it.

But not yet.

I centered the highest part of her back and shoulders against the wall and gradually lifted the bottom of her dress, revealing the most gorgeous legs.

What separated us was a lace thong.

Instead of slipping it down her body, I wanted to see the way she would react when I ripped the sides and shoved the flimsy undergarment into my pocket.

"Oh God," she panted the second it was freed from her body.

That sound, that burst of air from her lips, was one I hadn't experienced yet—and one I very much liked.

I kissed my way down her body, each press of my lips thought out, deliberate. I studied each spot I landed on, putting it to memory as I continued lower.

When I reached her center, I got onto my knees, my face close enough that I could take in her smell. An aroma that was just as tropical but even more pronounced down here.

Her hand ripped at my hair, trying to pull me closer, silently begging for my tongue.

But I didn't move.

I stayed inches away.

Dreaming about what she was going to taste like, what her wetness would feel like when it hit my mouth.

What kinds of sounds would fill my ears.

I wrapped one of her thighs across my shoulder and rubbed my nose over her slit. "Yes. Hell yes." I spread her wetness across my face. "You're so ready for me."

Several moans came out. "I told you."

Since I had her balanced, I took my wallet out of my back pocket and fumbled through it until I found the condom I kept in there. I tucked it into my hand while I used the other one to trace around her entrance.

I didn't give her a finger.

I just moved the tip in a circle.

Teasing.

Urging.

Testing.

Her nails reached my scalp, digging into my skin, trying to press herself against my mouth.

Each time she did that, her attempt at earning herself more, I went slower. I kept my tongue locked in and used only my nose and finger, sketching her with my skin, allowing her to crave me to the point where she could no longer stand it.

Until her thirst became so much that I said, "You want my tongue . . ."

"Please." She dragged the word out, letting it last several seconds. "Mr. Boston . . . *please.*"

I glanced up, her lace-rimmed lips parted, her gaze pointed at me, both so hungry.

That look of desire caused me to stick my tongue out, and starting at the top, I licked all the way to the bottom.

"Goddamn it," I moaned. "Just like I thought, you taste like heaven."

"Oh!" She rocked her hips back, meeting my tongue, grinding over it. "Yes!"

To give her even more, I dipped my finger inside her, sliding past her walls, going in as deep as my knuckle before pulling out and doing it again. And while my hand plunged in and out, circling within her, I focused on her clit, lapping, sucking.

"I can't." She swallowed. "I can't . . . This feels so good."

It did for me as well.

In a way that took me completely by surprise.

In a way that made me want to kneel on this ground all night, worshipping her, and even though all I could think was *ticktock*, I didn't want to stop.

I wanted this for me as much as I wanted it for her.

I wanted to savor this taste.

I wanted it rolling down my throat, where I could store it forever.

So I gave her more, a fierce combination of my hand and tongue, until I sensed she was getting to a point where she wouldn't return, and that was when I rose. I didn't bother taking my pants off—time was far too limited at this point. I just unzipped them, my hard-on popping through the hole of my boxer briefs and out the fly of my pants. With an urgency I hadn't felt before, I tore off the corner of the foil with my teeth, and once I had myself covered in the latex, I growled, "I need you. Now." I lifted her legs, wrapping them around my waist. And while I continued to aim the back of her shoulders against the wall, I slowly thrust in. My head fell back. My balls clenched. "You're so tight."

"And you're huge," she hissed. "Jesus, Mr. Boston."

I stayed buried, not moving at all to allow her to get used to me.

While she constricted around my shaft, her breathing turned labored, her nails now digging through my jacket and shirt.

I sucked her bottom lip into my mouth and held it with my teeth.

She didn't have to tell me when she was ready. I felt it—the release of her nails, the way the pulsing inside her body began to die down.

That was when I reared my hips back and stroked in. "There's only one thing I want to hear from you."

She exhaled against my face. "What?"

"Your fucking screams."

She wrapped her arms around my neck, holding me close, her body tensing, her legs squeezing my waist. "I'm almost there."

I increased my speed, my power, driving through her narrowness. "That's not good enough. I want you shuddering against my cock."

With the way I was holding her, I was able to free up a hand, and I moved it to the front of her, slipping a finger onto that spot I had just licked, rubbing back and forth.

"And now . . . I'm lost."

I'd released her lip, but I nipped it again. "Love, I want you to come. Now."

All it took was that command, that hard buck into her opening along with the tap of her clit, and she was quivering.

"Ahhh!" She inhaled. *"Yesss!"*

I felt each wave because it came with a pulse, a tightening, her body clinging to me, like I was going to leave her.

But I wasn't going anywhere.

I had eight minutes, I roughly estimated, and I was going to use every one of them.

"Mr. Boston!" she screamed. "I'm coming!"

And that only made me go faster.

If she wanted to remember this night forever, I was going to make sure that happened.

I was going to make sure there was only one man who had ever made her feel this way, and that was me.

A desire that I wasn't sure I fully understood, but one that felt vital.

She gasped. "What have you done to me?"

"I'm not done yet."

When the ripples in her navel began to still, I pulled her off the wall and put my back there instead. "You better hold on," I warned. She rotated her arms around my neck, and I thrust her into the air, bouncing her over my length.

Each stroke turned stronger.

Deeper.

Harder.

Her sounds got louder every time, her head even falling back, her lips opening and "Oh. My. God" pouring out of them.

With her throat exposed, I started at the base, feeling her swallow, and kissed up until I met the lace at her chin. "Now you're going to come again."

"I can't—"

"You will." My hand returned to her clit, and since I was bearing her weight with only one arm, I demanded, "Hold me even tighter."

The moment I really touched that spot, my thumb rubbing it back and forth, her reaction ignited my own orgasm.

That sound—that goddamn scream.

I couldn't get enough.

Her head rested on my shoulder, and she whispered, "I'm there again."

"I know," I roared. "I can feel it. I'm going to pound it out of you."

And that was what I did, slamming into her, hurling my hips back, and hammering in.

Over and over.

Her face stayed on my shoulder, her lips pressed against my neck, and with each drive, she got louder.

Her walls closed in on me, forcing my orgasm to bubble through my balls and into my cock, and just before I shot my first load, I took her lips, consuming them. "Love," I moaned. "You're milking me."

The feel of her told me she was in the same place.

Hearing "Oh yes" only confirmed it.

I plowed through her, the slimness inside taking hold of me, and both of our bodies shuddered together.

When there were only breaths left, I held her in my arms, staring at her masked face.

Love sighed. "I don't know what that was, but my God, the things you just did to me, I'll never recover from."

I gave her the softest kiss. "Maybe it was just the beginning."

"Mmm."

I kissed her again, circling my tongue around hers. Even though it didn't last as long as I wanted, even though I pulled away after a few swipes, I still retained every detail.

The feel of her mouth, the taste.

The sound she made when I ended our kiss.

I locked our fingers together. "This won't be the last time I do that."

"Kissing me or"—she shifted, reminding me that I was still inside her—"this?"

"Both."

"Both, huh?" She smiled, stretching the lace. "I would say you've earned yourself a second shot."

Pleasure spread across my hidden face as I set her on her feet, where she instantly pulled down her dress and adjusted the top, checking to make sure the lace on her face was in place. She held out her hand. "I believe you have something of mine."

Her thong.

Something I'd never kept from any other woman, but the urge with her was strong. So strong, I had no desire to give it back.

I wanted tonight to end with something of hers in my possession.

Something I could touch whenever I wanted.

Something I could smell when I . . . missed her scent.

I didn't know what was happening.

Where these feelings were coming from.

But they were there.

I gripped the back of her head, pulling our faces together. "Now I'll be able to get a whiff of you anytime I want. So, no, you're not getting it back."

She laughed. "Ruthless."

"Maybe when I get that second shot, we can negotiate."

"I'm up for that challenge." Her hand went to my chest softly. Our stares locked, her holding my gaze like she didn't want to let it go. And then she rose on her toes, her mouth eventually reaching mine, where she gave me the gentlest kiss. "Ticktock."

The moment her mouth and hand left me, I looked down to pull off the condom and zip myself up, and before I could say another word, she was gone.

CHAPTER FIVE

Me: Love, I can't get you out of my head, which means I'm ready for that second shot with you. But, this time, I want the mask off. I want to see your whole face. I want to see what you look like while I'm making you scream.

SaarasLove: Hiiiii.

SaarasLove: Hottest text award goes to: youuuuu.

Me: Is that a yes?

SaarasLove: Mr. Boston, it sounds like you've missed me.

Me: I had a good time the other night, so yes, I've missed you. And, like I said, I've thought about you a lot.

SaarasLove: Just curious, if I gave you another fifteen minutes, what would you do to me?

Me: Maybe I would spend every one of those minutes with my face between your legs. You seemed to really enjoy that. Or maybe I'd flip you around and point your ass up in the air and start there. Or maybe I'd spend every one of those seconds just talking to you, gazing into your eyes, learning, listening.

Me: Which would you enjoy more?

SaarasLove: Whoa. That's a tough one.

Me: Notice, you didn't say no . . .

Me: Give me a date, Love. How about sometime this week?

SaarasLove: You're going to think I'm playing hard to get. I swear I'm not—even though that does sound like fun—I just can't hang this week. I'm traveling for work, I'm juggling class and homework. I've reached the overwhelmed stage with all of that.

Me: I'm calling you. Pick up.

SaarasLove: You mean through the app?

The call feature had been part of our beta testing and had launched with the app. Since our emphasis was always on security and anonymity, we thought this would be an extremely popular element among users. Users wouldn't have to give out their phone numbers, and if things didn't go well with the person they Hooked, it was one less piece of personal information they had.

Rather than typing a response, I clicked on the "Phone" icon and waited for the call to connect.

"Wow," she said when she answered, "you don't waste any time, do you, Mr. Boston?"

"Not when I want something as badly as I want you."

Her laugh was short but sweet. "I like that about you. This incessant need to have me, yet when you got the chance, you didn't rush—you savored. I appreciate that."

"Admittedly, I like everything about you."

"Oh yeah? Like what?"

I moved to the window in my bedroom, staring out at the street below, wondering if she was doing the same, or if she was pacing her room, playing with her long, dark hair, if there was a heat moving through that gorgeous body of hers. "I like that we both have small tattoos that mean everything to us. I like that we both love to travel, and we're obviously dedicated to our careers because we're balancing school at the same time. I like the way your teeth bite into your lip right before you're going to come. I like that your scream goes a little high-pitched before you drag it out for multiple syllables. I like that I now know what your hand feels like when it's locked in mine."

"You're fascinating."

I rubbed my fingers across my lip, back and forth. "Tell me something that no one knows about you."

"Something no one knows," she repeated. "You mean sexually? Life-wise? Career-wise?"

"Anything."

"Well . . ." She turned quiet. "Aside from the physical satisfaction I hoped to gain from this app, taking my mind away from the place it's currently in—giving me some mental freedom, if you will—I'm also interested in studying the way you guys think. The mind of a man is something I'm completely intrigued by."

"How so?"

"Our sexes are so opposite. To me, that's completely captivating."

I pushed my back against the window. "You must be a psy major?"

She laughed.

"I need more details," I told her.

"Well, for starters, I think most men can have uncommitted sex and immediately move on to the next woman without any feelings getting involved. It could be the most amazing, intense, bonding experience ever, and they can move on without so much as a second thought. Not women. Most of us would want to duplicate that night over and over."

"You're forgetting something."

"What's that?"

"I asked for a second shot."

"I'm not forgetting. I'm trying to figure out why." There was movement in the background, the sound of her breathing coming through the speaker until she seemed to get settled. "What is it that makes me different than the last woman you slept with—which, I assume, was a one-night stand, no?" She paused to see if I'd contradict her. "That's what I thought."

Man, she was cute.

"She was, yes," I admitted. "But she didn't have this mesmerizing quality that you have. How every time you unravel a new piece about yourself, I want to dig deeper. I want to see what's underneath it. Like what wrist you had tattooed, which I didn't have a chance to check when I was with you, whose initials were inked, and why that person means so much to you. Before you left me in the stairwell, that last kiss you gave me. It was more special than all the others. Why? What words were you trying to speak with your lips?" I exhaled. "What I've tasted so far, in person and through the app, has only made me want more."

"You didn't crave those things with her?"

"No. I didn't even know her, Love, nor did I take the time to know her."

"*Ohhh.*"

I laughed. "You like that answer?"

"Mr. Boston, must I remind you that this app is for the kind of man and woman who don't want a second round. It's for adults who have the ability to move on without getting involved."

Her tone told me she was teasing, flirting, trying to draw a reaction out of me.

A side of her that was completely adorable.

I couldn't hide my smile. "Are you shooting me down, Love?" I didn't wait for a response and continued, "Are you afraid I could give you everything you've ever wanted and you might develop feelings that are incredibly strong? I'm talking all-consuming, mind-blowing love, and suddenly . . . you want to run?"

"*Ahhh,* two can play that game, huh?" I heard her grin. "I'm not afraid of anything, especially not love—I just don't know that I've ever felt it before."

I nodded. "Now that's an answer I can appreciate."

"Why?"

"Because I'm not afraid to try anything once," I told her. "If that means going for a second round or following a feeling or chasing love, then I'm up for it."

"Have you been in a relationship before?"

"Not one that was heavy enough to discuss."

"Let me see if I have this right . . . In the short time you've known me, things are already different than anything you've experienced before, they're deeper, and that's why you're interested in a second round?"

I left the window and went over to my bed, where I flopped down and adjusted the pillows to mold around my neck. "Yes. Much different. And already much deeper." I rubbed my hand over the top of my head, stopping to ask, "Does that surprise you? Because I get the sense this isn't one-sided—you feel it too."

"Surprise, yes." She paused. "I went into this needing to unplug, escape, and I had this burning desire to learn more about men. You could call it a focus group of sorts, giving me a moment to breathe from my life while scoring myself some rock star sex. I surely didn't see this happening."

"What do you want in a man that you've never been able to have before?"

She took several seconds to respond. "Trust. Monogamy. Love." She idled and I could tell she wasn't done speaking. "I've looked for it, and apparently, I've searched in all the wrong places. But if I'm being honest, even if those three things slapped me in the face right now, I don't know if I'd feel it. This moment, this present period of time—it's a hard one."

I understood that. Although I hadn't lost anyone close to me, this new stage of life wasn't easy to navigate. Still, I was intrigued by the three elements that meant the most to her.

Things that, after our evening together, seemed almost too easy to achieve.

I wondered what that meant.

For us.

For a future.

If I could really be the man who could constantly make her smile.

A smile I was dying to see, but I wouldn't ask for a picture or even a video.

When I saw that smile again, I wanted it to be in person, without any lace covering her face.

I focused on the desk across from my bed, the stack of books piled on top, knowing I had a paper to write for tomorrow and an exam to study for and at least eight more hours of Hooked work ahead of me before I would be getting any sleep.

But if Love told me she was available, I would meet her.

"Can I tell you something I've never said to anyone before?"

"Yes," she said.

"You're already changing me."

CHAPTER SIX

"Look who wants more," I said as I held the phone to my ear, answering Love's call through the app.

There was a slight giggle, and then: "Guilty. I want to hang. Are you free tonight?"

Free.

Something I wished for more than anything right now, especially after our last conversation and after she'd taken the initiative to reach out less than forty-eight hours later, when she'd told me she was busy the whole week.

"You're not going to believe this," I told her, "but I'm actually on a last-minute trip to Manhattan."

"Fun! What are you doing there?"

I didn't want to tell her that we were meeting with an advertising agency in the morning that would help us generate more revenue for the app. A meeting that hadn't been planned for a few more weeks but had been moved up by the Hooked team because we were doing so well.

"A bachelor party," I told her. "A buddy of mine is getting hitched next weekend."

"Did they meet on Hooked?"

Now it was my turn to laugh. "Hasn't the app been around for only a couple weeks? I hope they wouldn't be getting married that fast."

"Hey, you never know these days. Some people wed in Vegas after only meeting a couple hours before. Anything is possible."

"This is true."

"So, what are you doing?"

I glanced around the hotel room, then down at the towel wrapped around my waist. "I just got out of the shower."

Holden was at a bar, meeting up with a cousin who lived in the city. Grayson had Hooked a girl a few hours ago and was probably at her place. I'd stayed back to get some work done and planned to meet up with Holden in a little bit.

"You're telling me you're naked?"

I unwrapped the towel and dropped it on the floor. "Yes."

"Oh. *I really* like the thought of that."

Even though I could turn this conversation into something much more personal, using it to unravel more information about her, I was going to roll the other way.

A way that would show just how much she really liked the thought of me naked.

A way that would hopefully take care of this raging hard-on she'd already given me.

"Why don't you tell me what you're wearing, Love."

There was a brief pause. "Well, I just got back from a run, so I'm in a pair of running shorts and a tank top. Sneakers. Socks. I wish I could say I was in something sexier, but this is reality."

"Athletic clothes are one of my favorite things on a woman, so I would guarantee you look sexy as fuck right now."

"What's so hot about running clothes?"

"Well, for starters, I'm sure the shorts are cropped high, showing your unbelievable legs." I grabbed my dick as I made my way over to the bed. "I'm hard just thinking about the way you look in them. And then there's your tank top that gets more see-through as you sweat, showing those perfect tits and the curve of your waist and dip of your ass." I took a seat on the bed, leaning back against the headboard. "I bet your nipples are hard, and I bet you can see them through the tank."

There was movement, rustling, and then: "Oh my God. You're right."

"Tell me what you see while you look at yourself."

She sucked in a deep breath. "Well, the tank top is glued to me, stopping a few inches above my waistline, showing off my belly button."

"Mmm." I shook my head. "That's so sexy."

"And my nipples are definitely erect."

I smiled. "The run could have done that, but I'm going to take the credit and say it's from the sound of my voice."

"It is."

I'd been rubbing my cock but halted to say, "Are you dripping?"

"With sweat or . . ."

"I already know your skin is. What I want to know is if you're wet between your legs." I chewed my lip as I waited.

"Are you telling me to slip my fingers down my shorts?"

"Yes."

She half laughed.

"I want fifteen minutes," I demanded. "You'll be surprised how loud I can make you scream over the phone."

"They're all yours—the minutes and the screams."

"I want you to strip off everything you're wearing and tell me when you're naked, lying flat on your bed. I know you're sweaty, I don't care."

There was moving in the background, a change of breathing, and then: "I'm here."

My hand resumed stroking my shaft. "Hold the phone with your shoulder and run both palms around your tits. Just the outer edge of them while occasionally grazing your nipples."

"I've never had phone sex before."

I slid my thumb across my tip, wiping away the glistening bead there. "When you're touching your tits, I want you to think that it's my mouth, sucking your nipples. When you're rubbing your clit, I want you to think that it's my fingers, scraping back and forth across it, the way I did when I was inside you. And when you're fingering yourself, I want you to think it's my dick, thrusting in and out of your tightness."

"Oh God. This feels even better now."

"Can you handle pain?"

"I don't know. I'm not sure I've experienced anything like that either. I mean, aside from how big you are."

I chuckled as I wet the backs of my fingers and focused on my crown, holding it tightly. "I'm going to change that when we meet again."

"Should I be scared?"

"Didn't you tell me you weren't afraid of anything?"

"You remembered," she moaned.

Of course I remembered.

I wouldn't forget a single detail about her.

"When you add in pain, it brings in a whole different dimension," I said.

"All right, then tell me what to do."

"Pull your nipples." I balanced the phone on my shoulder and the pillow, running my hand over my chest and down my abs. "And when you've pulled them a few times, I want you to twist them. Not the ends. I want you to hold your whole nipple between your thumb and pointer finger, starting at the base and twisting as you circle out toward the end."

"Ohhh."

"You like that?"

"Yes," she exhaled. "You know what else I'd like? To know you're touching yourself."

"I am."

She released a long breath. "That's sexy."

I worked my way up to my tip, circling, squeezing, and dived back down. "I'm going to devour you when I see you. Fuck, I wish you were here right now." I gripped harder, wanting to punish myself for this trip. "Tell me what you're doing to yourself."

"I'm rubbing my breasts, tugging my nipples. Twisting. Just like you told me to do."

"So obedient . . ." My eyes closed and I pictured her incredible body. The bareness of her navel. The contour of her hip. What was in between those gorgeous thighs. I pumped as I said, "Keep one hand on your tit and run the other down the center of your body. Use just the tip of your fingers and slide slowly—so goddamn slowly—to your clit." My eyes opened. "I can't see you. I can't read your face, so I need you to tell me how it feels. How much pressure you're using. How wet you are when you get there."

"My back is arching off the bed as my fingers crawl down."

My thumb swiped over my mushroom head, switching to my palm, rounding across it. "That tells me the anticipation is getting to you."

"Yesss."

"Are you still pulling your nipple?"

"I haven't stopped."

"Good. Don't." I went to the center of my shaft before dropping to my sack. "In fact, I want you to flick it. Hard. And then rub it with your palm to ease the sting."

"Oh!"

"Another thing you like . . ."

"Yes."

"Quick bursts of pain . . . They can do so much."

She gasped.

The sound caused me to stop. "What's wrong?"

"I've reached the spot."

"And?"

"I'm dripping."

"Yes!" I smiled. "Now, using the pads of your fingers, add a small bit of pressure to your clit. Don't go lower. I want you right there, at the top, the same place I sucked, and I want you gently rubbing it sideways—back and forth, like it's my tongue."

"Oh God."

"Are you getting wetter?"

"Mm-hmm." She went silent. "My legs are spreading . . . The sides of my knees are resting on the bed."

The back of my head hit the headboard. Again. And again. "You're ready for me . . ."

"Why can't you be here?"

That tone.

That neediness.

I couldn't get enough.

"If I could, I'd be there in a second." All that whining, that wanting, had earned her a finger. "Keep your thumb on your clit and turn the rest of your hand so you can circle yourself with your fingers. Don't finger yourself, I just want you teasing that area."

"I'm"—she pulled in air—"soaking."

I wanted to see that again.

I wanted to taste it.

I wanted to swallow it down my throat.

"How easy would it be for you to slip in a finger?"

"I wouldn't even have to try. It would go right in."

"Goddamn it." I was stroking harder, faster. "I want you circling, staying on the outside. Go all around, spreading your wetness. And while you're doing that, add more pressure to your clit."

"Ah!"

"Feels good, doesn't it?"

"I . . . want it."

"Tell me what you want."

"My finger. I need it."

"Because you want to come?"

She moaned, "Yes."

The image of her legs open and wide, her hand between them, her finger on the verge of entering—there was nothing hotter.

"Do it," I ordered. "But just one, not two."

"Ahhh."

"Is it all the way in?"

"Yesss."

"Are you dipping it in and out?"

Her breath came out labored when she said, "I'm moving quickly. I can't stop. It feels too good."

So was I.

My balls were already tightening as I fisted my dick. I normally used lube, lotion—whatever. I didn't have that right now, but it didn't matter because I was in so deep, visualizing her wetness.

"Push down on your clit, like you're swiping the screen of your phone."

"Oh shit." She hissed. "Can I have another finger?"

She was asking permission.

Damn, that was sexy.

"How badly do you want it?"

"You. Have. No. Idea."

The emphasis of each word told me she was close to coming.

"You can have it under one condition."

"Anything," she promised.

"You need to arch those fingers up, aiming them toward your stomach, and that's the angle you need to move in each time you thrust inside."

She got louder, until it sounded like she blew a burst of air into the phone. "Oh my God. What is . . . *that.*"

"Your G-spot."

Obviously a place she'd never found on her own, and no guy had ever touched before.

Round two—whenever that happened—was going to rock her whole world.

"Every time you drive those fingers into you, I want them arched in that direction, so you're caressing that spot. And after a few pumps, I want you to keep your fingers lodged inside."

"One, two."

I assumed she had stilled.

And then I heard, "I had to give myself one more—three."

"Rub that area. Circle it. Use your palm on your clit if you have to. Just make sure it's getting friction. I want you to feel it from every angle."

"The combination—I can't."

"Wait until I do this to you and use my tongue at the same time."

"I'll probably die."

"But it'll be worth it. Every lick." I clenched my cock, slowing down my orgasm. "Start moving again. Fast. Pound yourself."

"You're going to make me come."

I nipped my lip at the thought. "That's the whole point of this." I spit on my palm, knowing the rubbing would eventually turn me raw, and I went right back to work, rising to my tip, twisting, and gliding to my base. I wasn't gentle. I wasn't calm. My hips began to buck, as though those gorgeous thighs of hers were wrapped around me. "Tell me what it feels like. I want to hear you."

"I'm lost." She inhaled loudly. "There's tingling and almost this swishing. My whole body is"—she stopped to moan—"being taken over. A feeling—it's incredible."

"Don't let up."

"I can't." She gulped. "Because the second I would, it would be over, and I need this feeling. I want more of it."

"Pick up your speed." I took my own advice. "Pat your clit. Slap it if you have to."

"Slap?"

I growled, "Try it."

"Ah!" She went still. *"Ohhh!"*

There was no better noise.

No better feeling than hearing pleasure come out of her mouth.

"Harder," I demanded. "I want to hear you come."

"I'm there."

"So am I . . ." The burst erupted in my balls, taking them prisoner as the sensation lifted higher, driving right through me. A tightening followed. So did a wave of tingles. "I'm going to lose it."

"Same. Now!"

"Let me hear you. Let me fucking hear you!" The moment the last word left my mouth, I positioned my free hand over my tip, and I shot my first load, squeezing my crown, draining myself into my palm. A second stream followed. So did a third. The white, creamy liquid pooled over my skin, and as the amount built, I grunted louder, each shot sending another pulse through me.

"Ahhh!" Her gasp was erotic, sensual, a final syllable that was dragged out in different octaves. "Oh God!"

And I sat frozen on the bed, listening, taking in each beat of her orgasm.

It wasn't just seductive—although it was definitely that.

There was something wildly beautiful about it.

When she began to quiet, I whispered, "How did that feel?"

"I . . . can't even breathe, just like the night in the stairwell."

"Are you still inside yourself?"

"Yes."

"Put the phone by your hand. As you start to wind down, I want to hear the wetness hitting your fingers."

There was movement, and then I got the sound I wanted to hear.

The drips of wetness, the impact they made when they collided with her skin.

"Goddamn it." As I took in that noise along with her moans, my dick threatened to get hard again. "You're amazing, Love."

There was a bit of stirring, and then: "I slid out."

"Is your body feeling sensitive?"

"Extra."

I held the phone with my shoulder as I walked to the bathroom to wash my hands. "How else do you feel?"

"Well, here's a bit more honesty for you. No one has ever made me feel this satisfied. And this need . . ."

"A need for what?"

"More."

I turned off the water, staring at myself in the mirror. My cheeks flushed. My hair half-dry. My pupils expanded, almost dilated.

But underneath those physical changes was something else.

A feeling.

A feeling that equaled exactly what she wanted.

More.

What is Love doing to me?

I shook my head, returning to the moment, and said, "Are you telling me I'm the best you've ever had?"

"Yes."

"You know, the more I learn your body, it's only going to get better."

"I'm afraid of that."

I still focused on my reflection but paused my movements. "Says the girl who isn't afraid of anything."

She was quiet for a moment. "I wasn't . . . until you."

CHAPTER SEVEN

Me: Good morning, gorgeous. I'm back from Manhattan and I'd love to see you. Are you free tonight? Tomorrow?

Me: Or maybe this weekend?

Me: You there?

Me: Shit, you really are playing hard to get now, aren't you? 😒

Me: I'm going to stop bugging you. Call me when you return.

SaarasLove: Hiiii!

Me: Wow . . . long time no talk, sexy girl.

SaarasLove: Life has been a little on the wild side, and I haven't had any time to get on the app. I'm so sorry.

Me: You went MIA on me. What's it been, about a week?

SaarasLove: It was a me thing, not a you thing. I promise.

Me: Yeah, I assumed something was up. Things good, though?

SaarasLove: Do you want to hear something funny?

Me: Always.

SaarasLove: Now I'm in Manhattan for work. You wouldn't happen to be here again too, would you?

Me: I wish.

SaarasLove: Damn. I guess I'm not that lucky.

SaarasLove: I just had some downtime at the hotel. Thought I'd get caught up on all my social media, it's been a min since I've done that.

Me: Will timing ever be on our side for round two?

SaarasLove: Life should be calming down over the next couple of weeks and I'll be in Boston more. How about you? Do you have any travel coming up?

Me: I'll cancel it if that means I'll get to see you.

SaarasLove: You're sweet.

Me: Nah, I just want you.

I waited for a response.

When I didn't get one and still craved more of her attention, I hit the "Phone" button and said once she answered, "I'd much rather hear your voice."

"Hello, stranger."

Since the guys were working beside me in our living room, I went into my bedroom and shut my door. "Why are you so far away?"

I wasn't ready to admit that every time I opened the app, I looked to see if the green light was next to her name, telling me she was online. That underneath her icon, it showed how long it had been since she'd logged on, a number I checked every day.

That I wasn't sure how or why, but I missed her.

Even though I'd never seen her face.

Even though I knew such a limited amount about her.

But that one taste hadn't been enough.

"One of us always seems to be," she replied.

"Have you thought about me?"

Silence grew between us, until: "Yes."

"What do you think about?"

Her exhale was short, but loud enough to hear. "The things you've done to my body—twice now. The way you've made me feel."

"And what's your conclusion?"

"You're a very dangerous man, Mr. Boston."

I took a seat on my bed, staring out the window. "Only with you." My thumb traced my bottom lip. "There's a reason we matched perfectly. I'm destined to figure out why that is. And in the meantime, I'm going to keep enjoying you and learning more about you and finding every possible way to make you scream."

"You make it sound easy."

"I told you, men can change. I already have because of you. If trust and monogamy and love is what you're looking for—I believe it's all possible."

There was movement, a breath, and then stillness. "Then let me ask you this . . . I know you told me that you just started a business with your best friends and you're Boston-sports obsessed, and then there's your username, but I still have to know: Are you married to Boston?"

I thought about her question. "You mean, would I move somewhere else?"

"Yes."

"No," I replied quickly. "You're right about everything you've said. My work is here. My passion is here. My family is here. My whole life is in this city."

"That's what I thought."

Her tone had softened in a way I hadn't heard before.

Why did that make my chest ache?

Why did I suddenly feel that question had moved us to opposite sides of the same path?

I ran my hand over my hair. "I want to see you."

"I . . . want that too."

I pulled up the camera on my phone and positioned it high in the air, turning my face to the side as I snapped several pics. I chose the best one and cropped out certain features to make me less recognizable, only because when we finally revealed our faces, I wanted to be able to kiss hers immediately after.

"Check your messages," I told her.

There was a pause, and then: "I knew it."

"Knew what?"

"You're as perfect as I remember."

I had a feeling she wasn't done, so I waited.

"Mr. Boston . . . this one is going to hurt."

I didn't ask her to elaborate. I didn't try to change her opinion.

I didn't say anything.

In my mind, there was no way I was going to cause her a single second of pain, so the only hurt that would come between us was what I planned to do with my fingers the second they touched her body again.

CHAPTER EIGHT

"I swear you just walked by me," Love said as I held the phone to my ear.

I chuckled as I rushed to keep up with Grayson, who had now gained a lead since I'd stopped to answer my phone. "What makes you think that?"

"I'm sitting outside a coffee shop in the Back Bay, sipping an espresso, and this guy passes my table. He has a heavy amount of scruff on his cheeks, strong jawline, sharp nose. Just like you. We catch eyes at the very beginning, you know, when he approaches the start of the sitting area. It can't be more than ten or twelve paces long, and the whole time he gives me this soft grin. The kind that spreads across your face when you know something about someone, but you don't want to let on. Do you know what I'm talking about?"

"Yes."

"He continued to look at me that way during those ten paces, holding my gaze until he was gone."

A weird, unexplained, unfamiliar pang hit my chest.

A feeling that came out of nowhere.

I'd never been jealous of another man . . . until now.

"And then what happened?" I asked, turning at the stop sign, where I followed Grayson down a packed sidewalk, my height an advantage that allowed me to weave to the spots where the congestion thinned.

"He kept walking."

"You didn't stop him?"

"No."

"So you let him walk right by, never knowing if that was me or not, living with a lifetime of regret."

There was silence, and then finally: "Was it you?"

"No."

"Then I have no regret." It was too loud to be sure, but I swore she sighed.

That sound, that response . . . it didn't solve the issue that Love would have let me walk by without stopping me. The need to potentially meet me with my mask off, spend unplanned time with me, hadn't been strong enough to send her to her feet.

A thought—a realization—that really made me ache.

Before I could reply, she said, "Wherever you are, it sounds busy."

I dodged a group of tourists holding their phones on selfie sticks. "I'm in San Francisco for work."

"Of course you are. The day after I fly home, you're gone."

Grayson and I had come out here to meet a team of coders. We needed to hire at least one more, possibly two, and since we were in Silicon Valley, we'd signed up to take a class. Not that either of us had any intention of coding, but we needed to learn the basics and at least speak the language.

I wanted to address what was bothering me, so I asked, "Can I admit something to you?"

"Please."

I moved back onto the sidewalk, Grayson now a few people ahead of me. With all the noise, there was no way he'd hear me, though I didn't care if he did. The guys were now well versed in all things that involved Love, and despite Grayson giving me endless shit about it, I'd stopped listening.

"I wish it had been me who had walked by your table. Except I wouldn't have kept walking. I would have gone inside the coffee shop and ordered you another espresso, first learning how you take it—with creamer, without, with sweetener, or black. That way, I'd never have to ask you again. Once I had the drink in my hand, I would have returned to your table and taken a seat next to you. And then . . ."

"And then?"

I stopped along the side of a store, rested my back against the building, and closed my eyes. "I'd lean into your ear, and the first thing I'd say is your real name."

"*Ohhh.* Something you don't have. Does that mean you want it?"

I really thought about her question.

In my mind, Love was her name, and it fit for so many reasons.

But if she gave me hers, I would have to give her mine, and a quick Google search would show her all the recent articles written about my best friends and me since Hooked had exploded. Being a cofounder of this app was a conversation I didn't want to have now or over the phone. It was a talk that needed to happen in person. The last thing I needed was for her to think I'd targeted her somehow or that I'd manipulated the match results.

"I want it when I see you again," I told her. "When I can hold you in my arms and look into your eyes and process what I'll now be calling you. It's going to be hard to give up Love when that couldn't be more perfect for you."

"You don't have to give it up, just like I'll forever call you Mr. Boston . . . as long as that's okay?"

"Of course."

"Good. I love that. Now after you say my real name, what would you do next?"

"I'd whisper something . . ."

"I'm afraid to know what those words would be."

My eyes finally opened, showing the large building was up ahead, but our arrival wasn't the reason I smiled. "Don't be."

61

CHAPTER NINE

"Are you trying to win a contest?" Holden asked.

His question, which broke the silence in the room, startled me. I shook my head, glancing away from the screen of my laptop to look at him, both of his palms pressed against the top of his light-brown, shaggy hair. "What are you talking about?"

"That's the longest I've ever seen anyone smile." He nodded toward me. "You're going on twelve minutes straight. I've timed you. And you do realize that, within those minutes, you haven't moved, you've barely breathed—you're just sitting there with your fingers on your keyboard, smiling. What the hell is going on?"

I was on the floor of our living room, my laptop on the coffee table in front of me. But he was right: my hands had been frozen on the keyboard, my whole body still.

Love was dominating my thoughts.

Not just the obvious need of wanting to be with her again, but a recap of the conversations we'd had lately. The one about the coffee shop and her lack of chasing me, something that still stung. Along with the talk we'd had about whether I was married to Boston and the answer I'd given so quickly.

The answer that had been nagging me since I'd said it.

I couldn't help but consider what would happen if I did move out of this city.

If I should be more open to the idea, even if it wasn't possible. But something about Love made me consider possibilities I never had before.

I pulled my fingers away and clasped them in my lap. "I've got a lot on my mind."

"Good things, obviously. Feel like sharing?"

Grayson came in, eating a sandwich, half the meat falling out the back of the bread while he took a bite. "What are we talking about?"

"Why Easton has been smiling for the last twelve minutes," Holden said to him.

"That's some impressive shit right there," Grayson said. "But that's not the first time he's done that. I saw him the other day, gazing out the living room window, looking all flushed and heart eyed, like an emoji I would never use. It's pretty obvious that motherfucker is already married to Love."

I slid away from the table until my back hit the base of the recliner, and that was where I stayed. "I'm thinking about her a lot, I'm not going to lie."

"What's the deal with you two?" Grayson took a seat beside Holden on the couch, wiping the mustard off his lip. "I know you guys hooked up at the masquerade party. You've been talking a shit ton. Now what?"

I took a deep breath and swallowed. "I don't know. I guess we're just seeing where things go. We haven't been able to meet up again. Something is always getting in the way of that. But we're still talking and texting a lot."

Holden smiled, the whites of his teeth gleaming from the sun that came in through the window. "You like her."

I groaned, knowing Grayson was going to unload several rounds of bullshit I didn't want to listen to, but there was no reason to deny what my best friends already knew.

How had things changed so drastically in the little time since we'd launched Hooked?

How had *I* changed so much?

I didn't even feel like the same person.

The guy who had developed an app to make women more accessible, to make one-night stands less daunting. The guy who had a fishing hook tattooed on the inside of his bicep to signify the way we'd founded Hooked.

Yet here was the same guy about to admit something he never had before. "Yes." I sighed. "I really like her."

"And you're worried we're going to give you shit for admitting something we've already assumed," Grayson teased.

"Worried?" I mocked. "*I know* you're going to give me shit."

Grayson smiled before he shoved in the rest of the sandwich. "You're damn right about that." He finished chewing before he continued, "Just like you'd give me shit if I got locked down by a chick." He kicked his feet onto the coffee table. "But you got the hardest part of the battle out of the way. You've told us—or me, since this one"—he nodded toward Holden—"is loving every second of this. Now share all the details, so I can amp up the level of shit I'm going to give you."

"Asshole," I barked.

"Just ignore him," Holden said to me. "I'm the nice one, remember? The forever romantic who wants you locked down. So just tell me and pretend he's not here."

I raked my hand through my hair, the gel sticking to my skin. "The whole thing is honestly wild. Like I said, we've texted a ton, we've spoken on the phone—things I never do with women. And then we met up at the party, and the fire between us"—I let out a hissing sound—"it was so fucking hot. We've been trying to get together again, and it just hasn't worked out. I mean, aside from some phone sex. But . . ."

"But you've got feelings for her that you can't explain," Grayson said, scratching his beard. "And it's so unlike you and you've never felt this way and she's different than any girl you've ever been with." He paused. "Am I on the right track?"

"You nailed it."

"I know," Grayson replied. "I see it all over your face."

Those same strands on my head, I now pulled. "I don't know what the hell I'm doing. This isn't me. I don't even recognize myself." I rested my elbows on my bent knees. "I told her how she's changing me, and now here I am, already whipped and thinking about her non-fucking-stop."

A few seconds of silence passed before Holden rubbed his hands together and said, "I'm going to say something pretty bold."

I sucked in my bottom lip, bit it, then finally released it to reply, "All right. I'm listening."

"I said it before, but I really mean it this time: maybe Hooked was created so you could meet her."

I let that set in. "You really think so?"

Holden looked at Grayson. "We know how many women you've been with, and we've seen you after every hook-up. You've never acted like this before. So whatever the reason is, it doesn't even matter. You've found her. And, my man, I'm so happy to see it."

I glanced between them. "I'm lost. This is unknown territory for me. I have no idea what I'm doing." I got up and moved to the window, placing my back against it, my hands on the warm, sunbathed glass. "Not too long ago, she asked me if I was married to this town, hinting that she was going to be leaving it soon."

"I hope you said yes," Grayson shot back. "Leave? No. Fuck that. You're BostonLifer for a reason. All three of us are."

I glanced between them. "She's on the verge of graduating and already has a job. What if it's taking her away?"

"The fact that you're even thinking of that just proves how real this is," Holden said.

His words hit.

And then they hit harder.

My brain conjured up an image of me holding hands with Love, walking toward a coffee shop that wasn't in the Back Bay, placing an order, and joining her at the table, where I whispered something into her ear. The skyline above us was one I didn't recognize, and part of me was okay with that.

I wrapped my hands over my stomach, the ache already there even though she wasn't gone. "What do I do?"

"That's easy," Holden said. "You don't let her go."

CHAPTER TEN

I reached for my phone as it rang on the coffee table, the screen showing that the call was coming through Hooked, Love as the caller. I held the phone to my ear and said, "I was just thinking about you."

"Oh yeah?"

"I just got back from California, and I have a free night, so yeah, I was going to text you and see if you're available—"

"I'm actually calling for a different reason."

Her tone was one I didn't recognize. There was a hint of sadness to it—and something else. Whatever that something was, it caused me to get up from the couch and go into my bedroom and shut the door, giving myself some privacy from the guys. "What's wrong, Love?"

"I don't know how to say this . . . but . . . we've run out of time."

I paused two feet in front of my bed, my chest suddenly throbbing. "What do you mean?"

"I'm not going to be around much—if at all. I've decided to quit the app."

Her words didn't come across as a warning. They were more like a promise.

A finale.

And with that came this unexpected emptiness. A feeling that burrowed its way out of my body, leaving a gaping hole behind.

I didn't understand where it came from.

Why there was something about this woman that I couldn't shake.

That I couldn't get enough of.

That I constantly craved more of.

And while I didn't necessarily understand those feelings, I knew that this wasn't the end of us.

It couldn't be.

"Listen, I get it." I paced from the window to my bed. "My life has gotten unexpectedly busy as well. It's actually been kind of wild lately. I'm saying this because I can appreciate what you've got going on. But I don't want things to fade out when they haven't had a chance to even get started."

I processed the idea of losing her, and I couldn't stand it.

I wouldn't let that happen.

I pulled up our chat box on the app and quickly scrolled through the messages we'd sent each other. Some were just random words we'd exchanged during the day. Some were parts of lengthier conversations. The date and time listed next to each one showed that, for the last month, I'd spoken to her almost daily.

"I know, but . . ." Her voice hadn't lightened at all. "My life is going to be changing drastically. I'm not sure what it's going to be like, aside from a lot of stress."

"I won't add any pressure. That's the last thing I'd want to do."

She made a noise, like she was eating something delicious. "I love that about you. You never need, you just always want."

I finally sat on the end of my bed. "You. Your body. Your happiness. All of it."

She laughed, but that was the only response I got.

"Why don't you take my number," I said. "We don't have to go through the app anymore—as long as you're cool with that. When things loosen up and we can make a date work, we will. And if that doesn't happen, at least we can still talk. There's no reason for that to stop, right?"

"Okay."

I read my number off to her, and within a few seconds, a text came through.

Hiiii, it's me.

I laughed as I read her signature introduction. "That was fast." I saved her info in my phone. "Are you in Boston now? Maybe we could meet up today for a coffee or something."

"I'm at the airport."

I sighed. "Never in the same place at the same time."

She was quiet for a moment, the background filled with a mix of chatter and gate announcements. "I want you to know, which I've already said to you before, but I never expected to find someone who makes me feel the way you do."

"Honestly"—I shook my head, the truth hitting me hard—"no one is more shocked about that than me." I gripped the edge of the bed, bearing all my weight on one arm. "Is everything all right? You've never sounded this way before, and we've talked enough for me to know the difference."

"It's nothing."

"But if it's something, you can talk to me about it."

Silence filled the space between us until she eventually said, "How do you know you're making the right decision when you're faced with something huge?"

"Ah. A crossroads. Those are tough, and it's impossible to know." I moved the phone to my other ear and shifted my weight to my opposite arm. "I can tell you that not too long ago, I had to make a massive professional decision. A risk that was going to change my life. And not just mine, but my best friends' as well. Do we follow the dream and open the business? Do we dismiss the whole idea? What about the financial burden of it all? And everyone else who will be affected—our employees, our families, who we borrowed money from. God, it's a lot, and decisions like that are fucking brutal."

"Has it paid off?"

I wanted to tell her all the ways in which it had.

This phone conversation was one.

Instead, I replied, "It has so far, and in the long run, it'll be greater than any of us dreamed."

"How did you know it was the right move?"

I glanced out the window, remembering how many times over the last seven months I'd stared at the same lone erect tree outside our building, searching for an answer. "Your gut will tell you. Listen to it."

"It's shouting at me."

I smiled. "Then it has a lot to say. Keep listening."

She turned quiet again for several counts. "Thank you."

"I didn't do anything."

"You're wrong." There was movement, almost like she was turning breathless. "You became more than just a man who wants to get me naked. You showed me trust is possible, and you know I've never had that before." Another breath hit the phone. "But now, I have to go."

"We'll talk soon."

"Bye."

I tucked my phone into my pocket and returned to the living room, where I took a seat on the couch. Since this had become my office, my laptop was already in front of me, and I logged on to the database, searching for Love's profile. She had signed up exactly thirty days ago. At midnight last night, the system would have sent her an email, asking if she wanted to move from a thirty-day trial membership to a subscription. If she made the switch, she would have to provide her name, address, and payment information—things we only collected from paying users. If she ignored the email and didn't sign up for the subscription or if she canceled her trial, her status in the database would turn from active to idle.

I was just clicking on her username when the change happened.

Idle.

The cancellation request appeared on her account then, her username locked until she returned—if ever—to Hooked.

She'd warned me that she was going to quit. I wasn't surprised, but I was something else—something I couldn't place aside from the emptiness that was gnawing a bigger hole.

I had her phone number.

I had the ability to reach out whenever I wanted.

Nothing was going to change between us.

So I didn't know why I was feeling this way. Why I was so worried about her tone as I replayed our conversation in my head. Why I feared that this hard place she was in would be too much for her.

As I listened to her words echo over and over in my mind, I pulled up the app and clicked on her profile. Even though I could check her status in the database whenever I wanted, I still set a notification so that if she ever turned active again, I would be alerted.

I wasn't sure why that mattered.

But something in my gut told me that it did.

Me: Just checking on you. It's been about a week, I think, things going well? Any chance you're in town?

Love: So much has happened in the last seven days. I feel like I've aged ten years.

Me: Good things, I hope?

Love: You were right, you know. About everything. It's been such an adventure so far, but it's all working out.

Me: You were faced with a hard decision. You obviously made the right one. I'm happy for you.

Love: Thanks for your help.

Me: Some friends and I are going out tonight. We'll be hitting up the Back Bay if you feel like getting a drink.

Love: Yeah . . . about that.

Me: I figured it was a long shot.

Love: More than that—it's sadly almost impossible at this point. But here's what I can promise, if I ever make my way back to Boston, that answer will be yes.

As I stared at her text, I began to nod, my lips grinding together.

There wasn't a single word she had typed that shocked me.

Deep down, I knew.

I knew this was what she was referring to when she told me this was going to hurt.

In her head, she saw our future, how this was all going to play out, and long distance—for Love—wasn't an option.

But not long ago, I'd envisioned what leaving would look like—a new skyline, our hands clasped, two coffees sitting in front of us.

Maybe I should have thought about it for real.

Maybe I should have dug deeper and considered the possibility.

What I'd kept telling myself was that Love was a woman I'd seen only once, someone I hardly knew. Besides, she'd never even asked me to move; she'd only asked if I was married to Boston.

Had I been given an invitation, maybe the result would have me feeling much differently. Maybe then I wouldn't feel the way I did now.

Because now she was gone, and my mind was tearing that vision to shreds.

And for me . . . that hurt.

◆ ◆ ◆

Me: I swear you just passed me at JFK. I would recognize that back and those gorgeous hips anywhere. Or maybe I'm just wishing you'll appear at the airport, and I can smuggle you onto the plane with me and take you home.

Love: I just landed at Heathrow. Opposite sides of the pond, I'm afraid. But my bestie is passing through JFK today and we have similar body types. Wouldn't it be wild if it was her?!?

Love: And hiii, btw.

Me: I've been thinking about you a lot. Too much, probably.

Love: You're making me blush.

Me: A color I never got to see on you, there was too much lace between us.

Me: Is life good? It's been what, a month since I've heard your voice.

Love: Something like that. I've lost count of the days . . . months . . . even the year at this point. Things have become such a blur.

Me: You better be squeezing in some fun.

Love: What I needed to squeeze in is a smile . . . and you just gave me one.

CHAPTER ELEVEN

Me: Just got another tiny tattoo and it made me think of you.

Love: Ohhh. What's it of?

Me: A whoopie pie.

Love: You're kidding?

Me: Yes. I'm kidding. It's a tiny replica of Sugarloaf Mountain.

Love: In Maine?

Me: Yeah, my favorite place to ski.

Love: You're a wicked New Englander, Mr. Boston.

Me: Do you miss it?

Love: I'm learning to live without it.

CHAPTER TWELVE

Me: Dude, are you alive?

Love: Hiii! Yes, sorry. Life has been hectic, and it seems to be getting busier by the second. How are you? How's life? How's Boston?

Me: We're both waiting for your return.

Love: Ha! You're cute. But you know that isn't going to happen.

Me: One can still hope.

Me: I've missed you.

Love: ☺

CHAPTER THIRTEEN

Me: I know it's been a while since we've talked, but in a couple of hours, it's going to be the new year and the thought of you popped into my head. It's been a hell of a year for me, and you were a huge part of that. Wherever you are, I hope you're safe, and I hope you're having fun.

Undelivered.

I stared at the text, unsure why the message was coming back as undelivered. We had the same kind of phone. My blue box of text appeared on the right side, and her white box of text appeared on the left, everything looking completely normal.

Until the exclamation point showed up in bright red.

She had no reason to block me, so that couldn't be it. But if she had, I was positive the message would still look as though it had gone through—at least on my end.

I knew she hadn't reactivated her account on Hooked. I had this strange habit of checking every few weeks, even though I'd set up an alert to be notified. I just feared that the alert, for some reason, wouldn't go through and Love would be on the app and I wouldn't know.

But at this point, would it matter?

Six months or so had passed since we'd texted. The last few occasions had been because I'd reached out to her, and her replies—short, unemotional—had shown she'd already pulled away.

I wondered what had changed.

Distance, regardless of where she was, seemed so trivial when you had a connection like ours. When we'd matched so well. When we had so much in common and the most explosive chemistry.

I tried sending the message again, curious if I happened to be in a dead spot or if she was experiencing an outage.

Undelivered.

I needed to make sense of this, so I gave it one more shot. I found her number in my contacts, pressed her name, and held the phone to my ear. Within a few seconds, a recording came through the speaker.

The number had been disconnected.

What the fuck?

I tried again and the same recording repeated, the identical question filling my head.

It wasn't like we were anything, but Love and I had been something.

Something that mattered to me.

Something that made me care about her.

Something that made me miss her.

And now, we were nothing.

If I had her name, I would look her up on social media. But we'd never exchanged that detail. It was like staring at her face and never seeing the color of her hair. A name was just blonde or brunette or red to me—and I loved all three.

But what I felt in my chest, that feeling was all her.

So was the image I saw in my head and every single detail that followed.

Despite our communication fading over the latter part of this year, I hadn't anticipated her wiping me out of her life.

But that was what had happened.

Even if that wasn't what I wanted.

Even if I wasn't ready for it.

Maybe it was that realization that hurt the most.

Or maybe it was the fact that I'd fallen for a woman who hadn't fallen for me.

PART TWO

They say to get right back up once you've been knocked down.

But do I stay kneeling on the ground, looking up the skirt of every woman walking by?

Or do I get on my feet only to fall . . .

Again?

CHAPTER FOURTEEN

Easton

Five and a half years later

I hung up the phone with Rachel, our recruiter, and carried my coffee and the résumés down the long hallway of the executive floor of our building in the Back Bay. My first stop was Holden's doorway. "Do you have a second?"

He looked up from his computer. "For sure. What's going on, my man?"

I held up a finger. "Let me see if Grayson's busy. I'll be right back." I continued to the end of the hall, leaning against the frame of Grayson's doorway while I looked inside his office. "Can you meet with Holden and me?"

"You do realize it's month end and I'm in the middle of hell, don't you?"

I maneuvered the papers so I could flip him off. "That makes two of us, asshole. Your hell isn't any worse than mine. Get up and follow me to Holden's office."

Instead of waiting, I walked there alone and took one of the empty seats in front of Holden's desk. "He's in a mood."

"Isn't he always?" Holden replied. When Grayson walked in, Holden added, "Ah, there's Mr. Sunshine—we were just talking about how happy you are today."

"Fuck the both of you." Grayson slumped down in the chair next to mine. "Can we hurry this up? I don't feel like sleeping here tonight, and at this rate, that's going to happen."

I set the résumés on Holden's desk and wrapped both hands around my mug, wishing more than anything it was a tumbler half-filled with a single malt, aged at least twenty years. "I just got off the phone with Rachel, and she's found three solid candidates to fill Marvin's position. I need you guys to look these over because our assistant is going to be setting up interviews."

Marvin, our director of app development and engineering, had resigned a few days ago. It was imperative that we replace him, not just for the future of our company but because we needed someone to manage and mentor our large team of coders and developers. In addition, Hooked was presently a national app. Whoever took over this position would be launching the app internationally, something Marvin wasn't capable of doing, and that was the reason he'd quit.

Grayson crossed his arms over his chest. "I hope you gave Rachel shit for not renewing her Hooked membership."

"Thanks to Hooked, she found someone, so there's no need to renew it," I told him.

"Hell yeah," Holden said. The forever romantic was even more of a relationship softie now that he was a single dad to Belle. He held up his hand to high-five me. "Another relationship in the books due to our genius invention."

Since launching, many things about the app had changed, and that included the addition of two other divisions. When users created a profile, the first question they were asked was whether they wanted to only hook up, whether they were looking for a long-term commitment that could result in marriage, or whether they were single parents searching for a partner with children, like Holden.

"I don't know why you're celebrating," Grayson said to him. The dude was still hotheaded as ever and completely allergic to monogamy. "The only reason she settled was because she was tired of waiting for Easton to fuck her."

I shrugged. "Truth."

"I don't care," Holden said. "I'll still take the victory."

When Holden lifted the résumés and began to read them, I said, "Rachel's favorite is Drake Madden, the one I placed on the bottom. I guess he's a tech rock star, über talented, has all the credentials we're looking for."

"Hire him," Grayson said. "Offer him the world. Whatever it takes for him to say yes. Because the second Marvin leaves, which is in, like, three days, I'm taking that spot in the interim, and I don't know a goddamn thing about coding or framework or any of that shit."

"Get our boy a drink," Holden said to me. "Quickly."

"Both of you need to pipe down," I ordered. "Grayson isn't getting a drink yet. It's not even ten in the morning, and we have a long day— and night—ahead of us. And"—I paused to look at Grayson—"we're not hiring Drake without interviewing him and the other candidates. All three deserve a fair shot, and hell, we might like one of the others better."

"Do I need to remind you that in exactly three days, I'm going to oversee our entire coding department, ensuring every user among all three divisions has a friendly and efficient experience on our app? That their payments are properly processed?" He raked his hair. "What the fuck do I know about friendly?"

"At least he's got that part right," Holden mumbled.

I laughed.

But the truth was, we'd hit a growing pain, and it was a good problem to have. The first time we'd felt this kind of stretch was when we came up with the idea to launch the two new divisions. Now we were here again, and we were taking this app to a place that no other competitor had ever reached.

With that came complications.

We'd figure it out. We always did.

Grayson was pulling at the collar of his polo, like the fabric was strangling him.

I grabbed his shoulder, shaking it. "Don't worry. We'll find someone, and Holden and I are here to help you with the department. We're not going to just throw you to the wolves."

"Isn't that nice of you," he barked back.

I reached for the résumés, taking them from Holden's hand, and held them where everyone could see them. "Look, we have Ralph, who graduated from Carnegie Mellon and runs the backend system of Lyft."

"Impressive," Holden said.

I flipped to the next sheet. "Julia, who graduated from Stanford and does the same kind of work for Godiva."

"Does Godiva have an app?" Grayson asked.

I thought about his question. "I don't know. We'll get that answer before she comes in. I'm assuming it must or Rachel wouldn't have recommended her. However, she's certainly qualified. That's one hell of an achievement list she has."

Holden eyed Grayson and me. "I just want to remind you gentlemen that whomever we find to be the most qualified candidate for our team, they're off limits."

"Huh?" I huffed.

"I'll spell it out for you," Grayson said. "Holden doesn't think we know how to keep our dicks in our pants."

"Whether they're man, woman, part horse—I put nothing past you two," Holden said.

"Dude"—I shook my head—"we're not fucking animals."

"Yes, you are," Holden said. "And I'm not sure which one of you is worse."

"Why are you even bringing this up?" I asked.

"Why? Because I want to remind you of the drama that went down between our old assistant and one of the coders. Remember when we caught them fucking on your desk"—Holden pointed at Grayson—"and then their nasty breakup a few months later when she sent our whole staff a pic of his dick?"

"*Ohhh* shit," Grayson moaned. "I forgot about that. I don't know how, since it cost the company over a grand to get my fucking office sanitized and disinfected."

"Exactly," Holden said, leaning into the edge of his desk, crossing his hands on top of it. "I'm the father to a five-year-old little girl. I want nothing more than to bring Belle into our building and show her how deserving candidates of all sexes are equals in this workspace, where women can have an office as big as her dad's—or even bigger—and prove to my baby that, one day, she's going to rule the world. Let's never forget that, fellas, all right? Let's use Belle as our inspiration and make sure that what happened with our old assistant and coder doesn't ever occur again." He scanned my face, then Grayson's. "Relationships need to stay outside these office walls. This space"—he circled the air—"is all about business."

"We don't do relationships," I told him, my foot tapping the air, my hands getting slightly sweaty as I thought of Love. "I think you're forgetting that."

In fact, the division of the app where Rachel had found her match was created out of necessity, not because Grayson and I had any desire to use it.

After Love, I had no interest in dating, monogamy, or settling down. Rachel knew that.

Hell, all of Boston knew that.

"Can you read between the lines, perhaps?" Holden challenged. "I'm talking all things—kissing, touching, marrying, whatever. And that goes for everyone in this building, not just the two of you."

"This motherfucker"—Grayson nodded at Holden—"needs to get laid."

"Moving on," I groaned, and showed them the last piece of paper. "Finally, there's Drake, who"—I grinned when I saw his education—"is one of Boston's finest, graduated from MIT, and currently works for Faceframe in a senior management role."

"Sold," Holden said.

I was, too, based on Drake's experience, but I wasn't going to let on. I wanted Holden to take his own advice and weigh the candidates equally.

"I think I'm Team Julia," I told him. "Her credentials are pretty serious, and Godiva, I believe, is international. I think she could offer a lot to us."

"I agree," Holden said as he took Drake's résumé from me. "But an MIT graduate? Who works for Faceframe, the biggest social media site in the world, having a massive international interface? Does it get any better than that?"

"Point for Drake," Grayson said.

I didn't need a fucking scorekeeper—I needed someone on equal ground. "Julia has a hell of an education. Excellent job history. Longevity at each company with plenty of management experience. She could probably do this international rollout with her eyes closed."

"Point for Julia," Grayson said.

"We've lost some amazing employees to Faceframe," Holden continued, reminding us of David and Brennon, our original coders. David we still employed, but Brennon had gone to work for the tech giant when we couldn't afford to pay him what he wanted. "Therefore, we know what they expect out of their employees and the type of qualifications that are required. If Drake has spent his entire professional career there, and it looks like he has, then he's the right candidate for us."

Again, I didn't disagree. I just liked to challenge the single dad once in a while, since he was notorious for trying to keep Grayson and me in line.

"Not to mention"—Holden pointed at Drake's résumé—"he's done part-time consulting for LinkedIn along with Amazon."

I couldn't deny that was a remarkable employment history.

"He makes our résumés look puny," Holden added.

"Hey, speak for yourself, asshole," Grayson said, and then he looked at me. "Keep your gun in its holster, but I'm Team Drake."

I glanced between my best friends as Holden's grin spread, knowing he'd won this battle. "All right, I hear you. I like Drake too. But I want you to go into these interviews open-minded. Who knows? Ralph or Julia could be really great for Hooked, and I don't want to miss out because the two of you are ready to get on your fucking knees and give Drake the best blow job of his life."

CHAPTER FIFTEEN

Drake

Home.

That warm, fuzzy thought vibrated through my body as I walked through my favorite city toward Hooked's Back Bay high-rise. After all these years, I had finally returned to where I'd grown up. The place where I'd experienced so many of my firsts.

My first educational achievement.

Kiss.

Heartbreak.

I'd been anxious to come back for many reasons. It wasn't that I didn't enjoy my job at Faceframe or living in Palo Alto.

I actually loved it.

But the desire to return to the East Coast was stronger.

My heart couldn't continue accepting California when it ached for Massachusetts.

So when I started to put out some feelers, a colleague recommended Rachel, who had earned the title of one of the best recruiters in the tech field. I sent her my résumé, and during one of our many phone chats, she brought up the available position at Hooked. She described the company as having a relaxed environment. Plus it was based in my favorite section of the city and was run by three best friends, who had graduated with MBAs from Harvard.

It sounded perfect for me.

Despite Rachel saying that formal attire wasn't necessary for the interview, I still leaned toward professional and dressed in a suit and heels. Fortunately, the walk from my best friend's apartment wasn't more than a few blocks, so I hadn't even broken a sweat from the unseasonably semi-warm spring day.

I had just started finger-curling a long, dangling lock, trying to work through my nerves, when I felt my phone vibrate. I pulled it from my pocket, checking the screen before I said to my best friend, "Hey, Saara. I'm, like, twenty steps from where I'm interviewing. What's up?"

"I just wanted to wish you good luck, babe. Nail it, like I know you will. And show them why you're beyond fabulous and they'd be morons not to hire you."

Her voice made my face heat. "I'm on it, girl."

"Good. Now, love you hard, kick all the ass, and I'll see you tonight."

"Deal."

I hung up just as the security guard greeted me, practically singing, "Good morning, can I help you?"

I halted in front of her desk and handed her my ID, smiling. "Good morning. My name is Drake Madden. I'm here for an interview with Hooked."

She scanned the ID into her computer and reached for the phone. "Drake Madden is here for her interview." She hung up and returned my ID to me. "Ellen, the receptionist, is on her way down to get you."

I thanked her and moved to the side of the desk, waiting less than a minute before the elevator chimed, the woman who stepped out making her way over to me. "Drake?"

I nodded, still grinning. "Yes, hi, that's me."

She stuck out her fragile hand. "I'm Ellen, it's nice to meet you. You're here for the director of app development and engineering position, yes?"

"It's really nice to meet you, too, Ellen. And, yes, I am."

"Wonderful, please follow me." She brought me over to the elevator, joining me inside. "Hooked now occupies the top three floors of this building." She hit the button for the thirty-third floor. "We're about to take over our fourth floor."

"Wow. Sounds like things have come a long way. That's amazing."

The door to the elevator shut, and with it came a draft of cold air.

She buttoned the top of her cardigan and rubbed her arms. "Will it ever be summer? Jeez." The thick grooves around her mouth deepened when she smiled.

"I hate the cold too. I don't know how I'm not living in Florida right now."

"That makes two of us, darling." She winked. "Anyway, I joined the company when it was only five months old, and I've been here ever since. I keep saying I'm going to retire, I'm just too old to be doing this, but the boys won't let me."

I could see why. She was lovely, and motherly in every way.

My hand clutched the strap of my bag, the leather turning slick from my sweaty palm. "I don't blame them one bit."

"Thank you." The elevator buzzed upon our arrival. "Please come with me."

She took me through several open workspaces, where there were standing desks and beanbag lounges and employees' dogs snoozing on fluffy beds—very reminiscent of my current office. The difference was the large panes of glass that showed the city's stunning skyline.

When we finally settled in the conference room, she asked, "Can I get you anything to drink? Water? Flavored seltzer? A latte, perhaps?"

"No, thank you, I'm fine."

She swept the air with the back of her palm. "All right, then. Make yourself all comfy and the partners will be in shortly."

I was suddenly alone in this oversize space, wishing it made me feel tiny.

But it did just the opposite.

I took a seat along the side of the oval table and continued to shift around until I found a comfortable-enough spot. My hair was the first thing I attacked, the top needing to be flattened from the hint of humidity that had caused it to rise. I then moved on to my jacket, pulling at the bottom to make sure it was low enough but loose around my stomach. I circled my lips, checking for excess gloss, along with the corners of my eyes to wipe away any leaked liner.

Am I ready?

Ready as I could be.

But I was still alone, so I tried to busy myself by looking at the wall decor—framed articles from the *Boston Globe*, *Forbes*, and *WIRED*, photographs of the partners shaking hands with celebrities and famous CEOs.

They didn't just have an impressive office; these guys were the real deal, with quite the reputation in the tech arena. According to my research, they had launched the app during their last year of grad school, the articles emphasizing that they were exactly the demographic they were looking for in a user.

To me, that equaled single and horny.

Multiple sources had even reported that Easton Jones, the CEO, had developed the app to make his dating life easier and less time-consuming. They called him a genius, innovative. Some even said legendary.

I'd say the ultimate bachelor had certainly struck gold.

And what the partners needed now, what they desired in a candidate, was something I knew I could provide for their company.

Once I heard the door handle turn, my neck straightened, my body stiffened. The heavy wood slowly swung open, and after a few hard blinks, I connected the face with the pictures I had seen online and across the walls in this room.

Easton Jones.

As he came in, his focus was on the piece of paper in his hand. "Drake, hi, it's nice to meet—"

His voice cut off the second his stare connected with mine. Each of the three men had a distinct look about them, but Easton's was pure sex.

Even more so in person.

A detail I wished I hadn't noticed.

But it was impossible not to.

Just like it was impossible to miss the shock that came across his face.

"I'm sorry . . ." He glanced down, returning to the paper he was holding. "Either I have the wrong room, or you do."

The . . . *wrong room?*

"No, I'm sure it's me—yikes, I'm sorry about that. This is just where the receptionist brought me for the interview." My voice was scratchy enough that I cleared my throat to fix it, my hands so unsteady in my lap.

He stopped halfway between the door and the table.

When he looked up, licking his lips, my breath hitched in my throat.

A hint of familiarity tugged at me.

Something I couldn't place or figure out.

"Which position are you interviewing for?" he asked.

I continued to dig through my memory, trying to locate those lips, and continued to come up blank, so I pushed those thoughts away. Whoever this position reported to, I hoped the boss wasn't as sexy as Easton.

I smiled. "Director of app development and engineering." I pointed at the door. "Should I go back to the reception area and find out where my interview is?"

"You're Drake Madden?" His brows lifted, and so did the corners of his mouth.

"Yes."

The noise he let out sounded like a half cough, half sigh. "I apologize, it's just . . ." The intensity in his gaze continued to build with each second that passed. "It doesn't matter. You're in the right room. I'm Easton Jones, it's great to meet you." He moved closer, his hand outstretched.

The moment our fingers locked, two things happened.

The first was a feeling.

A hot, spicy tingle that shot through my entire body, humming as it circled my chest.

The second was the way his scent enveloped me, how it reminded me of a night in the mountains, an aroma of burnt citrus with a heavy dose of fall.

My God.

"Nice to meet you as well," I replied when my voice decided to return.

He released my hand, and as he moved to the head of the table, I took my time studying him. Six three, I estimated, with hair as dark as black ink and eyes that were lighter than baby blue. They were piercing, fierce, the shade of ice, like a husky's. His strong, square jaw was covered in thick, delicious scruff. He had broad shoulders, arms so wide that his short sleeves hugged them, with forearms that were just as muscular and veiny.

As if that weren't enough, he smiled.

That expression caused the humming in my chest to erupt, adding to the slickness on my palms and the jitters in my stomach.

This man wasn't just hot.

He was beautiful.

And his eyes hadn't left me.

Eyes that . . . I was positive I'd seen before.

But that was impossible. I was sure I was just recalling all the photographs I'd seen of him during my research; that was the only explanation for this familiarity that still nagged at me.

"My partners will be joining us any second." He rested his hands on the table, folding his fingers together. "While we wait, I must say, your résumé is impressive. MIT graduate. You worked for Faceframe during your senior year of college—if the dates are correct?"

I smiled back.

It felt necessary.

Almost . . . important.

"Yes, well, they started recruiting me my sophomore year and offered to pay for the remainder of my education if I transferred to Stanford and came to work for them full-time."

He glanced at the paper, which I could now see was my résumé. "But you didn't?"

"No. I finally agreed that I would join them my senior year as long as I could stay and graduate."

"Drake, that's quite the offer to turn down."

"Yes, well, I was dead set on graduating from MIT—it's something I promised my mom before she passed."

"I'm sorry."

"No, no, it's fine. I just wanted you to know why I declined the social giant. But in the end, they got me anyway."

Just as his lips parted, two more people walked into the conference room, dragging my attention toward the doorway.

"Drake," the first one said, his eyes widening as he took me in. *"Oh."*

The confusion on his face somewhat resembled the shock that had been on Easton's. The other partner looked about the same as he gawked at me.

"Yes," Easton said to them, "*this* is Drake."

Something was off here.

I had a feeling I knew what it was.

I smiled and said, "Let me guess, you thought I was a man?" I shifted my gaze to Easton. "And when you came in, that's why you thought you were in the wrong room." I stopped to laugh.

"Guilty," Easton agreed.

One of the others gripped the top of a chair to pull it away from the table. "It's extremely surprising to see you're not a man, yes." The thickness of his beard, a staple in each of the pictures I'd seen online, told me it was Grayson.

"What Grayson means is—and please don't take any offense to this—we did think we were interviewing a male, only based on your name, but we're very pleased to meet you," the last one said.

I figured that must be Holden. He was just as tall as the others, but there was a gentleness about him that Easton and Grayson didn't have. Light-brown, almost golden, hair that looked windblown and a shirt that had a few wrinkles in the sleeves, like a man who was always in a rush. I wondered if that had anything to do with his being a father, something I'd learned during my research, or if he was just the more tender alpha of the group.

I laughed. "No offense taken. It honestly happens all the time." I grinned. "For some unknown reason, my mom named me after her father, and as much as I love the uniqueness, it can be quite confusing at times, so I get it." I shook both of their hands before they sat down.

"Thank you for coming in and for handling the name mishap with grace," Holden said. "I'm not sure what Easton told you before we arrived, but I'd like to say I'm blown away by your accomplishments."

Before I could respond, Grayson asked, "Why don't you tell us what you know about Hooked."

His voice was cold, demanding. Definitely the broodiest of the trio.

I had one hand resting atop the table and the other on my lap. I moved them together and squeezed. This was where my attitude needed to match my black suit. "I must say, you've built quite an infrastructure from a technical standpoint. Your design is clean. Easy to use and follow. There's compatibility and seamlessness between the different operating systems. Is there room for improvement? Always. I've also noticed your app is only US based, and that's a change I would make if it's something you'd even consider."

Easton glanced at the other two and then said, "Are you a member of Hooked?" When I didn't immediately respond, he added, "Why I'm asking is that certain aspects of the app can't be accessed unless you have a membership. I'm just curious if you saw it all or half or if you only concentrated on one of the divisions—say, the dating and marriage section."

"Let's put it this way," I started. "I may be in management now, but I began my career in coding, and I'm highly skilled and highly trained in that arena. I don't need to be a member to access your app"—I offered them another smile—"as I can slide through any unprotected pathway."

"Oh shit," Grayson groaned. "Should we ramp up security if we're that easy to hack?"

I laughed. "What you have is adequate for the average user, but, yes, I would increase security because if I'm able to get in, others can, too, and that addition is something I would do immediately if I was given this position."

Holden moved his chair closer to the table. "One of the things we liked most about your résumé is your international experience. As I reviewed the different positions you've had at Faceframe over the years, I see that part of your responsibilities has been to utilize data to create better experiences for the user."

"Yes," I confirmed, the sweat finally starting to dry on my hands. "For the last year, it's been one of my main focuses. I've traveled all over the world to make our interface as friendly as possible within each market."

"That's exactly what we're looking to do and one of the main reasons we're hiring for this position." Easton's hand lifted from his chest, his fingers rubbing through his scruff. Fingers that were causing the strangest sensation to enter my body. "We're launching the app internationally."

The sound of his skin brushing through his whiskers reached me on the other side of the table.

So did his gaze.

Neither was letting me go.

I coughed to clear my throat. "What I've learned during my years at Faceframe is every demographic has a different experience while using the app, and that expands across all countries and languages. We conduct rigorous testing, thoroughly researching these markets to understand them better, constantly tweaking the interface to meet their needs and expectations."

"Let's talk about travel," Holden said. "Would you be open to representing our brand at international conventions?"

"I love to travel—it's a huge passion of mine," I replied. "So yes, I would absolutely represent your brand at conventions. That's also something I did at Faceframe."

"Were you at the convention in Austin last month?" Holden asked.

"I was and, admittedly, had the best barbecue I've ever eaten in my life." I smiled.

"Was that your first time trying Texas barbecue?" Easton inquired.

My stomach tightened from his voice. "Sadly, yes, but now I find myself craving their brisket and ribs, and I need to find my way back there very soon." I laughed. "But I want to also say that in addition to conferences, something else I did for Faceframe was when the data showed a feature wasn't working on the app, I would be the first person to get on a plane to analyze the market personally."

"Without breaking your NDA, could you give us an example of that?" Grayson asked.

The excitement from my most recent discovery caused my pulse to hammer. "Of course. We launched a new messaging feature in Israel, and it wasn't being used. I was dumbfounded. I couldn't figure out why, after conducting all this research, it was being ignored. I flew to Tel Aviv and spent days working with test groups and analyzing data, and the problem immediately became apparent." I tucked a chunk of hair behind my ear, my mom's bracelet grazing my skin. "Hebrew is read from right to left. The message feature was in the wrong spot, and it wasn't aesthetically pleasing for those users. Now, for a US-based user, it would have worked perfectly, but this was a case of understanding the market and adapting to it."

"What happened once you moved the button?" Easton asked.

I shook my head, feeling my face light up. "Exactly what you'd imagine—the usage increased over eighty percent."

"That had to be a fascinating find," Holden said.

I nodded. "Those are some of the things I would do for Hooked. I would get you answers, like why are users signing up for their free one-month trial and quitting after only a week. Did they match and find the One that quickly? Maybe. But it's more likely that their experience wasn't what they wanted or what they were looking for." I glanced at each of their faces. "You need someone who doesn't just understand different audiences, but someone who knows how to target them, how to create an experience that will result in an increase of revenue, not a loss or a missed opportunity."

"The person who's currently in that role does none of that," Grayson said.

We were speaking candidly here, so I replied, "In their defense, they probably don't realize they have to. Your membership rate has continued to grow, am I right?" When I received a nod from Grayson, I continued, "You started with a solo focus and you expanded to include more offerings, therefore you've been on an upward trend. Things have been going amazingly well. The director just needed to help maintain that, and I'm sure they have. But I'm assuming you've reached the point where things are starting to plateau—every app hits that point right around the five-year mark, and you're beyond all that. You can increase ad spend, but something tells me you probably tried that. You can lower the membership fee, offer discounts, sales—enticing language that will result in only short-term gains. Or you can broaden your audience, and that's why I'm sitting at this table with all of you."

The ideas were already flowing.

A few days inside their network, reviewing, testing, and I would have an entire presentation to share with them.

I rested my arms on the table, letting it bear some of my weight, and I gave my closing argument. "I'm positive you have other candidates for this role, some you've most likely already interviewed. What sets me apart? I could say my experience, maybe. Most people in director-level roles have an impressive list of bullet points and achievements that match mine. What I'm going to say instead is my work ethic. I will treat this company as though it's my own. You can count on me to show up, you can count on me to be here and be present, and you can count on me to fight my hardest for you as owners and for the empire you've built." I glanced at my hands for just a moment, and when I looked up, I continued, "If you call any of the references I've provided, my direct reports at Faceframe and the CEOs and managers I've worked with during my consulting, that's the first thing they'll say about me. The second thing they'll say is that I won't let you down. Ever."

CHAPTER SIXTEEN

Drake

"Drake Madden," Easton, my new boss, said as he walked into the elevator but stopped in the doorway so it couldn't slide shut. "Your expression tells me you're having a moment with that Diet Coke you're guzzling. Should I leave you two alone, or do you mind if I join you?"

I swallowed, almost choking on the carbonation as I laughed. "Oh, we're definitely having a moment. Only I wish this soda had a few shots of rum in it—and I don't even drink liquor." I waved him forward. "Come on in. Please join us."

As he moved to the far side of the elevator, checking that the button to our floor was already lit, his scent hit me. That same burnt-citrus aroma, almost spicy, that I'd noticed during my interview tugged at my memory, hinting at a time when I'd smelled something similar.

"I'm assuming you're having quite the day?" he asked.

I nodded, sighing. "Nothing has gone right, but it's okay . . . I don't quit. I fight back—with soda."

"This is, what"—it appeared that he was mentally calculating—"the end of your second week? Everything is kicking in and kicking hard, totally normal." He reached inside the small brown bakery bag that he was holding and took out a piece of something that he popped into his mouth.

I chewed the corner of my lip. "Are you having a day like me?"

"See, you go for soda, which is commendable. My poison of choice is doughnuts." He held the paper bag in my direction. "There are three in there. Two I plan on devouring and an extra in case things get wicked hairy in the next hour. Help yourself to it."

I shook my head.

"Trust me, that doughnut will turn your whole day around. I was in your shoes six years ago, when we were trying to figure all this shit out. I swear, I was ordering these by the dozen."

I smiled. "If you get me hooked on these, you're dead." I reached inside the bag, the dough and sticky glaze immediately gluing to my fingers.

"Attagirl. Enjoy."

I took a bite, practically moaning as the glaze dissolved over my tongue. "Yep. You're dead."

His smile grew. "But it's so worth it." He looked up at the monitor that showed our progress as we passed each floor, the most recent number telling me we were halfway there. "How'd the move go? I don't think I even asked you."

He hadn't. That wasn't to say we hadn't spoken in the last two weeks. We'd done plenty of that. And even more—like the smiles as we passed each other in the hallway. The small talk whenever we crossed paths in the kitchen. The way he lingered a little longer at the end of each executive-level meeting so he could say a few extra words to me.

Nothing Easton did went unnoticed.

In my eyes, at least.

But it was *his* eyes that I couldn't get out of my mind.

His lips.

His personality, which reminded me so much of someone from my past—I just couldn't place him.

"*Ahhh*, about as fun as a cross-country move could go," I told him. "Which includes a broken bed frame, and my entire box of bathroom stuff went missing. I didn't realize that until I got out of the shower and had to air-dry and then rush to the store to get myself some deodorant."

"Damn those movers."

I waved my sticky hand in the air. "I needed new towels anyway."

"But the bed frame, that's a real bummer."

"Eh." I shrugged. "Maybe I needed a new one of those too."

"A new frame?" His brows rose. "You must have a pretty active bed."

Active?

I almost snorted.

My bed was a dead zone, but I certainly wasn't going to discuss that with the man whose eyes were constantly dipping down my body, who lit my skin every time I was in his presence.

Who was one of the three people I reported to.

And that, combined with all this bed talk, was the reason my cheeks were reddening.

Fortunately, I was saved by the door, which swung open as we reached our floor.

I held up the rest of the doughnut. "Thank you for this. You're right, it did turn my whole day around."

Or maybe that was just Easton.

Something I didn't want to admit to myself.

He returned my grin before I walked out. "I'll see you in twenty."

"Twenty?" I asked, facing him.

"The executive meeting."

I quickly checked my watch. "Oh crap, that's right. I guess I'll see you there."

I rushed down the hallway and into my office, shutting the door behind me. I was out of breath, and I was positive it had nothing to do with how fast I'd walked to get here.

That man took every bit of air out of my lungs, even if I continuously tried to fill them.

I tried to ignore that thought as I sat at my desk, returning just a handful of emails before I had to go to the conference room. Everyone was already seated when I got there, and the only spot available was, of course, the one next to Easton.

"Drake, why don't you start and give us an update on how everything went this week," Grayson said from the head of the table.

The team was usually pretty honest during these meetings—at least the few I'd attended so far. But I wasn't sure it was appropriate to tell them that only eight hours had passed since I'd arrived for work but it felt like a year and a half.

Man, I was exhausted.

"She's doughnut high at the moment," Easton replied before I could answer.

"Dude, you gave her a vanilla glaze and didn't get me one?" Grayson barked.

Easton pushed the bakery bag toward the head of the table. "There's one left. It's all yours."

"What about me?" Holden asked.

"And me?" the head of HR said.

"Sucks to be the both of you since I don't share," Grayson said with a full mouth. His gaze sauntered over to me as he added, "Tell us, Drake, are things good? Stressful? Are you in need of three more doughnuts?"

I laughed. "Yes. Yes. And *yessss*." This environment was so casual, there were times—like now—that aside from the tiredness, I forgot I was even at work. "You know I'm in the process of evaluating my entire team to make sure they're adept for the rollout. It's been a daunting process, but I believe I finally have some results."

"What are your findings?" the head of finance asked. Her sweater hung across the back of her shoulders and tied around her neck, and she tightened the knot, making sure the heavy garment didn't fall.

I glanced down at the notebook in front of me, reading the notes I'd taken during the solo meetings with my team. "About fifteen percent will need to be replaced with candidates a bit more qualified." I shifted my eye contact, avoiding Easton. "I expect a lot more than their previous director, and for the model you're presently running, they're fine. But for what I plan to do, I need more qualifications."

"I'll get in touch with our recruiter, so she can replace the coders you deem unfit," the HR director said.

I nodded at her, smiling. "I'm happy to assist with the hiring."

Only a brief period of silence followed before I heard, "Not wasting any time. I like it."

There was no mistaking who had spoken those words.

Maybe that was because Easton's voice was already in my head.

And after two weeks, it clearly had no plans to leave.

But that wasn't the only thing I felt as I looked at him.

There was his smile.

His sweet, sultry, beyond-likable presence.

And as I unraveled each layer, my body reacted.

Except what immediately followed was the realization that I couldn't think of my boss this way. My work ethic and reputation were all I had, and I wouldn't jeopardize that for anything.

Or anyone.

Not even the devastatingly handsome Easton Jones.

And that was assuming those wandering eyes and sexy smile were even trying to win me over—and I wasn't sure that they were.

"My plan, as of this morning, is to have Hooked go international within the next six months." I'd glanced away, but as I returned to him, I instantly wished I hadn't. Those eyes—they weren't gentle. "I also plan to start testing different options within the app to see if I can improve membership retention. So, as you can see, I don't have time to waste. I need the support, and I need to make sure the team is suited to meet my expectations."

"Will we see the options you plan to test?" Grayson asked.

"Would you like to?" I tucked a lock of hair behind my ear as the room turned quiet. "Let me say, I realize at this point I haven't gained your trust, so if you want to approve all testing, I'm happy to send you my plans. But I want you guys to know my only goal is to grow this company, and every decision I make is to accomplish that." I moved my gaze to Grayson.

The head of finance shifted in her seat, drawing my attention away from him. I watched her look at each of the partners, her expression telling me she was impressed.

"I like the idea of Drake knowing what she's allowed to test and what requires permission from the partners," the HR director said. "And that's surely something the partners could work on—that way everyone feels comfortable and there are limits in place."

"I agree," Holden replied.

"This is new to us," Easton said. He waited until I looked at him before he added, "You're new to us. We'll get you exactly what you need, don't worry."

When he began to lick his lips, I glanced away.

His tongue inspired far too many thoughts.

And memories—although I couldn't piece those together and they didn't make any sense.

The timing was perfect because Grayson said, "I'll talk to the fellas, and we'll come up with something within the next few days. Cool?"

"Yes," I replied. "Thank you."

"Anyone else have anything to add?" Holden inquired. When several seconds of silence ticked throughout the room, he continued, "Great, then I'll meet you all at the pub next door in an hour."

I inventoried each of the faces around the table before I replied, "Even me?"

"Especially you," Holden responded. "It's month end, and it has become a tradition in this office that we celebrate with a drink. One more month that Hooked has been alive—we toast to that."

"Hell yeah, we do," Grayson sang.

"It's always a fun time when we all go out," the HR director said. "It'll be a blast, I promise."

A drink.

Something I wanted more than anything right now.

But they were meeting in an hour, and that meant I would get minimal work done over the next sixty minutes. There were piles on my desk that needed to be read, and plans for tomorrow's testing that had to be sorted out. I had at least forty emails to reply to.

"I know you're slammed," Easton said. "We've put a lot on your plate and you probably had every intention of staying late to get some work done, but there's always tomorrow to complete those tasks."

"That was my intention," I admitted.

"Would it persuade you if I said they happen to have the best french fries in the world?" the head of finance said, smiling at me. "I know I'd love to get a chance to chat with you, so I hope you can make it."

Most of my team at Faceframe had gone out for drinks once or twice a month. It went a long way for morale to be with the crew outside the confines of the office, so I knew the benefit of meeting up after work.

Plus, this would give me the chance to see how everyone acted in an environment that was even more relaxed than this one.

Even Easton, *oh God.*

The last thing I needed was to find myself a few glasses of wine deep, loose-lipped and confessing just how attractive I found him, that I'd been fantasizing about his mouth since the moment we'd met.

That would be disastrous.

"What do you say?" Holden pressed. "Are you in?"

I couldn't say no.

I didn't have it in me.

"Yes." I smiled. "I'm in."

CHAPTER SEVENTEEN

Easton

We hadn't been seated in the bar for more than a minute when a waitress approached our table, her eyes on Drake as she asked, "What can I get you to drink?"

"Sauvignon blanc," Drake replied.

"No rum and diet?" I asked from the seat next to her.

Drake laughed at me. "That's only elevator talk. Bar talk, I'm a beer-and-wine girl."

"And for you?" the waitress said to me.

"I'm not a beer-and-wine girl." I winked at Drake and requested vodka on the rocks from the waitress.

I couldn't say it was a coincidence that I was sitting next to her, that there just happened to be an empty spot beside her. My move, when we'd arrived at the bar, had been far more strategic than that.

I just needed to be around her.

I needed to be closer.

Because never in all my life had I seen a woman as gorgeous, intelligent, and charismatic as Drake Madden.

She was the type who didn't need makeup; there was a natural, warm glow that came over her face, lighting her rich, mocha-colored eyes, emphasizing her lips, a thick pout that I couldn't stop staring at, that made my body burn every time it parted.

Individually, her qualities were mesmerizing.

As a whole, she was perfection.

Dark, coffee-colored hair that I wanted to wrap around my wrist and pull, elongating her neck, which I'd been dying to smell since the very first day, when her coconut perfume had taunted me. An hourglass figure with curves and dips that I wanted to run my hands over.

That I wanted to take my time devouring.

The sweater she wore had a wide, open neck that had stayed in place all day. Since arriving at the bar, the neck had shifted, falling off her shoulder, tormenting me with a view of that creamy, soft-looking skin.

My dick had been hard the moment I sat beside her. A mere tease of her velvety flesh and I was fucking aching for her.

Two weeks—that was all it had taken.

A total of fourteen days and I was already enamored.

So out of character for me, so fucking risky because she was a director at our company and someone I wasn't supposed to want, someone I wasn't supposed to touch, someone I wasn't supposed to desire.

Did this make me an asshole?

The worst CEO in the world?

But shit, there was something different about this woman. Something I couldn't quite put my finger on. Something that just seemed so . . . familiar.

Like I'd passed her on the street, and we'd shared a smile.

Like I'd sat next to her during an international flight, and we'd spoken the whole ride.

Like we'd spent an hour together in a dark, hidden alley, drawing the loudest moans and mind-blowing orgasms from each other's bodies, our sexual desires trumping our need for conversation.

Whatever the case was, I couldn't get her out of my head. Every thought I'd had of her during the interview—the questions, assumptions—had been solidified once she'd begun her employment and I'd gotten to know her a little more.

And each time I was around her, I noticed something new.

Like now, as I studied the gentle curve of her collarbone, how her neck dipped to that delicate spot, the skin stretching to meet her bare shoulder.

A place I wanted to kiss.

Taste.

Bite.

Inhale.

But, *goddamn it*, I'd told Holden I wouldn't hook up with any of our employees.

That was a promise I didn't want to renege on.

And going against that promise wouldn't just disappoint Holden— it could potentially ruin things for Hooked if Drake couldn't handle us hooking up.

I didn't want to fuck up one of the best things that had ever happened to our company.

But still, I stared at Drake while she spoke to our head of finance, who sat on her other side. Their voices were so low, I couldn't hear what they were talking about, but Drake's fingers circled and twirled the stem of the wineglass that the waitress had just delivered.

Even her profile was gorgeous. The peak of her plump lips, the arch of her nose, long lashes that fluttered open and closed.

There was only one other time in my life when I'd thought about a woman as much as Drake, and that had been Love.

And that was why I questioned if a hook-up with someone as spectacular as Drake would be enough.

Or if it would lead to me wanting more.

More.

A feeling that had turned to pain the moment Love was gone.

It was that unanswered question, that haunting memory, that was consuming me when Grayson said, "I need to tell you about the customer service inquiry that came in this morning."

I shook my head, clearing my thoughts for him. "Go on."

But within a few sentences, I stopped listening to him and shifted my focus back to Drake, waiting for an opportunity to interrupt our head of finance so I could steal Drake's attention.

Fortunately, I didn't have to wait long.

Our head of finance got up, presumably to use the restroom, and Drake sat unoccupied, sipping her wine. I waited until Grayson finished his detailed explanation of the complaint that he had fielded today before I turned to Drake and said, "Can I ask you something?"

Her head slowly turned, her teeth nipping the fatter of her two lips as she faced me. "Of course."

"What really brought you back to Boston?"

I'd tried and couldn't piece it together.

I needed to know why she'd given up such a successful career at Faceframe. Was it to be a larger fish in a smaller pond? To make her own mark on a company that wasn't as well known as the social giant she'd once worked for?

Or was the reason much more personal?

Her head fell back just enough that she was able to gaze at the ceiling, revealing the column of her neck, the way her throat sank down, the cords that led to her chin. Simple movements that she made look so stunning. "I told you during my interview that my mom died. The honest answer is, I just wanted to feel closer to her. Boston was her place. I was quick to leave it. But as time went on, I realized how much I missed this city." She held the wine against her chest, her gaze now fixed on mine. "There's literally nothing better than sitting in the Green Monster during a Sox game. Or walking down Newbury Street after a few mimosas. Or shopping for ridiculously overpriced shoes in the Pru."

I smiled. "I've purchased shoes all over the world. No one has quite the inventory of the Pru."

She laughed, resting her hand on my arm for just a moment, knowing my response was full of shit.

The moment passed too quickly, and her fingers were gone.

"I love it here. I can't help it."

I took a look around the bar, at the framed memorabilia on the walls, the TV playing a Sox game, and listened to the chatter filled with our famous accent. "I do too."

"Besides, my bestie lives here. She's all the family I have, and it feels good to be close to her again."

I didn't want to ask.

But I did.

"There's no dad?"

She slid the thin, fragile, gold-woven bracelet around her wrist. "Who needs a dad when you have the best mom ever?"

"You couldn't be more right about that." I pointed at my eyebrow, the tiny scar that sat above it. "That's what my dad gave me."

Her eyes widened. "You mean, he hit you—"

"No." I shook my head, laughing. "Nothing like that. I just happened to be a really chubby baby, and I was wiggling like crazy. I fell out of his arms and hit my head on the high chair."

She covered her mouth, giggling as she said, "Oh my God."

That laugh.

That smile that lit up her face.

Fuck me, she was beautiful.

When she finally quieted, she said, "Tell me about some of the things you guys do around here. It's been so long since I've lived on the East Coast, I forget." She took a sip of her wine and set the glass on the table.

"The guys and I are into outdoorsy things. In the winter, we go skiing almost every weekend—Maine, Vermont, anywhere we can get to fast, and then we add in a few trips to Colorado, Utah, and Montana. The summer we spend mountain biking. Hiking. Wakeboarding. Camping. Finding a beach and parking my ass in front of the ocean."

Her brows pushed together. "You camp?"

"Sure." I tilted my head. "That surprises you?"

Her hand returned to my arm, this time my bicep. "Honestly . . . yes."

"Why?"

"You have to promise me you won't take this the wrong way, okay?"

"For the record, nothing good ever leads to a conversation that starts that way." I winked. "Go on."

Her teeth scraped across her lip. "I just assumed you were more of the bougie type. A private jet, a penthouse in the Back Bay, your own personal chef, a driver. I can't envision you spending a weekend in a tent in the middle of the woods without a toilet in sight."

I shook the ice around in my glass. "All right, all right. You've got a point. But what if I'm a little of both?"

"That still surprises me."

I had this burning desire to tell her more about myself.

And with that emotion came another.

It didn't feel as though I were talking to a colleague or even an acquaintance. It felt like I was talking to an old friend.

Someone who had already seen hints of my foundation.

Someone who had already peeked beneath the button-down and jeans I had on.

Regardless, there was no way she could know any of this, so I wanted her to understand. I wanted her to hear it from my mouth.

Even though I didn't know why.

"I'm the youngest of three with two older sisters," I told her. "My parents couldn't afford to put us all in summer camp, so the five of us would go camping on the weekends. Even now, there's something to be said for stripping away every amenity and sleeping under the stars." I held the back of my neck, rubbing the muscles that suddenly felt tight.

"I've gone on trips where the tents have bathrooms, and I've slept in a sleeping bag outside in the woods." I grinned. "I'm trying to earn the title of Mr. Versatile. How'd I do?"

"I'd say you succeeded." She shifted around in her seat, our knees briefly grazing, a heat instantly soaring through my body. "I'm sort of embarrassed now to admit that I've never been."

"For any particular reason?"

She shrugged, breaking eye contact. "Mom appreciated bathrooms. Then came college and work and California, and the opportunity never presented itself. Traveling, yes. Camping"—she shook her head—"no."

"I think you'd like it."

A hint of a smile crept over her mouth. "What would give you that impression?"

My gaze wandered over her as I exhaled. "Think of what it would feel like to be in a place that has no cell service. Where you're completely unreachable. I can imagine that type of break would rejuvenate someone who works as hard as you."

"And here I thought you were going to tell me that I'm the type who can really rock a long weekend of using dry shampoo."

I chuckled. "That too."

"Thank you for both compliments." Her eyes lightened in a way I hadn't seen before. "So let me ask this"—she leaned a little bit closer to me—"you're cozy in front of the campfire. The beer, wine, whatever, is going down like water. At some point, it's time for bed and you're all comfy in your sleeping bag until the urge to pee wakes you out of a dead sleep. You tiptoe out of the tent and there's mama bear checking out the s'mores you made a few hours before. What then?"

Damn it.

The sexiest woman alive was showing me her adorable side, and I was eating it up.

"Let me make sure I understand the real question here. Are you asking where you would go pee in the middle of the night or what you'd do about the bear?"

She laughed. "I can't believe I'm going to say this—or that I even brought this up, it's the wine's fault, I swear—but both."

I wanted so badly to move the hair that was now sticking to her glossy lip, but touching her, getting too near, wouldn't help me fight the urge I was already battling.

"For starters, there's bear spray. You don't go camping without it. It'll deter the bear if it's used correctly, and in most cases, they'll back off." I took a long drink. "As for the peeing, that's definitely a little trickier for women, but I've dug some pretty elaborate holes for Belle—that's Holden's daughter—and she's managed just fine."

"You take her camping?"

"We take her everywhere."

"Oh yeah?" She glanced at her left and then her right. "I bet she's quite the woman magnet at the bar."

"Well, mostly everywhere," I corrected. "But she's always a crowd-pleaser." I reached into my pocket to take out my phone, tapping the screen to pull up my photos. I enlarged the one I'd taken on our recent ice cream date and handed her my cell.

"Look at her little purple glasses and those curls and the dimple in just her one cheek." She gave the phone back. "Okay, I'm officially melting, she's the most precious little girl I've ever seen." She paused. "And I love that you're the proud uncle."

I hadn't called Belle my niece out loud—Drake had come up with that on her own.

She was listening.

Processing.

Fuck, I liked that.

She took a few sips of wine and said, "I'm curious. Do you see me as the bougie type?"

"No." I crossed my legs. "I think you're the type of woman who would be down for trying anything once, especially if it involves a challenge, like camping. I don't see you being competitive with other people. Rather, I see you as someone who competes with herself."

She turned her head, looking at me now from the corner of her eye. "Interesting."

"You're a leader when it comes to your professional life, Drake, but in your personal time you're more of a go-with-the-flow type. Someone who would prefer showing up than making the plans . . . as long as it involves a bathroom and running water."

Her laugh was even lighter this time. "It's fascinating to hear your take on me when you've only known me for two weeks."

I held the glass near my lips, staring at her, taking her in. "I don't know why, but it feels like I've known you for much longer than that."

CHAPTER EIGHTEEN

Drake

Since the bar was too loud to have this conversation, I carried my phone outside, holding it to my ear while I waited for Saara to pick up. "Don't kill me," I said once she answered.

"You're not going to make it, are you?"

Two hours ago, when I'd first arrived here, she'd texted that she had returned early from her business trip and wanted to have me over for dinner. I'd agreed, never thinking I'd spend more than a couple of hours at the bar. But after some wine and lots of conversation, I wasn't ready to leave.

"I'm so sorry, Saara."

"Don't be, babe. You're bonding with your coworkers, and that's exactly what I want to happen. We'll meet up tomorrow night, it's no biggie at all."

I could envision the warmth on her face as she said that, her sapphire eyes staring back at me, the flash of her hot-pink nails before she grabbed my hand to squeeze it.

"Thank you for being the bestest."

She laughed. "Someone's on her third glass of wine."

I pushed my back against the exterior of the building, relieved to hear she wasn't upset. "You can tell?"

"I know you better than you know yourself. So, yes, I can tell, and also, keep drinking and have as much fun as possible. And, girl, that's an order."

I bent my knee, pressing my heel against the wall. "But getting slurry with my coworkers on our first outing is not an option. I'm done after this glass."

"I'm sure they're feeling as tipsy as you, so don't feel bad about it. Keep chugging."

"You're a bad influence."

"The worst, I know." There was movement in the background, followed by the sound of her swallowing, and then she said, "Just poured my first glass. See, you inspired me. Hey, is Mr. Hottie there?"

I rubbed my thumb over my lip, chewing the corner of my nail. "Yes."

"And?"

Mr. Hottie had been a main topic of every conversation I had with Saara since my interview. In fact, one of her favorite things to do was bring him up. Most of the time, I would brush it off, acting aloof and changing the subject. There was nothing to discuss, nothing for her to dwell on.

What I hadn't told her was that I'd looked up Easton on social media and checked out his pictures on Instagram. It took only a few months' worth of photos to learn more about him, how much he enjoyed traveling and going out to eat, spending time with his family and friends. The shots also confirmed that he was as outdoorsy as he'd said earlier tonight. I didn't think there was a sport missing from his collection of photographs.

"And . . ." I glanced across the street at our office building, the moon reflecting off the mirrored windows of the giant high-rise. "We talked tonight at the bar."

"I need more."

"And I learned more about him."

"Why aren't you giving me any juicy details and instead acting all, *We talked about the current drought New England is experiencing and our love for French macarons.*" Her voice had lowered, mimicking an old, distinguished gentleman. "Come on, babe, we both know you went deeper than that."

I laughed. "We just talked and sorta eyed each other up. I found myself grabbing his arm way too many times." I thought about his lips. His eyes. Scanning my memory, flipping through all the people I'd met during my career. "I don't know, there's just something about him that makes me keep reaching for him."

"Keep reaching. I have this gut feeling that he's a good guy."

"Ignore your gut." I rubbed the back of my head against the brick behind me. "He's my boss, Saara. He stays in that category."

"Let's not forget I once dated my boss, and even though it didn't work out, it was one of the best experiences ever."

My head tilted and I blinked hard. "*Ummm*, you had to get a new job."

"Not because of him, girl. The company got bought out and we ended up going our separate ways when he relocated to the new head-quarters, and I took a position elsewhere. But those sixish months we were together . . . whoa, they were hot. Boss sex might be my fave."

"You're not helping the situation," I told her.

"Drake, Easton is hot—let's focus on that."

"And he's also anticommitment."

She sighed. "How do you know that?"

"Hello, must I keep reminding you that he cofounded Hooked? His Instagram doesn't show one photo of a woman who isn't related to him, and I've found zero pics online where he's brought a date to any public event or gala."

"Busted." She giggled. "So, you have been snooping on him, huh?"

I groaned. "Stop it."

"Well, it's the truth. You dug because you're interested, and you're interested because he's making you all hot and bothered, and you're hot and bothered because all the pics I've seen of him—oh yes, bestie, I've googled—makes him a total smoke show."

I blinked hard, keeping my eyes squeezed shut. "I may have taken a peek at his accounts, but that's it, it ends there, there's no reason to read into any of this."

"Mm-hmm."

My eyes flicked open. "I'm serious, Saara."

"You know what I'm serious about? My best friend putting herself first, and if that means grabbing that man at the bar and laying one on him, then do it. Don't hold back. The unimportant things, like what will happen after or your rule about workplace dating or if he's ready for monogamy, will all get figured out. Don't stress about them."

I pushed my hair away from my face. "You do realize those are huge items, right? Things I can't really see past?"

"*Shhh.* Go enjoy your time with the hottie. We'll talk tomorrow, when you bring over a pint of ice cream because I'm pretty sure I'm going to inhale my last pint while I take a bath."

"Love you, Saara."

"Love you more."

I slipped my phone into my purse and walked back into the bar, catching a glimpse of our table and how everyone was congregated around it. Drinks were in their hands. Conversation flowed from their lips. My focus shifted to Easton, the way he was laughing at something the head of finance said, his hand combing the scruff on both sides of his mouth.

That man.

He made even the smallest gesture look so incredibly sexy.

And once again, my body was failing me.

Tingling.

Bursting.

Aching.

Before he noticed me gawking, I decided to make a stop at the restroom, turning my back to the group and heading to the other side of the bar. Once I found my way into a stall, I played the hover dance, balancing over the toilet to make sure nothing fell or touched until I was safely at the sink washing my hands.

I was just adding soap when I caught a glimpse of myself in the mirror. I definitely had the buzzed look going on—flushed cheeks, eyes wide and observant. A smile that wouldn't leave my lips. Movements that were slightly overexaggerated. The little makeup I'd worn was long gone, and the collar of my sweater had fallen dangerously low down my arm, showing my entire shoulder.

Easton's eyes had wandered there a few times throughout the night.

Easton . . . my boss.

Someone I shouldn't be so personable and forthcoming with. Someone I shouldn't be staring at from across the bar. Someone who shouldn't be in my head at all.

But from the moment we had arrived here, I'd felt his gaze.

And even though I'd found myself in other conversations tonight, some with Holden and Grayson, the heads of HR and accounting, during those chats, I'd still caught tiny glimpses of Easton's delicious lips and the way they parted to sip his drink. The way his fingers traced the top of his glass made me wonder how his hands would feel on my body.

I couldn't stop my mind from strolling through the possibilities.

I couldn't stop fantasizing.

But . . . I needed to stop.

I needed to concentrate on the now, and that was fixing how frazzled the day had made me look. I ran my hands through my hair and adjusted my sweater, adding a quick swipe of gloss from a tube in my bag. I turned away from the sink, and just as I was walking toward the door, it opened.

The sight caused my feet to immediately halt.

That mouth. Those eyes. That haunting grin.

Oh God.

He looked so beautiful, I could barely breathe.

But why was Easton in the ladies' room?

Had he come in to look for me?

I tried to ignore the smile playing across his lips when I asked, "What are you doing in here?"

He stopped only feet away. "I should be asking you that question."

"Me?"

He nodded toward the left, causing me to look in that direction, where I noticed a row of urinals. "You're in the men's room."

"I'm . . . *what?*"

I turned in a circle, checking out the small space. Dumbfounded. Blinking repeatedly to make sure he wasn't joking with me and that my eyes weren't playing tricks. But each time my lids opened, every detail inside this room only proved that he was right. "Oh my God, Easton." I slapped my hand over my mouth. "I swear, I thought this was the women's restroom. I'm such an idiot."

"You're not an idiot. It's an easy mistake to make."

The intensity from his eyes, the way they bored through me, made me start to sweat.

"How humiliating." I took a side step. "I'll go so you can . . . you know."

"You don't have to go."

A set of words that caught me off guard, that stilled my feet. "Why would I stay?"

"Maybe you're not done."

I thought about his question.

Was I . . . *done?*

The butterflies in my stomach mixed with a bit of nervous energy would have me ordering another glass of wine as soon as I returned to the table.

My fourth.

I knew that would be a mistake. It was best that I head home, where I wouldn't say something stupid, where I wouldn't regret anything in the morning.

"No, I'm . . ." I glanced away, the sight of him becoming too much. "I'm going to go home, I think."

"Now?"

I nodded.

His movement caused me to look at him again, seeing that he was checking the time on his watch. "It's too late for you to walk home alone. I'll order you a car."

I laughed. "That's sweet, but I only live three blocks from here."

"Then I'm walking you home."

"Easton, no—"

"Then you're staying." He smiled. "Which are you going to choose, Drake?"

I filled my lungs, debating the lesser of two evils. "Home it is."

He went to the door, holding it open for me, his voice extremely gritty when he said, "After you."

CHAPTER NINETEEN

Easton

I was hoping the chilly air and the fact that I was wearing short sleeves would be such a slap to my skin that my erection would die down the second Drake and I stepped outside the bar. But once we did, my hand went to her lower back, ensuring she didn't trip over the curb, and I was suddenly even harder.

Fuck.

I knew I was being overly protective by walking her home. This was Boston, a city that never slept; she certainly wouldn't be alone on the sidewalk, unchaperoned during her short commute. Not to mention, the Back Bay was one of the safest parts of town, almost guaranteeing me she'd be just fine.

That wasn't the point.

The point was, she wasn't leaving unless my eyes were on her.

And that just so happened to score us more time together.

"I think you'll see a few of the team members trickle in a little late tomorrow," I said as we made our way to the end of the block. "Don't feel like you have to rush in. We're not sticklers when it comes to arrival and departure times. Work from home, at the office—wherever, as long as the work gets done."

"I'm an early bird. I'll be up anyway."

"Oh yeah?"

She attempted to slide up the neck of her sweater, covering her bare shoulder for just a moment before it fell back down again. "I used to go into Faceframe around five."

"Shit, that is early."

"I'm nuts, right?" She laughed, and *damn it*, I loved that sound. "But yes, I liked to get there before my team, so I could actually get work done."

"That's admirable."

"And certifiably loco, I know." She glanced at me as we reached the stop sign and smiled. "Why do I feel like you live around here too?"

I raised my arm and pointed at the high-rise on the next block. "Right there."

Her eyes moved across my chest and arm, slowly following my finger. "You're kidding?"

"No . . . why?"

"That's where my bestie lives. Her apartment is on the fourth floor."

"Then your bestie has good taste in buildings."

We made our way past the crosswalk, her bare shoulder rubbing against my arm as she neared to avoid a crowd of people. We stayed that way for a few paces, until we got closer to the curb, where she added space between us.

"I'm assuming you have a penthouse?" she asked.

"I bought it three years ago. Three months after I went into escrow, Grayson purchased the penthouse right next to mine."

"Best friends, partners, and neighbors. Do you ever get sick of each other?"

I chuckled. "It hasn't happened yet, but give it time—we're only thirty."

"You know, we're also neighbors." She nodded toward the upcoming street, where a building stood at the beginning of the block. "That's me right there."

I liked the idea that she lived so close to me.

What I didn't like was that this walk would be over in a few minutes.

But I just wanted to keep her talking.

I just wanted to know more.

"How's your apartment?" I inquired.

"I love it. As soon as my lease ends, I'm hoping to buy one in the same building."

"You really do want to stay in Boston."

She rubbed the sleeve of her sweater, like she was trying to warm herself up, the wind making the chilly air even colder. "I suddenly feel . . . married to this town. So why waste money on rent when I can afford to buy."

Married.

A word that hit me and ricocheted in my chest.

"That's an impressive decision," I told her.

It certainly wasn't every day that a twenty-eight-year-old—an equation I'd done during her interview—could afford a condo in this city, never mind this particular area, especially without help from their parents.

Support like that was something Drake didn't have.

But her salary was quite substantial, and based on the negotiations we'd had several weeks ago, I knew she had done just as well at Faceframe. What that also told me was that she was extremely smart with her money, a quality I found sexy as hell.

"You know, the crew enjoyed getting to know you a little more tonight," I said. "It's too bad they're not as lucky as me and they didn't get to catch you in the men's room."

"Lucky?" She smiled, a redness moving across her cheeks. "More like embarrassing as hell."

"The incident itself, maybe, but the irony of it—yes, that does make me lucky."

She stopped at the next block and turned toward me. "I don't understand."

I couldn't blame the vodka.

I'd had only one glass, and it would take at least two more before I felt a buzz.

This was me.

Wanting.

Needing.

Desiring.

"Listen, if I'm going to walk into a men's restroom and see a woman standing there, I'm just saying, I would want it to be you."

She searched my eyes while she gnawed away on that beautiful bottom lip.

"Have I confused you, Drake? Or have I made you speechless?"

She mashed her lips together. "Both."

"Are you really that surprised? I'm positive you've felt my eyes on you long before tonight." I glanced at her building, estimating that we were about twenty yards away. "Honestly, I've thought about doing this since your interview."

"Doing . . . what?"

"Kissing you." Since I was much taller, I gazed down, holding her cheek to point her face up at me, and I swiped the lip she had been chewing.

Her gloss stuck to my skin, but that didn't stop me from doing it again.

And then again.

"I don't know why, but I can't get you out of my head. I've tried. Fuck me, I've tried." That gorgeous mouth on mine was everything I wanted, but I wouldn't ravish those lips until I knew it was all right. "Drake, tell me it's all right to kiss you."

I waited for her response. A movement, confirmation—anything. But she was frozen, staring into my eyes until I finally heard, "Yes. It's all right."

I dipped in closer, but not toward her mouth. I stayed near her neck, pausing, whispering, "Coconut. I've been . . . dreaming about this scent."

This spot, the nearness—she was setting my body on fire.

The flames licked up my fingers as I gripped her tighter, dragging my nose up her throat on my way to her jaw. I stayed there, breathing, knowing my exhales were rushing across her face. And when I finally lifted, my lips hovered above hers for just a second longer before I closed the distance between us. I fucking moaned the second our lips touched and again when my tongue collided with hers.

A taste that must have been in one of my fantasies because I remembered it.

And as I took in more, it was like returning home.

Since we were at the start of the crosswalk, blocking anyone who wanted to get by, I wrapped my arms around her waist and lifted her into the air, holding her against my body as I carried her to the building behind us.

I didn't stop kissing her, even when I set her down. We stayed locked, breathless, our lips tangled, our tongues exploring, my arms above her head, caging her in. "Drake . . ."

It wasn't a question.

It was a reaction.

A feeling I had to release before my palms traveled down her sides, taking in those incredible curves, the arches of her body that I wanted to ravage. My cock craved to be inside her as I rounded her rib cage and lowered to her navel, each section as seductive and enticing as the one before.

And with each spot I discovered, I kissed her harder.

Deeper.

I gave her more of my tongue.

What that eventually earned me was her touch, first on my stomach, where those small, delicate fingers slid across my abs. She took her time, getting well acquainted before she rose to my arms and shoulders, gradually cupping my face.

That was where she halted.

Where her hands began to study me as though my scruff were whispering every one of my secrets to her.

I closed my arms around her, our bodies flush, until I pulled my mouth away. "If I don't stop, I'm going to carry you inside your building and . . . never leave." I licked her off my lips. "Unless you want that too?"

She dabbed her mouth like she was drying it, even though it wasn't wet, her eyes widening at the same time, her chest panting. "I . . . should go."

Her stare told me otherwise.

It showed me an emotional struggle.

A fight.

A worry that was also settling into me, the weight of it heavier than I anticipated.

Her chest rose, her throat bouncing as she swallowed. "Easton . . ."

"I know," I whispered. "And I know I'm your boss and I know everything you're feeling right now."

But I didn't want one of those feelings to be regret.

What I wanted instead was for her to think of only our kiss, so I gave her another. Softer this time. Less needy. Healing her mouth after I'd just roughed it up.

When I released her, I stepped back until she was too far to hold, my hands dropping to my sides. "Go." I took in that stunning body one more time. "I'll see you in the morning."

She still rubbed her fingers over her lips as she walked away from the building and headed for the crosswalk, waiting for the signal before she went across the street and disappeared into her high-rise.

Once the door closed, I decided not to return to the bar, where I assumed the guys were still hanging out. I went to my condo, pouring myself a scotch as soon as I got through the door.

I stood in my living room, staring out the floor-to-ceiling windows, taking in the view of the city, hoping the liquor would tame this hard-on. But I finished the glass and a stiff second pour, and my cock continued to fucking ache.

For her.

I carried my glass into the bathroom and stripped off my clothes, leaving them in a pile on the floor. I turned on the shower, and the multiple streams of water that came from the ceiling and the back wall, even a few from the floor, caused the glass to steam.

I stepped inside, set my drink on one of the shelves, and squirted some soap into my hand, rubbing it over my shaft. My other hand pressed against the wall in front of me, reminding me of the way I'd caged Drake tonight, the look on her face while I stared down at her.

My head tilted back, my eyes closed, and a growl erupted in my throat as I began to stroke my dick, the sensation taking hold of me.

I didn't need to search for an image to beat off to.

They were already there.

The way Drake's hips had swung as she'd walked away from me, the way her sweater had lifted in the back, just enough to show me that perfect, heart-shaped ass. The way her scent had gripped me, swallowing me in a cloud of coconut.

Shit, this felt fucking good.

It would feel even better if I were brushing my tip around her clit, teasing her, spreading her wetness.

The last time I'd been this drawn to a woman, I had ended up fucking wrecked. That feeling, that memory—both should be strong enough to make these thoughts of Drake completely dissolve from my head.

But even if I was uncertain about where this could go, I couldn't dismiss how I was feeling about her.

It was too strong.

I tightened my grip as though I were entering her, and I pumped to my base, then circled my crown.

I wanted our bodies aligned again, goose bumps rising across her flesh, following each of my kisses, her nipples puckered as I breathed over them.

Licked them.

Bit them.

How her clit would harden as I pressed my nose against it, inhaling her before I gave her my tongue. But once I did, I wanted to take my time. I wanted to cover myself in her scent. I wanted to live in that intimate spot, relishing in her.

Slowly giving her a finger, and then a second one.

My hand pushed into the slick shower wall as my speed increased, my balls starting to tighten, the memory of her smile at the forefront of my mind. The sound of her laughter. The way she had tasted when our lips touched.

That . . . familiar kiss.

"Ahhh," I moaned as the wave soared through me. The tingles exploded. My hips rocked forward as I aimed toward the drain and shot my first stream. "Fuck me." I twisted as I stroked, driving my palm across my length, draining every drop of cum onto the shower floor. "Mmm."

As I emptied my sack, I shook my wet hair under the water and caught my breath.

Jesus fuck, what has this woman done to me?

The scalding water banged my chest and stomach, but I didn't move. I wanted the heat to burn me. I wanted it to give me clarity.

I wanted to make sense of these feelings.

Emotions.

The agonizing awareness that something was there, and I just couldn't grasp it.

Tonight wasn't a mistake; I knew that much.

What I didn't know was how Drake was feeling. How she was processing what had happened. What result she was coming up with.

This was only her second week at Hooked.

Before she closed her eyes for the night, I wanted to give her reassurance.

I wanted her to go to bed without worrying where my head was at.

I stepped out of the shower, found my phone in the pocket of my pants, and located the number that I'd saved—we all had—since her first day of employment.

Me: I can't stop thinking about that kiss . . .

CHAPTER TWENTY

Drake

The elevator wouldn't move any faster. I slammed my finger against the button to my floor repeatedly, as though each hit would force the speed to double.

But it didn't.

As the lift rose, the pace was more like a crawl, and I wished, just in this moment, that I'd leased an apartment on a lower level—anything that would get me home quicker.

Because . . .

That taste.

That feel.

That . . . mouth.

My other hand brushed my lips, back and forth, as though I were memorizing the texture of my skin. But instead, with each wipe, memories were exploding in my head.

I'd studied two weeks' worth of data—expressions, gestures, scents—and the results were so apparent after tonight, especially once he'd pointed toward his building and I'd caught a glimpse of his tattoo.

The one on the inside of his bicep.

The one that confirmed every other sign I'd witnessed.

And felt.

I no longer had to test.

To analyze.

I knew.

And I'd been staring at the answer the whole time.

I didn't know why I hadn't seen it, why I'd refused to see it.

Or, maybe, why I didn't want to believe it.

I just needed one more layer of confirmation and—*oh God*, I didn't know what would happen then. What truth I would be facing at that point.

But first, I needed to get to my computer.

Finally, I reached my floor, the elevator door just starting to slide open when I squeezed through the tiny crack, running down the hall and waving my fob in front of the reader beside the door. Once I was inside, I rushed into my office and shook the mouse to awaken my monitors, typing my credentials into Hooked's system.

The database of all users.

I sucked in the deepest breath as I entered BostonLifer into the search bar. The system took less than a second to provide the user's information.

Name.

Address.

Billing date.

All the data we collected and stored on members who were both active and inactive but had exceeded their thirty-day trial period and become full members.

Something I'd never done. I'd quit before I had to provide any personal information.

But BostonLifer had provided that data.

My cursor flashed next to his name at the top of his user profile.

Easton Jones.

My hand slapped over my mouth, my lungs now barely able to fill.

Was this a surprise?

I didn't know.

But I knew I'd felt something.

Those eyes.

Those lips.

I couldn't place them—or maybe I could and just didn't want to. I didn't believe that a coincidence like that, so real, raw, heavy, could really happen.

But it had and the reality was gazing back at me.

And now, after tonight, following a kiss so passionate my body ached, a whole new feeling was pounding through my chest.

What am I going to do?

I couldn't sort these feelings. They were too messy. Too muddled. So I pulled my phone out of my back pocket, ignoring everything on the screen as I searched for Saara's number and called her.

She answered with, "Why aren't you making out with Mr. Hottie right now—"

"Saara . . ."

Silence ticked.

And then: "Oh fuck, babe. What's wrong?"

I continued to stare at my monitor, my heart leaping, trying to break through my chest, each beat hitting the back of my throat. "I knew." I swallowed. "I think I felt it—I don't know."

"What are you talking about?"

I shook my head, but the name on the screen didn't change. "First, I saw his tattoo and it clicked, but it didn't, you know? And then he kissed me, and the second our lips touched, I was positive. I tasted it. Smelled it—that spicy scent. And once his hands gripped me, I was taken right back to that moment."

"Slow down, start from the beginning. You're not making any sense."

"Easton . . ." I walked away from my computer; I couldn't look at it a second longer. "He's Mr. Boston, you know, BostonLifer from Hooked. The guy I fell for all those years ago."

"Shut the fuck up! No!"

I went into the kitchen and found a bottle of white in the fridge, removed the cork, and took a long drink.

I didn't need a glass. I needed wine inside my body as quickly as possible.

"I wish I was kidding," I whispered, wiping my lips. "Or maybe I don't—Jesus, I don't know anything anymore."

"Okay, okay. Let's think this through."

This was why I'd called her. She would know what to do, how to move these pieces together, since everything was sticky and edgeless in my head.

I carried the wine to the couch. "Okay," I repeated, using her word because I couldn't come up with my own.

"You and Mr. Boston had something before you moved to Palo Alto and you were semi-obsessed with him, but the timing was all wrong and you were dealing with oodles of Mom grief and things died out."

"I don't know if I can describe it exactly that way, but yes, things ended."

"And then you took the job at Hooked and Mr. Hottie immediately gave you attention, almost from the moment you began working there. Things have built over the past two weeks, and tonight, the first time you've all gone out, he kisses you."

"Yes."

"That means he likes you, Drake, hello."

I brought the wine back to my mouth and guzzled, stopping to say, "I'm not sure that even matters."

"Why?"

"Because things didn't end so pretty between us. I did a lot of wrong there, and Easton is my boss at a job that I absolutely love—and please, for the love of God, don't compare my boss to your ex. The situations are completely different now."

"I won't, but it doesn't seem to bother Easton that he's your boss, am I right?"

I set the bottle on the table, sinking lower into the couch. "What are you saying, Saara?"

"I'm saying you have to tell him."

My chest tightened. My hand shook as I gripped the phone against my face. "What the hell do I say? 'Oh, *hiiii*, I'm SaarasLove, and this is just a giant coincidence. How's life been for the past five years and change? Yes, I'm the one you banged in the stairwell while we were both masked. And now I'm back in your life as a director at your company— oh, you want me to do your international launch even though I know you have the biggest dick I've ever seen in my life? Awesome, let's get that done.' *Suuure.*"

She laughed. "I love you so much."

"I'm freaking out, Saara."

"We'll get this sorted out. I promise. But, first, you have to tell Easton who you are. He obviously hasn't figured it out or he would have said something to you. Therefore, you need to be the one."

"Of course he hasn't figured it out. He's a boy, they don't pick up on detail like we do, and you insisted on setting up my profile and giving me SaarasLove, which at the time was kinda cute, but now I'm realizing it was a horribly bad decision. If you had gone with Drake-something, it would have been much more obvious."

"An obvious username wouldn't have helped either—you'd still be in the same position, you two just would have realized the truth a little faster."

She had a point.

"What the hell am I going to say to him?" I asked.

"Again, we'll work out those details when the time comes. But we can't do that unless you reach out to him and set up a time to talk."

She was right, but that didn't make this any easier.

And since I was out of words again, I mumbled, "Okay."

"This is going to be fine. I assure you. In fact, I'd bet everything I own that it's going to work out."

"Work out? Work out how?" I picked up the bottle of wine and held it near my lips. "I had feelings and then I took off and then I came back to Boston and now there's Easton and there are new feelings, but those feelings are really old feelings—"

"Take a deep breath."

I held the phone with my shoulder and pressed my palm against my chest to calm what was happening inside. "I'm just going to drink all the wine."

"I'm in love with that plan. Do you need me to have more delivered? Or are you well stocked?"

I glanced toward the rack in my kitchen. "I have plenty."

"Good. I'm going to call you when I wake up tomorrow, after you've slept on this, and we'll come up with a plan. But if you want to reach out to Easton in the meantime and set up a date, do it."

I agreed to talk to her in the morning and hung up, my thumb scrolling across the notifications that I hadn't looked at before I'd called her, pausing when I came across a text.

Easton: I can't stop thinking about that kiss . . .

Was that because my lips were just as familiar to him?

Because the moment that had just happened between us was indescribably perfect?

You have to tell him.

But scheduling a meeting just didn't sit right with me.

Still holding my phone, I swiped through several pages' worth of apps before I came across Hooked, an interface I was all too friendly with for many reasons. Because it had been so long, the system required me to log on again, my username and password already saved.

From there, I was promoted to start a membership or, since more than a year had passed from logging on, do another thirty-day trial, which wouldn't collect any of my personal information.

I chose the latter, and I went to my profile and found my last conversation with BostonLifer.

SaarasLove: Hey stranger, I'm back in Boston. Just wondering if you want to meet up for a drink.

CHAPTER TWENTY-ONE

Easton

As I sat at my desk, my head a fucking hurricane of thoughts, a chime came through my phone. It was that double ring, the same notification I'd set up all those years ago that would alert me when Love was live on the app. The first time I'd heard that sound was last night, shortly after I'd gotten out of the shower. Seconds later, there was a message in my inbox.

From her.

She told me she wanted to meet up for a drink.

I didn't know what to say. How to react. If I should even respond. More than five years had passed, and even though our communication had dwindled during those last few months, she was the one who had ultimately cut it off.

The sound going off now was to tell me she was online again.

And as I clicked on the app, there was a tiny green circle next to SaarasLove's username.

She was back.

Maybe for good.

Maybe just visiting.

But she was here, in the same city, and she wanted to see me.

Something I'd rejected in the early hours of the morning, after I'd drained several more glasses of scotch.

Even if it was just a quick meetup, a drink and possibly some closure, I wasn't interested. What happened, what we were, didn't matter, and I wasn't going to waste a second to figure any of it out.

A second notification filled my screen, this time with a message.

SaarasLove: Please, Mr. Boston, I just want to talk. Nothing more, I promise.

Another message popped up right underneath it, giving me a place and a time she wanted to meet tomorrow night. I set my phone on the desk, staring at the green dot until it disappeared.

I didn't have to look in the system, checking to see whether she had become a member or reactivated her trial membership. I'd done that last night. I already knew I had no access to her personal information.

That alone made me want to change the way Hooked collected data for trial memberships. I didn't give a fuck if they canceled before the thirty days were over. I wanted to know who they were.

I wanted to know her name.

I wanted just a tiny bit of information that would give me a clue as to who this woman was and why things had gone so wrong.

But Love owned only part of my thoughts.

The other half, the more dominant side, was Drake.

Not a single thing in my office—not my email, my ringing office line, not even the knock on my door—could pull me out of the trance I was in as I replayed last night's kiss.

Watching it over and fucking over in my head.

Knowing she was only down the hall, in her office, was driving me mad.

I wanted to see her.

I wanted to be around her.

I wanted to smell her in the goddamn air.

I didn't know why, when I'd climbed into bed long after my shower, I ached so goddamn hard for a woman I barely knew. But inside, somewhere deep, it felt like we'd spent years together.

Like I'd already kissed those lips.

I'd already grabbed that waist.

I'd already inhaled that scent off her skin.

And all that did was increase my desire to have more.

What would she look like in the morning as she cozied up on my chest, her body freshly fucked from a night of orgasms?

What would she sound like as I trailed my lips down her stomach just as the sun peeked through my blinds?

What would she taste like if I spread her across my kitchen counter after we shared the breakfast I'd made her?

"You want to talk about it?" I suddenly heard.

Talk about it?

I glanced up and Grayson was standing halfway between the door and my desk.

I hadn't heard him come in. I hadn't even felt his eyes on me.

"You didn't answer my knock," he said. "I knew you were in here, but whatever I was going to talk to you about isn't nearly as important as what's on your mind right now."

"Why would you say that?"

"Easton, look at yourself."

I was gripping the strands of my freshly gelled hair, my lip raw from the way I was grinding my teeth across it.

I dropped my hands onto the desk and released my lip.

"Go on. Talk. You need it," he said, taking a seat in front of me.

I didn't want to tell him about Drake. Besides, there was nothing really to say. We'd kissed, nothing more. And even though he wasn't the lecturer—that was Holden—I didn't know where things were going to lead, so it was stupid to even mention it.

"Something strange as fuck happened last night," I said. "I got home from the bar and there was a message from Love. She's back in town . . . and wants to meet."

I didn't have to remind him of who Love was. Both guys knew. She'd been mentioned plenty over the last five-plus years.

"Did you respond?" he asked.

I took a breath. "Yeah, I told her I wasn't interested."

He stretched his arms up over his head, bending his elbows, and finally held the back of his head with his palms. "Now that's some shit." His stare intensified. "What the hell is wrong with you? For what reason would you say no?"

I refused to mention Drake.

This wasn't about her, anyway. This was about Love.

"Because what would be the point?" I asked him. "Things are good, man. I don't need that wound reopened."

"Who says you have to reopen it? Why not just fuck her?"

I exhaled, shaking my head. "I have no desire to do that either."

"You've earned yourself a VIP medal for how many women you've found on Hooked. You've moved on after each one. Treat Love the same as all of them—"

"But she isn't the same. She wasn't from the moment we started talking or the moment she forced us to stop talking."

He leaned forward, resting his arms on his knees. "You're still torn up about this, aren't you?"

"Not about what happened . . . shit, that's in the past. But her popping up like this, out of nowhere—yeah, it stirs some memories."

"Are you looking for advice?"

I folded my hands, covering the screen of my phone as the notification came through, alerting me that she was online again.

He nodded toward my phone. "Is that her?"

"Yeah."

He smiled as he stood from his chair and headed for the door, stalling once he reached it. "Remember, if you don't go, you'll regret it. For the rest of your life, you'll always wonder what she wanted to say to you."

"Maybe."

"No, I'm right." He opened my door and glanced down the hallway, his stare returning to me. "Want to go to the bar tonight and get utterly shit-faced?"

"Fuck yes."

"Good, then I'll see you later."

Once he was gone, I opened the text box I'd started last night, gazing at the words I'd sent Drake.

I didn't want to bombard her with attention. I didn't want to go into her office and tell her how gorgeous she looked. I wanted to give her just a little space until I knew how she was feeling about all this.

But that didn't mean I was going to back off entirely.

Me: Your door was closed when I came in this morning. You weren't kidding, you are an early riser. Figured you were nursing a wicked hangover and needed some space. That's why I didn't knock.

Drake: You should have seen me with my coffee. It was quite a scene.

Me: I've seen you with Diet Coke. I can only imagine.

Drake: Lololol.

Me: But a night that was well worth it.

Drake: You're right about that.

Me: If you have to take off early and nap, I promise I won't judge you.

Drake: If you saw what my day looks like, I think you'd feel bad for me.

Me: I think you should feel bad for me . . .

Drake: Why is that?

Me: Because I'm dying to walk into your office and lean across your desk and ravish your lips and it's taking every ounce of willpower I have not to.

Drake: We're at work. Down boy.

Me: Except the thought of you makes that extremely difficult.

Drake: I'm blushing.

CHAPTER TWENTY-TWO

Drake

I sat alone at the same table I'd shared with Saara just minutes ago. The chunky ice cube was melting into water at the bottom of my glass, each sip now only full of the lemon and rosemary that had garnished the Manhattan my best friend had ordered me, the liquor much stronger than a small pour of sauvignon blanc. Saara's hope was that it would whittle away my nerves, making the prickles in my body less blunt, but it hadn't worked. The thought of Easton and Mr. Boston still turned me into a nonstop-talking, jittery mess.

As did the—*oh God*—questions.

I didn't even know where to start with those or how to process them.

Or what to even think.

But my best friend had been very strategic with her departure, leaving less than a ten-minute window before Mr. Boston's arrival. A few minutes before eight o'clock, the door to the bar opened with force, a familiar face walking through the entrance, his eyes scanning the large space, unsure of who he was looking for.

I had told him I'd be in red.

Fitting, I thought.

I stood, balancing my purse on my shoulder, gripping the strap like it was rope, and walked toward him. With each step, I squeezed the leather even harder, urging my courage out of hiding, forcing my emotion to the forefront of my heart, where it needed to stay, at least until I got through this.

I wanted to stop a few feet away and catch my breath, an attempt to calm the flutters.

But I couldn't afford to take the time.

He was searching the crowd, looking for red, and it was only a matter of seconds before he landed on me.

I placed my hand on the back of his shoulder, whispering just loud enough that he would hear me over the noise. *"Hiii."*

His body froze, like he was registering my touch, my sound, my signature word, and he turned.

His expression was full of confusion as he took in my face. "Drake"—his stare deepened, intensified, quickly dipping down my body, silently acknowledging the color of my dress—"what are you doing here?"

"I asked you to come and I'm so relieved you finally agreed to." I waited for the courage to surface, but the nerves were there, digging away at me, relentlessly. "Easton . . ." I glanced down, unsure of how to proceed even though I'd rehearsed this. Even though I'd thought about this moment countless times over the years. But now, here, as he stood before me, everything seemed more difficult. "I'm SaarasLove."

The news hit his face, causing his eyes to widen, his lips to part. "You're . . . *her.*"

It wasn't a question.

It almost sounded like he was confirming the truth in his head, sliding each of the pieces into place, the puzzle either what he had suspected . . .

Or hadn't.

"Let's go sit and talk." My fingers dropped to his arm. "I already have a table."

He said nothing as he followed me across the room, returning to the spot where I'd met Saara earlier this evening, silently sitting as we took the chairs across from one another.

"Before you say anything," I started, "I want to explain—"

"I think I need a minute." He pushed his back against the chair, his posture more erect, staring as though I were a mile away and he was straining to keep sight of me.

And while I looked at him, I saw everything that was happening through his eyes.

The rewinding.

Recapping.

Replaying.

"It's you." His voice was barely audible. "I thought"—he shook his head, holding his forehead as he gazed at me—"I thought I was finally meeting her."

"You are."

His hand fell to the table, his fingers clenching into a fist. "I've constantly compared you two and I felt every similarity . . ." His voice had turned so soft and faded. "But it's you. It's been you this whole time. This doesn't make sense . . . I don't think . . . I don't know." His lips closed but immediately parted again. "Did you know? Is that why you came to work at Hooked? Did you hack in and figure out it was me—"

"No." I reached forward, clasping my hand over his. "Since the interview, something has been nagging at me. Your hands, your scent, your eyes. Your voice. I recognized them, but almost like they were from another life, another time."

"They were."

I spread my gloss across both lips even though it was already evened out, and I nodded. "It wasn't until I saw the tattoo on your arm and we kissed that I figured it out. Those lips"—I inhaled slowly—"once

145

they were on me, I knew. Your kiss is something I've never forgotten, Easton." I let that admission settle. "When I left you that night, I rushed up to my apartment and looked into the database, and what I already knew was confirmed."

"Do you know how badly I wanted to look you up in that database? For years that thought plagued me . . . I just wanted to find out who you are. And I couldn't, because you didn't exist in our system."

"I know." I pulled my hand back, my heart throbbing in my chest. "As nuts as this sounds, even though I wanted to tell you the next morning, I thought you needed to hear it from Love, not me. That's why I set this up. That's why we're here now."

Before either of us could say another word, the same waitress from earlier came to our table and asked me, "Would you like another Manhattan?"

"Yes, please," I told her.

"What can I get you?" she asked Easton.

"You don't drink liquor," he said to me.

I gripped my empty glass. "I do tonight."

"I don't know what I want," he replied to the waitress.

I handed her the tumbler and said, "He'll take one of these too. Thank you." I waited until she was gone before I said another word. "After five-plus years, I came back to Boston and accepted a job with Hooked—the same place, in a sense, where I met you—and then it turns out you were the guy I fell for back then, and in two weeks we reconnected just as strongly as we had before." I rubbed my thumb over the grooves in the table. "It's hard to believe that two people who are so different matched at one hundred percent and hit it off not once, but twice." I analyzed his stare, first his left eye and then his right. "What are the chances."

He took a deep breath. "I don't deny that—or any of this. But I can't stop thinking about then, the way you just disappeared, changed your number, and gave me no way to ever reach out to you again. Why?" He added, "I didn't deserve that."

"No"—I shook my head—"you didn't."

"Make me understand."

When I filled my lungs, I held the air inside.

"And another thing," he continued, "you moved to California—a location I now know about but didn't then—without so much as a heads-up. One day, you were asking me if I was married to Boston, and it felt like the next day you just up and left, saying something like if you ever made your way back, we'll meet up for drinks. But you never asked me how I felt about trying things out long-distance."

While he broke eye contact to look at his hands, I whispered, "Easton, you never asked me how I felt about long-distance either."

He glanced up at me again. "You're right. I just assumed it wasn't what you wanted."

"And maybe I assumed the same."

He was quiet for a moment. "The truth is, if it was up to me, I would have called you every night. I would have flown out to see you. I started to feel like things were getting very one-sided and if I didn't keep reaching out, things would have been silent between us. And then you changed your number, ending everything before we had a chance to even be something." He crossed his arms over the table. "You could have seen me before you left Boston, maybe that would have changed things. You also could have given me your new number. You just chose not to."

There was a knot wedged so tightly in the back of my throat, I wasn't sure if I could speak.

Fortunately, the waitress returned with our drinks, giving me a few seconds to get my thoughts straight and to take a sip, squeezing the coldness between my hands once I was done. "I want you to understand something, Easton. I only planned to spend thirty days on the app. Saara, my best friend, whose name probably sounds familiar, convinced me to join, and she set up my account, hence the username she picked. Thirty days, Easton—that was it."

"Jesus." He analyzed my eyes. "Why?"

"I had just lost my mother and I was an emotional wreck. I was drowning in grief and homework and work for Faceframe. Saara wanted me to have fun before I took off for Palo Alto, and she thought the app would ensure that. Some meaningless, uncommitted sex, exactly what Hooked was designed for, to get me out of my head and give me some emotional freedom. That's why I joined, to just give me a break from life. I never expected to find you or to have the feelings I had."

His brows rose. "But I made it clear how badly I wanted you, especially after the masquerade party. What happened? What changed?"

"Like I said, I was on the verge of finishing school, and at that point I'd already accepted a position with Faceframe, and they were having me travel all over the country. I was so young, I was only twenty-two years old, and I had an opportunity that I'd always dreamed of. Once Mom was gone, that became my focus. It was all I could see—but then there was you. And you made things messy in my head. You made me question if I wanted to leave, and that scared the shit out of me."

"So you ran."

"I shut down, and yes, I walked away." My voice softened. "But, Easton, I was already going anyway. My lease in California had been signed, I had a move date. Was I wondering if I was making the right choice? Of course, and that's why I asked you for advice. But really, at that point, my decision was made. I just followed through without laying all the details on the table and being completely honest with you. And that was wrong, I shouldn't have handled it that way. You didn't deserve it and I'm sorry." When he said nothing, I added, "I want you to know that, in my head, I saw the way we were going to end if things between us continued. With us on opposite sides of the country, our time together stretched so thin, and it would have crushed me. I didn't want to break . . . even more than I already was."

He was quiet for a moment, moving his drink around but not bringing it up to his lips. "I was all about you, Drake. You were the one I wanted. The one I was going to change for."

"And you were the one I wanted, and that was terrifying. One month of texting and phone conversations and I was considering backing out of the job at Faceframe, staying in Boston, and turning us into more. Or, on the flip side of that, asking a man whose name I didn't even know and whose face I hadn't ever seen to give up his marriage to Boston and move to the other side of the country with me." I reached for him again, needing his skin, desperate for him to understand. "Our circumstances were hard and tricky. I had no idea how to navigate any of it. I just knew that I didn't want to lose what I'd worked so hard for, so I pulled back. I put more than just miles between us."

"But to change your number? That, I don't get."

I sighed. That day, like so many others, had hurt.

"Faceframe gave me a company phone and there was no reason to maintain two lines, so I got rid of my personal one. Before I did that, every morning I would wake up and look to see if there was a text from you. I was battling the loss of my mom, and I couldn't even distinguish grief from happiness anymore. I was just moving, keeping busy, burying myself as deep as I could so I didn't have to think about that permanent hole in my chest." I stopped to breathe. "I could have reached out, of course, but again, I didn't trust myself. I didn't trust what I'd say to you, what I'd promise you, what I'd ultimately do if you asked me for more. I wasn't in the right headspace. So I thought if I disconnected, if I made it impossible for us to communicate, I would be able to move on."

"Did you?"

I shook my head. "Not even close."

Silence ticked between us, but his stare was as strong as ever.

It didn't just hit my face.

It penetrated far below my skin.

"I regret not being honest with you and not giving you my new number," I told him. "That's something I have to live with, not you."

His thumb went over my hand, sliding to the inside of my wrist, rubbing the letters tattooed there. "Your tiny tattoo," he whispered. "L. E. M."

"Lilly Elenore Madden. My mom."

"I always wondered and never asked." He was silent for several moments. "Drake, I understand the regret you felt, but why wasn't it strong enough for you to rejoin Hooked and find me?"

Those words hit hard.

Enough that I had to look away, sucking my lip into my mouth, chewing the end of it. "It wouldn't have changed the fact that I was in California, you were in Boston, and neither of us were bending on that."

More quiet passed between us until he said, "You owned my thoughts for so long. I think, in some way, I tried to forget every piece of you. The tone of your voice, the scent of your skin, the way you look at me—the same way you looked at me that night at the party. Maybe I should have figured it out, maybe I should have known the second I walked into the conference room, but I didn't." He released my hand and tilted away from the table, pushing up the sleeves of his thin sweater. "I just knew that there was something about you that was achingly familiar, whether you were someone I'd hooked up with in the past or sat beside during an international flight or shared a smile with on the sidewalk. In some way, you weren't new, and neither were my feelings, and those started up again the moment you interviewed." His focus shifted all across my face, and he slid his drink to the side so not a single piece of glass sat between us. "Drake, you came clean, you told me all of this for a reason. What is it?"

CHAPTER TWENTY-THREE

Easton

As I stared at Drake, waiting for her to reply, my mind reeled, recalling the conversations we'd had all those years ago. The long, in-depth chats. The banter. The chemistry.

The stairwell.

The phone sex.

Our connection had been thick from the start. That was why I had pushed so hard to see her again. I wanted to know what it would feel like to take the mask off and memorize her face.

To touch her again.

To kiss her without lace rimming her lips.

To confirm what I already knew: that Love was going to be the woman who changed me.

She'd just never given me that chance to prove it to her.

But now, all these years later, she came back into my life. The same woman who had me thinking about her day and night. The woman who mesmerized me with her brilliance.

Her charisma, passion.

Sexiness.

And incomprehensible beauty.

Did I know it was her? Fuck, that was something I didn't think I could ever answer, but now there was relief that I no longer had to wonder why this gorgeous woman felt so familiar.

I would have done things much differently had I been in her position.

But at twenty-two years old, already buried with a shit ton of responsibility from her employer, trying to finish up her undergraduate degree, and having just lost her mother, she made the decision that felt best for her. At that age, I didn't know what it was like to feel alone in this world, to have to fully support myself financially. Just because I would have made different decisions, that didn't mean I was going to punish her for hers.

We all made mistakes; we all lived with some level of regret.

Drake's just happened to affect my life.

But fuck, it was hard to wrap my head around the fact that two prominent women had taken up most of the real estate in my mind.

And now . . .

They were one.

"Why tell you all of this?" she repeated, as though she needed to hear my question again. "I just wanted you to know. I wanted you to hear it from me before you figured it out on your own." She licked her lips, shaking her head slightly. "This is so much, Easton. I don't know what it all means or how to even process our kiss from the other night. I'm at Hooked, directing a vital role at your company, working beneath you, and I love my job more than anything. It's just"—she stopped to breathe—"a lot, like I said."

"We don't have to figure out anything right now."

She nodded gently.

"I just need to know one thing." I wasn't going to reach for her hand; I didn't want my touch to influence her decision. "I need to know if you have any feelings for me. If this is something—if I'm something—you want. I'm not saying we have to move straight into a relationship or dive head in. I'm not saying this has to instantly turn into something extremely heavy. What I'm saying is"—I felt my voice lower to a growl—"if I lean in to kiss you, would you let me have your lips or would you stop me?"

Emotion slid into her eyes.

"I've waited over five years to touch you again, Drake. First with Love. Now . . . you." I rested my arms on the table, my sleeves not high enough, so I pushed them to my elbows. "I don't know how much longer I can wait, because that kiss . . ." My voice drifted off. "It wasn't nearly enough."

She glanced down, her hands moving into her lap.

Her face was hidden, not allowing me to read it.

Fuck, it might as well have been covered in lace.

I didn't know what she was thinking.

How she was feeling.

I just knew what I felt, and I hoped it was enough.

"Easton . . ." she whispered, wrapping her arms around her stomach, eventually glancing up at me. "I don't know that I have any answers right now, but I do know one thing."

I waited.

It was fucking torturous.

Ticktock repeated in my head over and over.

"I want you."

Three words.

They slapped my chest so hard, I rushed up from my seat and grabbed her hand and lifted her from her chair. The closeness brought me her scent.

One that I wanted to fucking eat off her skin.

I surrounded her face with my hands, her lips breaths away from mine. Goddamn it, she felt so good.

Soft.

Beautiful.

Delicate.

I gripped her even tighter, and a feeling came over me.

That familiarity of the last time I'd held her so close.

Those stunning eyes that reminded me of a dark maple syrup.

Those pouty lips.

But there was more.

There was a hardness in my cock.

A need so deep, so strong, I pointed her face up to mine, taking in her features again to slow down the moment, to appreciate it for a few seconds more.

If she hadn't pulled away back then, if she had only kept her same number, this would have looked so different, and so would all those years we'd spent apart.

But she was here.

Now.

And I was promising myself one thing—I wasn't going to let her go.

As that thought simmered in my head, right before I pressed my lips to hers, I whispered, "I'm crazy about you."

Fuck me, there was nothing like kissing Drake Madden.

Tasting her.

Having my tongue circle hers.

I aligned our bodies, eliminating even the air between us, and it filled me with an overwhelming amount of heat. While I felt a pulse inside her, my hard-on rubbed against her.

Enough so that when I pulled her face away from mine, scanning her eyes, I said, "I'm taking you home."

"Do I need to worry about Grayson seeing us?"

"No."

Her shudder vibrated against me, her hand clinging to mine. "Then take me home now."

I didn't bother to look for the waitress. Instead, I reached into my wallet, took out $100, and slipped it underneath one of our glasses. As I shoved the wallet back into my pocket, I locked my hand with Drake's and headed for the exit. My arm wrapped around her waist as we stepped outside, her head resting against the side of my chest, and I breathed in her hair, filling my lungs with her scent, pressing my lips against that same spot.

I'd waited so long for this moment.

That was why, even though my building was only two blocks away, it felt like it took a goddamn eternity to get there.

We were greeted by my doorman, who held the entrance open for us, the elevator waiting as we walked through the lobby. I hit the "PH" button as soon as we got inside, and as the door closed, I backed Drake up against the wall, surrounding her with my arms.

"I need you," I roared before my lips touched hers.

This was a desire, a scorching need, that I'd never felt this intensely before. I was sure she knew that by the way I claimed her mouth. By the roughness with which I tackled her lips. By the way I held her strong and steady.

The only reason my mouth left hers was because the elevator had arrived, and I took Drake by the hand and led her through the small hallway and into my condo. I was already peeling off her jacket when the door slammed behind her. I tossed the coat onto my kitchen island, my gaze immediately dipping down her body, taking in the red, tight, incredibly sexy dress that hugged every one of her dips and curves.

"My God." I slid my palms down her back and pulled her closer. "You look gorgeous." I ran my fingers down her cheek, lowering to her chest, circling her navel. From there, I held her hips, slightly arching her back. "I'm obsessed with your body."

"It's all yours," she said softly.

"Mine." I traced the bottom of her tits and around her sides, my fingers stretching to her ass. "You're perfect, Drake. Every bit of you."

The dress stopped above her knees and bound her so tightly, if I set her on the kitchen island, I'd never be able to spread her legs. So I demanded, "Kiss me," and I lifted her into my arms and carried her through the living room and into the far wing of my place. When I reached my bed, I set her on the very edge.

The room was pitch dark.

Instead of flipping on any lights, I found the remote to the fireplace and turned it on. As the flames came to life, their glow flickered across her face, giving off just enough of a gleam that I could see what I was doing.

That I could take in that breathtaking face as it looked up at me.

There was no reason to hurry this. I'd waited far too long to rush through it now.

So I took my time lowering her zipper, giving her just enough space to slip her arms out, freeing her top half as I dragged the material down her torso, continuing past her knees until I could toss the dress onto the floor.

All that was left were knee-high boots, black lace panties, and a matching bra.

"Drake . . ." I moaned. "I always wondered what you would look like naked"—I shook my head—"but nothing, not a single image I could come up with in my head, compares to what I'm looking at right now."

She said nothing, her teeth just grazing the larger of her two lips, a hunger moving through her eyes.

I took the base of her boot into my hand, resting the heel against my stomach, and unzipped the leather, wiggling it off her. I did the same with the other boot.

Now only her undergarments were left.

I knelt on the floor in front of her, keeping her legs spread as I gazed up her body. "I could sit here forever, looking at you."

She was art.

The sexiest form of vulnerability.

She ran her fingers through my hair, pausing to say, "You are every form of flattery and then some, Mr. Boston."

"I'm not flattering you." I gave her another scan. "My compliments are barely denting what I see when I look at you."

As her legs dangled off the bed, I set her feet on the edge and gently grabbed the sides of her panties, gradually shimmying them down her thighs. Over her knees. And, finally, past her feet, flinging them somewhere behind me.

I didn't look between her legs.

I didn't break eye contact.

But while I stared into those eyes, which were even darker, richer in this fire-filled room, I again lifted her foot off the bed, and I kissed her ankle. The scent of coconut was just as thick down here, and I slowly made my way up her calf and around her knee. I focused on the inside of her thigh, and when I reached the top, I moved toward her center. That was where I stopped.

I paused.

And I took a long, deep inhale.

She watched me.

The desire building on her face.

"Do you know how badly I want to lick you? How that one time in the stairwell wasn't nearly enough?"

Air huffed from her mouth. "Easton . . . I'm dying right now . . ."

I surrounded her thighs and swiped my nose around her clit.

Followed by my lips.

And scruff.

Getting completely, entirely lost in her.

"Drake . . ." The breath I sucked in was full of her. "It's as perfect as I remember."

But before I returned to that spot I was craving, where I'd be so captivated, I wouldn't leave, I kissed around her hips. Consuming. Savoring. "And these are perfect." I licked each place after I kissed it, moving from that area to cross her stomach. "So is this." I settled there, traveling around her belly button, to the lowest point that was just above her center, and rose to her ribs. "And here." I moved slowly. Lovingly. Unhooking her bra and freeing her breasts, my mouth hovering above her nipple as I breathed, "Even more perfection right here." I dipped down her arm, ending at her wrist, where I kissed the black tattooed initials. Once I covered her other arm in tender embraces, I leaned back to take her all in. "You're a fucking dream and now you're here and . . . you're mine."

Despite the hunger, there was emotion, too, her hand tightening in my hair as she exhaled. "Easton . . ."

My position placed me close to her mouth. "You've haunted me, Drake. Every inch of you has."

When she pressed her mouth to mine, her kiss was different.

It was sentimental.

It came with a mood and a tone.

And it told me precisely what she wanted.

That was why, when she eventually pulled away, I returned to the V between her legs, holding her thighs apart, my gaze covering the bareness of her lips and the fold of her clit. "I'm one lucky man right now."

"You have no idea what you're doing to me."

I wiped my finger around her entrance, gathering the wetness there. "I can tell. I can feel it." I traced the skin on her inner thighs, and an explosion erupted in my body as my tongue landed on her clit. "Fuck, Drake. There's nothing like you. Nothing that tastes better. Nothing that I want more." I continued to lick, only stopping to say, "How badly do you want to come right now?"

As my question simmered in her chest, her teeth stabbed her lip.

An action that made my dick twitch.

That made everything inside my body start to tingle.

"Because I plan on taking my time." My nose rounded her clit. Softly. With just enough pressure to make her gasp. "Dragging this out as long as possible, until you're screaming for an orgasm."

Her lips parted, but she said nothing.

That look. That stare. That famine that moved over her mouth was more than I could handle.

"Never mind, Drake, I'm not going to give you a choice."

Her palm moved to my forehead, like she was trying to stop me from licking her. "What are you going to do to me?"

"Everything I've been fantasizing about." I peeled her hand away. "Starting with this." I flattened my tongue and trailed it across her clit.

"*Ohhh. Yesss,*" she moaned.

I allowed her to get used to the feel of me again, the texture of my skin. The way her wetness mixed with my spit before I gave her more. But when I did, I started with a tease, circling the tip of my finger around her opening, carefully going in as far as my nail to see how easily I slipped into her. "You're so fucking tight."

Something I remembered.

Along with the way she had molded around my dick.

How she had clutched it from the inside, pulsing around me when I finally buried myself in her.

"Easton!" She squeezed my strands of hair. Pulling, yanking them. She even went as far as twisting them as my finger dipped all the way in, my tongue flicking back and forth across her clit. "Shit!"

Her hips bucked.

Her fingers locked on my head.

From her sounds alone, I knew this wasn't going to take long.

But I wanted to worship her.

I wanted to bathe in her scent and soak myself in her wetness.

So I slowed down, giving her more friction with my finger, inserting up to my knuckle, and pulling back out. I repeated that pattern over and over. And each time, I swallowed her, reveling in her flavor as it flowed down my throat.

"Yes! Fuck!" she shouted.

The second my tongue increased in speed, her hips rocked, and she used more strength as she pushed against my face. She was building, closing in. Her clit hardening. Her moans loudening.

She was narrowing even more around my finger.

"You want to come."

Her eyes were already pleading with me as she gazed down between her legs. "Please."

I licked her even faster. I gave her more pressure, sliding in a second finger, aiming both toward her stomach so I hit that intense, magical spot.

The one that, before our phone sex, had never been touched before.

"Easton!" She tremored. "Oh! Fuck! Me!"

I kept my fingers plunged inside, caressing them over her G-spot. Her legs closed in around my face, but that didn't stop me. My tongue moved with the same ferociousness, alternating between flicking and sucking, as my fingers dived, circled, left, and stroked back in.

And all the while, I watched her peak.

She gave off every signal that she was moving toward that mind-blowing spike. Her hips ground, her clit turned even harder. Because I knew she was there, teetering that edge, I gave her every ounce of power I had, using a speed I hadn't reached before.

She gasped. "Oh my!"

I didn't pause.

I didn't even slow.

Not even when her stomach began to shudder and she screamed, "Easton," throughout my bedroom.

I just kept rolling, licking, devouring, until I sensed that she was coming down. That was when I eased up, knowing her body was on the verge of extreme sensitivity.

"Wow," she panted as she finally stilled. "I don't know what the hell that was, but . . ."

I lapped her, gently pulling my fingers out, sucking off the wetness that coated my skin. Before I lifted my face away, I gave that spot one last kiss.

At the very top.

Where it was the wettest.

Where I'd been licking.

And then I rubbed my lips over hers, knowing I could do this anytime I wanted tonight and again in the morning, and that was the best feeling in the world. I kept my mouth against her as I whispered, "Tell me you're ready to come again."

CHAPTER TWENTY-FOUR

Drake

Come . . . *again?*

I didn't know how that was possible.

I didn't even know if I could.

My body was still reeling from his tongue.

The only time I'd ever felt anything like that was the first time he'd put his face there.

And once again, he'd sent me to places I didn't think I could reach. Not just from his licking, which was the most incredible thing ever, but also from the way he was fingering me.

That spot. Deep inside. It was explosive.

But something told me that was just an appetizer. My screaming hadn't nearly peaked; my voice was going to go much higher and get much louder tonight. And that Easton hadn't even really gotten started—he was going to give my body even more experiences, sensations I'd only ever felt with him.

"Ready . . . to come again," I replied.

He was still kneeling between my legs. His mouth still appearing like it was hungry, getting ready to devour me a second time.

"Again, yes." He rubbed my thighs. "And again after that."

I'd dreamed about this. First with Mr. Boston and then with Mr. Hottie, as Saara had been calling him.

But it was a fantasy.

I wasn't sure—I didn't necessarily believe—that in either case it would ever become a reality.

"I"—I filled my lungs, inhaling as hard and as fast as I could—"don't know if I can."

He touched the center of my lips as though quieting me. "Let me determine that. You just focus on screaming."

He got onto his feet and began to strip off his clothes. I'd never seen Easton in shorts, never mind getting little slices of his uncovered body.

Which was happening now.

Rendering me completely speechless.

Except for when I groaned, "Holy shit," as his sweater dropped to the floor. He stared at me, never breaking eye contact as he began to unbutton his jeans. "You're not even real."

His arms had looked extremely muscular when I'd been sitting across from him at the bar and he'd pushed up his sleeves, and I remembered touching them when he'd held me against the wall in the stairwell.

But with his shirt off, I could see every ripple.

Every vein.

Every inch of definition.

My stare rose to his chest, his pecs etched, his skin tight and covered with a light dusting of hair that trailed down the center of his torso, where the dark strands met his abs. Each one was carved into his body, like someone had outlined them in black marker, until they disappeared below the waist of his boxer briefs.

Boxers that were now falling to the floor.

"I . . ." My voice cut off as I tried to comment on the view of his erection. One I could recall the feel of quite easily, but I hadn't been this close up, I hadn't seen it this way. My throat turned dry . . . and I was lost. Lost in the pleasure that I knew he would soon be giving me. Lost in thought of what this man—and his massive cock—was about to do to me. "Easton . . . I'm . . ."

"You're . . ." He chuckled as he moved over to me, naked, placing his arms on either side of me to align our faces. "About to get ravished. And I assure you, Drake. I'm very real. I proved that to you years ago and I will again."

I swallowed, attempting to take in a breath. "You're also perfect."

"You can't use my words."

"But you are. In every way. And I mean *every* way."

His eyes narrowed, an intensity moving through them. "Drop your feet to the floor."

I hadn't realized my knees were bent. That my toes were clinging to the end of the bed, like it was going to hold me up.

"You're blocking my view of you, and after all these years, Drake, I just want to look at you."

As my feet landed on the floor, his words simmered in my chest, his gaze reminding me of how I'd felt back then, in the stairwell, and how those emotions were even stronger now.

I nipped his thumb as it passed my front teeth and kissed it to soothe the hurt.

The grin grew across his lips, and it was so beautiful it made me ache.

Instead of replying, he placed his knee on the mattress between my legs, and as I reclined onto my back, he hovered over me. He held his weight with one arm, the other roaming my body.

His kisses weren't slow or gentle.

They came with hunger.

Need.

The moment he pulled his mouth away from mine, he moved to my neck, kissing around my throat and down my breasts. He stalled over my nipple, sucking it into his mouth, flicking the end of it.

My back lifted off the bed as he shifted to the other side. "That feels—" As I searched for an adjective, he gave me his teeth. The sharpness. The bite. "Amazing."

I remembered when Mr. Boston and I had phone sex and he'd taught me all about pain.

Something I'd never experienced before him.

Or after.

Until now.

Until I felt the scrape across my nipple.

Back and forth.

And with that came so many urges—the need to scream, the need to dig my nails into his skin, the need to wrap my legs around him.

I did all three.

And I instantly met the hardness of his tip as it pressed against my clit. "*Ohhh,*" I moaned, my head pushing into the mattress again.

He didn't move his dick. He kept it right there, at the very top, the same place he'd licked earlier, his crown adding pressure as he kissed his way back to my lips.

"One day, very soon, we're not going to use one of these." He reached toward his nightstand and opened the drawer, pulling out a foil packet. He ripped off the corner with his teeth and aimed the rubber over the top of his shaft.

I was tempted to say we didn't have to use one now. I was on birth control; I was sure he'd practiced safe sex in the past—at least he had with me.

But this was just the beginning.

Time was something we both needed to figure this all out, and whatever we turned into, condoms would either be a part of it or not.

What I did notice as he rolled the latex over his shaft was that I now had a front-row seat to every throbbing inch of him, even closer than I had been moments ago.

That all those inches were going to somehow, someway, fit inside me again.

"You look scared," he growled.

I hadn't realized he'd finished, that his hands were now strolling around my chest.

"I might be a little."

"If it's because of my size, then I can understand that fear, even though you know I'll be gentle at first, just like I was last time." His lips pressed against the side of my neck, tickling their way up to my throat. "But if it's because you know that I'm about to dominate your body, then you have no reason to worry. I am going to do that. For hours. But I promise, Drake, it's going to be nothing but pleasure."

He was huge, there was no question about that, but so was the size of his body, one that came with an immense amount of power and strength, and something told me I'd only ever felt a small portion of that.

"Trust me," he whispered against the center of my chest as he began to kiss toward my stomach.

He didn't stop there.

He went farther.

Pausing when he reached my clit, his tongue wide and wet as he swiped it.

"Oh! Yes!" I moved with him, my hips swaying forward and back, an orgasm already so close. My feet pressed against the bed, my legs spread, and I arched my butt high, pushing even harder against him.

I'd yet to find anything in my life that felt better than Easton's tongue.

The skill he used.

The place where he licked.

The way he knew just how to get me there.

And just when I neared that edge I wouldn't be able to return from, he lowered his mouth and began to focus on my entrance, even wrapping my legs around his neck as he slid his tongue in and out of me.

"Oh fuck," I cried.

A whole new sensation came over me, something I wasn't expecting.

While his tongue slithered into me, he rubbed my clit with his thumb, the combination igniting something wicked.

Something fierce.

"I can't get enough of you," he hissed.

And I couldn't breathe.

I positively couldn't see.

I gripped the blanket, squeezing it into my hands, and held on for dear life. "Easton!"

The intensity came to a screeching halt as he unraveled my legs from around his neck and rose to a standing position, pulling my ass to the very end of the mattress. He lifted my legs and circled them around his waist. And while my body was high in the air, his tip found me.

Bumping my entrance.

Teasing me.

"You know what I love about this position?" The desire on his face increased. It darkened, even. "I get to watch you. I get to see how my dick makes you feel while I'm fucking you with it." His thumb returned to my clit. "And I get to use both of my hands to touch you."

He went slow, steady, allowing me to adjust after each bit he gave me.

"You're so tight."

Hearing those words, seeing them move through his mouth, knowing I was squeezing him from the inside, was the most incredible feeling.

So was the way he looked at me while he worked his way in.

"The deeper I go, the tighter you get."

How could the truth be so sexy?

But it was. Every syllable. Every rise of his hips. Every flex of his abs as he continued to gently slide in.

Until his movements came to a stop and I heard, "You have all of me, Drake." His voice was deeper now. Almost animalistic. "I'm not going to move until you get used to me."

He cared.

That feeling, that raw tenderness. There was nothing hotter.

But there was something else, something I saw on his face, that told me he was holding back, straining not to move. That told me the second I was ready, I was going to get even more.

I was going to get all of Easton Jones.

And that thought, the fullness that was already dominating me, made my body pulse.

"I'm ready," I finally voiced.

"You're sure?"

"Yes."

He reared back to his crown, circling his hips before he dived in. "Fuck," he moaned, strumming my clit. "You feel amazing."

And so did he. *"Ohhh."*

Within a few pumps, I learned something.

Easton, once again, controlled my body like I was his possession.

Like I was his.

He moved in and out of me as though his only goal was to make me scream in pleasure.

And I did. "Easton!" My head tilted back, my hair splaying over the bed. "Oh hell, you're incredible."

Less than a minute had passed.

Yet I was there.

Already.

"Fuck yes!" I gasped. *"Ahhh!"*

He picked up speed, his hips grinding and rotating before he plunged into me. But that wasn't all the friction he was giving me—there was also his thumb. The way it switched, back and forth, like he was turning me off and on.

"A second orgasm—that fast. What did I tell you . . ."

I clutched the blanket, my limbs numb, my body completely owned by him. "Easton . . ."

"Let me feel it, Drake. Let me feel you come on my cock."

His order held no weight because, at this point, I couldn't stop it. I was too far gone.

Tingles were blasting through me, this fiery electricity that shot across my legs and into my stomach and up my chest. A build that was so strong, I was frozen, suspended in this sublime space, followed by a peak that made every part of me shudder.

"Ahhh!" I sucked in air. "Yes!"

Easton didn't stop.

He didn't let up.

He just pounded into me, rubbing across the spots that made me yell even louder, fulfilling this need I didn't know I had.

But I wanted.

And I wanted even more.

"Fuck me, that was gorgeous to watch," he roared.

I took in his face, a sight I almost wanted to avoid, the combination of passion and his stare too much for me to handle.

"Now let's do that again."

He pulled out and flipped me onto my stomach, where he guided me into doggy style. He stayed standing at the foot of the bed, leading my ass toward his tip. Once he found my entrance, he teased it, circling around several times before he eased in.

"Wow." This was different from the previous position. Fuller. Even more overwhelming. "Easton!"

"Let's see how quickly I can get you there."

Again.

A concept I couldn't even wrap my head around.

He gripped my hips, pulling me toward him. "You don't believe I have it in me . . ."

"Stay out of my thoughts."

"I can hear them loud and clear. But if tonight hasn't shown you how well I already know your body, then this will."

It was a warning.

And within a few plunges, I realized why he'd given me one.

If I thought I'd felt his ownership before, it was nothing compared to this.

This was power.

Domination.

And I was completely adrift, even more so when he reached around my side, his finger returning to my clit, stroking it at the same time his dick was thrusting into me.

I simply balanced on my hands and knees, and the orgasm began to bare its teeth.

"What are you doing to me," I exhaled.

"I'm worshipping you."

I believed that.

And just as I was closing in on that place, my body spiraling toward the summit, he was gone, moving toward the front of the bed while I stayed at the end. He sat by the pillows, resting his back against the headboard, his legs stretched out in front of him. His hand was behind his head, his abs tight while his other hand stroked his dick. His stare as naughty and delicious as his raging hard-on.

"Crawl to me, Drake."

Still in doggy style, my body was on complete display as my hands dug into the bedding, bringing me closer to him.

"Now I want you to ride me." He gripped my hips, giving my nipple a quick swipe with his tongue. "Take me wherever you want to go."

I straddled his waist, his crown penetrating me as I lowered over him. "Oh. My. God." My head fell back as I reached the bottom of his cock, fully submerging him inside me.

Each stance he'd taken tonight had felt entirely different. This was no exception. Especially as he angled me in a way where my clit rubbed the short hairs that fanned over the top of his dick. The way they brushed me added just the right amount of friction.

"You have no idea how gorgeous you are." He kept our mouths close, his hand on my cheek. "Or how good you feel in my arms." He gave me a small kiss. "How I never want to let you go."

"Then don't," I whispered.

It was my turn to own the movements, the speed. And while I managed both, his fingers roamed. They added more satisfaction to the fullness that was already settling in.

"Someone likes the power." He kissed me. Hard this time. "I knew you would."

I wrapped my arms around his shoulders, using his muscles to bounce. To gyrate over him.

He kissed down my throat and over my collarbone and held me even tighter when his lips pressed against mine. "You better slow down, Drake, or you're going to make me come."

I rocked over him. "That's what I want." I was an endless pit of pleasure tonight; it was only fair that I shared some with him.

"If I'm going to come, then you are too."

I arched my hips, rotating, swaying in both directions. "I'm close."

"I can tell."

There was nothing sexier in my mind than us getting off at the same time, so to make that happen, I gave him every bit of energy I had left.

"Easton!" I bucked, on the verge, and then—gone. "Fuck!"

"I can feel it, goddamn it." He clutched my back, ravishing my lips, taking over all the movements.

They were fierce, a blunt hammering that had me screaming, "Oh! Yesss!"

"You're tightening around me, milking me."

Just as my nails stabbed into his flesh, as he slammed into me, relentlessly, I felt the shudders.

Not just in my body, but in his.

We were trembling together.

"Fuuuck!" he shouted.

My eyes flicked open, not even aware that they had closed, and I saw this vast, scalding heat on his face, lust on his lips, thirst in his eyes—it was captivating.

Enticing.

And so erotic.

While my orgasm hit and I started the blissful descent, our breaths turned labored, our grips tightened.

Everything slowed until there was nothing left but stillness.

Instead of releasing me, he wrapped his arms fully around me, drawing me in even closer so our chests were pressed together. Our warm skin stuck, the heat from the passion we'd just shared keeping us glued.

"You have no idea how happy it makes me to look at you." A soft kiss followed. "To see your face, to know exactly who you are—whether that's Love or Drake, I don't care."

There was something so special about those words.

They hit me, hard, staying in my heart, squeezing it.

I licked him off my lips, raking my fingers through his hair. "You know, one of the best parts about tonight is that it doesn't have to end. Instead of going home, feeling alone, I get to wake up in the morning and kiss you again."

CHAPTER TWENTY-FIVE

Easton

I stood in the doorway of Drake's office, watching her type on her keyboard, reminiscing about this morning, when she'd been lying on my bed, naked, her long, dark hair spread across my chest, and I'd listened to her breathe. And now, hours later, while I hovered here, employees passing me in the hallway, I had to act as though I hadn't spent half of last night with my face between her legs. As though I couldn't still smell the coconut on my skin from when we'd kissed on our way to work. As though I hadn't held her against the wall of my shower and given her several reasons to scream this morning.

Her eyes finally flicked up, noticing me, and a smile spread across her face as our stares locked.

I walked into her office, whispering, "You look gorgeous," right before I took a seat in front of her desk.

She glanced down at her outfit. "No, I look like a mess. But you know one of the things I like most about you?" She set her arms on her desk, swimming in the baggy button-down that she wore, and leaned into the edge of the wood. "The fact that you saw me, what, two cups of coffee ago, and you're looking at me like this is the very first time you've ever seen me." A warmth dragged all the way up to her eyes. "You're a whole mood, Easton. I love it."

That was because I couldn't get enough of her.

And I didn't know if I ever would.

"If you weren't so beautiful and if I wasn't so grateful that you—Love—the both of you are back in my life, then this expression wouldn't be on my face."

"Stop. Look at what you're making me do." She pointed at her cheeks, which were reddening. "If anyone walks in right now, we're a dead giveaway."

"Speaking of that."

"Yes, speaking of that." She held up her hand, telling me she wasn't done. "I know we talked about this very briefly at the bar, and then all hell broke loose the second you kissed me, but we need to discuss it."

"Is that how you'd describe what I did to your body? Hell breaking loose?"

She shook her head, grinning. "You're so distracting."

"I want to lock your door and ravish you on this fucking desk right now."

She glanced away, fanning her face, laughing. "This is serious and you're not helping."

I leaned back in my chair, crossing my legs. "All right. Serious side. Hit me with it."

She didn't immediately answer, collecting her thoughts first. "I've already expressed to you how much I love this job. But you're my boss, and your level of authority over me makes me a bit nervous. There are just so many unknowns with that." She paused, searching my eyes. "Easton, I've never done anything like this before—I didn't date anyone from Faceframe or any of the companies I consulted for."

"I get it. I really do."

"Good, then you understand why I want to take things slow. I want to figure this out together. I want what's best for us and Hooked and for both of us to feel comfortable with what that looks like. I'm not pausing, I'm not rushing, I'm just taking the steps that feel right for us." She clasped her hands, looking so genuine when she said, "I really care about you, and I want this to work."

I softened my voice. "I do too."

And because of that, I had zero issues with her being employed here. With her working beneath me.

But I understood there were levels of authority, and that affected her job and, quite possibly, her performance.

I could handle slow only because that would eventually lead to Drake Madden becoming all mine.

"I don't want to say anything to the guys," I told her. "For now, this will be our secret. When we have a better understanding of what we are and how this is going to look at the office, then I'll talk to them about it."

"You have no idea how much I appreciate that."

Now that the hard shit was out of the way, I rested my hand on the back of her desk. "I want to see you tonight."

"Is that taking things slow?"

"If I was moving fast, I would have asked you out for lunch."

She laughed and glanced down at her phone as it dinged on top of her desk, and when she read the message that filled her screen, her expression instantly changed.

"Is everything all right?" I asked.

She sighed. "Yeah, it's just a colleague from Faceframe. An issue came up and they need my help. I'll deal with it later." She slipped her phone away and slowly looked at me. "Sorry I got distracted—what were you saying? Something about tonight?"

"Do they reach out to you a lot?"

She shrugged. "Enough."

I sensed the topic added stress she didn't need, so I leaned closer to her desk, skimming my bottom lip as I imagined all the things I would do to her when she came by my place tonight. "Back to tonight, I'll cook and we'll eat naked."

"Naked?" Her brows rose. "What if I spill something? That'll really burn—"

"Oh good, you're both in here," Holden said from behind me.

I quickly turned around and pushed my back against the chair as I watched him walk into Drake's office.

"Now I can tell you guys at the same time." He took a seat next to me.

"Tell us what?" I asked.

He handed me a tablet, and I briefly read the information at the top of the screen. "There's a conference in Berlin in three weeks. I want Hooked to be there."

"I know of the conference," Drake replied. "I attended every year while I was at Faceframe."

"Excellent, then as long as you don't have anything on your calendar that you can't reschedule, I'd like you to go," Holden said to her. His forehead scrunched as he stared at her. "Is that Easton's shirt you have on?"

Fuck me.

"Yes," I quickly chimed in. "She spilled coffee on her dress this morning, so I gave her my shirt to cover up the stain."

Drake had been extremely self-conscious when I'd lent her the button-down that she wore over the top of last night's dress. It was a look that drove me wild, especially because I knew she'd be smelling me all day, that my fabric would be wrapped around that delicious body. Because I hadn't let her out of the shower, devouring her not once but twice while we were in there, and she had an early meeting, she hadn't had time to go back to her apartment to change. Even though this combo was overdressed for our environment, I assured her no one would notice.

Of course, the hopeless romantic who dressed an extremely picky and overly opinionated little girl every morning had picked up on it.

"What a good man," Holden said, clasping my shoulder before he took back the tablet. "Anyway, I hadn't planned on us going, not while Marvin was in Drake's role. Now that I have confidence we're getting much closer to an international rollout, I think it's vital that we're there."

"Me too," she added. "And I'm excited to attend."

"I want Easton to go with you," he said.

Nothing made me happier than the thought of having Drake all to myself during an international flight on our private plane and three-plus days in Europe.

"Sounds good to me," I told him.

"I'll have our assistant work out the details and book the hotel."

"Have her plan an extra night at the end of the trip," I suggested. "I've never been to Berlin. I'd like a little time to explore." I looked at Drake. "I don't know how you feel about that since you've already gone. We can have our assistant book you a commercial flight back if you'd rather leave early."

I wanted to give her an option.

I also wanted Holden to see me come up with the idea in front of them so he wouldn't suspect anything was happening between us when I randomly extended the trip.

"I've only spent a little bit of time there," she admitted. "An extra night will be kind of nice."

"I'll take care of it," Holden said.

He left the office, the two of us now alone. I checked my watch and stood up. "I'll see you tonight."

She said nothing until I got closer to the door. "Easton?"

I turned around. "Yeah?"

"I saw what you did back there, Mr. Slick." She was grinning.

I returned the expression. "Are you saying it was a bad idea?" As her smile grew, I added, "I didn't think so," and I walked out of her office with a raging hard-on.

CHAPTER TWENTY-SIX

Drake

I stood in front of the refrigerator, checking each bottle of creamer until I found one flavored with vanilla and made of oat milk. This office certainly didn't lack for options when it came to food or drinks, an amenity I appreciated, among so many others. The moment I spotted the blue carton, I grabbed it off the shelf, and as I turned around, I collided with something.

Something as hard and dense as brick.

Something that smelled incredibly spicy.

My gasp silenced as I met Easton's stare, and I peeled my face off his shirt, a material that was the same color as his eyes.

"I didn't even hear you come in," I said softly.

He rubbed his short beard against my cheek before he kissed it. "I know. I can tell."

"You're lucky I didn't scream."

"Baby . . ." His fingertips nipped my waist. "Maybe that's what I wanted."

I gently hit his arm, shoving him away. "We're at work . . . *remember?*"

He laughed as he backed up to the other side of the kitchen, leaning his butt into the edge of the counter as he looked at me.

Why did he have to be so handsome?

His hair was still wet from the shower we had shared this morning, a routine that seemed to happen whenever I stayed the night. The vintage T-shirt he'd put on clung to his chest, showing his muscular pecs. Past the short sleeves were well-defined, veiny arms that had lifted me a few hours ago, like I weighed nothing more than a feather, and moved me into all the positions he wanted me in.

They bent me over.

They held me against his body, the wall, the bench under his shampoo shelf.

I could still feel the burn of his whiskers on my face.

On the insides of my thighs.

Oh hell.

I buried those thoughts and spied the mug in his hand. "Didn't you grab coffee on our way to work?"

"I needed an excuse to come into the kitchen and see you."

I added the creamer to my coffee and returned the carton to the fridge since Easton drank his black. "Sneaky, sneaky." I lifted the warm brew to my lips, stopping to say, "Why are you smiling like that?"

"You're the reason." His voice was smooth, enticing. "I'm thinking about this morning. Last night. This past week."

The combination of his gaze and each of the times he'd mentioned caused my heart to take off as though I were several paces past the starting line. It wasn't a steady increase of thumps—this was an explosion of beats, my pulse hammering away in my neck.

"Why do I get the feeling you're remembering this morning too . . ." His stare started at my feet and slowly rose, taking in every section of my body, inch by inch, the same way he had done just hours ago with his tongue.

"Because . . . I am."

And those memories were setting me on fire.

I was even finding it hard to breathe, to stop myself from jumping into his arms and begging him to carry me into his office, where he'd fuck me against the locked door.

Slow was still my preferred speed, but Easton and I were spending more time together. In fact, in the last week, I'd stayed only two nights at my apartment—the rest were with him. And each day at the office, I was learning to not let situations like this affect me. To not let his smiles and presence and each time he walked by my doorway get in the way of my job.

Because the minute that happened, something would have to change, and that was the last thing I wanted.

He took a drink. "Wait until you see what I'm going to do with you tonight."

"What do you have in mind?"

He shifted his stance, crossing his feet. "Maybe the Jacuzzi on my rooftop. Or maybe homemade sushi that I'm going to eat off your body. Or maybe chocolate fondue." His lips puckered, like he was envisioning the latter. "I'm leaning toward the chocolate."

"We're at work," I reminded him again. "We can't talk about this now."

"Why?" His gaze dropped once more, stopping near my waist. "Because I'm making you wet?" He walked toward the door. "I'd hate for that to happen, especially because I can't lick it away."

Once he was gone, I stayed frozen in the same spot. My coffee untouched. My mind a mix of fantasies that he'd strategically planted, knowing exactly what he was doing and what that would do to me.

"Good morning, Drake," Grayson said as he entered the kitchen.

The sound of his greeting pulled me out of my thoughts. "Morning."

"Long night?"

I knew Easton hadn't said anything to him, so the fact that I was standing in the corner of the kitchen, looking very dazed and confused, had to give that away.

"Why do you ask?"

He went over to the coffee machine and pressed several buttons. "Whenever I have that expression on my face, I either had a hell of a date the night before or I polished off a bottle of scotch when I should have stopped at a few glasses."

I pushed away from the counter and pointed at my temple, giving it a quick rub. "Guilty."

He smiled. "Coffee cures every kind of hangover."

Just before I took a sip, I said, "I hope you're right about that." I left the kitchen and went into my office, wincing as I took a seat at my desk.

Every part of my body ached from Easton.

Something I'd never had before, but was getting used to the more I was with him.

I shook my mouse, waking my monitors, and saw that an email from Easton's assistant had just come in. It was the itinerary for our trip to Germany, the arrival and departure times of our flights, the two rooms that had been booked at the hotel, and the details of the conference. The last bit was a full description of our extra day in Berlin, including the private car that had been reserved and the tours that had been scheduled.

I picked up my office line and, after hitting a few numbers, held the receiver to my ear.

"Miss me already?" Easton asked as the call connected.

"Two things. One, you can't leave me like that in the kitchen. Grayson walked in seconds later and I was having a hard time hiding—"

"How turned on you were."

I sighed. "Yes."

"And what's two?"

"I'm looking over the itinerary for Berlin, and I see your assistant has put a lot of time and effort into our trip."

"Is that what you think?"

I tapped a pen against my desk. "Is that not the case?"

"She was merely the messenger. That last day, those plans that have been made, they're all me."

A flutter moved into my stomach, its long tendrils rising to my chest. "All you, huh?"

"My assistant doesn't know the things you're into or the places you'd like to see."

I scanned each of the spots we were visiting.

"For example," he continued, "when we were at your place the other day and you were in your room, packing up your overnight bag to take to my condo, I checked out your bookshelf. There were a few titles about World War II—both fiction and nonfiction on there. So I booked us a tour of the Jewish Museum, thinking you would enjoy that as much as me."

My eyes closed, my head shaking.

This man.

My God.

"Mr. Boston, you're quite the thoughtful one."

"I accept all forms of appreciation as long as they involve your mouth."

"You're too much," I said, laughing, and I hung up.

The moment I set my phone down, I reached for my cell.

Me: He saw the books I have in my apartment about WWII and booked us a tour of the Jewish Museum while we're in Germany. Can you even?

Saara: I live for him.

Saara: And didn't I tell you dating your boss is the BEST? Now, you can tell me how right I am and how incredibly amazing I am . . . I'm waiting.

Me: Lolol. I love you.

Me: Seriously, Saara, the man reeks of sex and dirty talk and I'm so here for it, but then he does something so sweet and generous, and the combo has me melting.

Me: It's also prevented me from getting a single thing done this morning.

Me: Let's add distraction to his list of qualities.

Saara: Efficiency is overrated.

Saara: Besides, you didn't mind his distracting ways last night, did you?

Me: I have a rollout. An international rollout at that. The partners will kill me if I don't make the date I've promised.

Me: Wait, how did you know about what he did to me last night?

Saara: It was just a guess, you sex-reeking minx.

Me: Saara, he's wild.

Saara: Another reason I love him.

Saara: And how wild are we talking? And does he have a brother?

Me: Two sisters . . . and I can barely sit down.

CHAPTER TWENTY-SEVEN

Drake

Never once during our flight over the Atlantic, where we'd spent almost every one of those hours in bed together, or in the ride to the hotel or while we'd been checking in, had Easton mentioned anything about going out to dinner. The conference started at eight the next morning. I assumed we'd be eating at the hotel and going to bed early, jet lag already setting in. But after a long nap and shower and catching up on some work, we were walking through the lobby, hand in hand, to make our reservation.

Easton halted once we came out of the hotel, his face tilting up toward the sky. "Should I grab us an umbrella? Just in case?"

I hadn't checked the weather; I didn't think we were going out.

Nor did I look up before I said, "Let's risk it."

He pointed at my right. "Then the restaurant is that way."

I matched his pace, my shoulder brushing against his arm as we moved down the walkway, as narrow as the street it lined.

"What do you like most about this city?" he asked.

I felt his eyes on me, but I didn't gaze back. I absorbed our surroundings instead, the modernist architecture mixed with buildings from the Bauhaus movement, the art that hung in the gallery windows, the energy in the people.

"The beauty." The sun had already gone down, but the sky was still aglow, so much so that the streetlamps hadn't yet switched on. "It's as pretty at night as it is during the day. You'll see on our way back from the restaurant." The area was starting to look familiar, the hotel I'd last stayed in just a block from where we were. "When I came last year, my coworker had a wicked case of morning sickness that went from day to night. When we weren't at the conference, she was in her room. Unfortunate for someone who was dying to see the city."

"Did that stop you from exploring?"

"No." With the dampness causing my hair to curl, I tucked some locks behind my ear. "I'd get up extra early, before the conference, and go for walks. And since it wrapped up before dinner, I wandered out each night, eating all the German cuisine, soaking up every second of culture. That's one of my favorite things to do." I finally looked up at him. "But at the same time, I'm happy if you stick me in a park with a cup of coffee. Like, say, the Public Garden—that's one of my most treasured places in Boston."

"That park doesn't get enough love."

I squeezed his hand. "You think so too?"

"There's so much to love about that little slice of the city. The view, the landscape, even the ducks and swans that come during the warmer months."

I smiled. "Yes. All of that."

We'd reached the end of the block, waiting to cross, and there was a store directly across from us. In Boston, it would have been called a bodega. Here, it was known as a Späti, and it was one I'd frequented the last time I was here.

I turned toward him. "How married are you to the idea of going to a restaurant?"

"Unattached." He faced me. "I'm down for whatever you want to do, Drake. I just didn't want to stay in the hotel tonight."

"I have an idea. Follow me." My mouth watered the moment we stepped inside the Späti, the scent of bratwursts strong in the air. "I'm going to grab us some snacks."

I waved to the older woman behind the counter, the only other person in here, her cheeks so weathered they looked like mini accordions. She gave me a slight nod and I went to where the prepared foods were stored, filling my arms with containers of potato salad and cabbage salad. I combined those with some sausage, bratwursts, and a double serving of sauerkraut.

"Give me a job, Drake. I'm just standing here, useless."

I laughed at his description and nodded toward the beer section. "Pilsner. Find us a good one. And stick with cans, so we don't have to fuss with a bottle opener."

He disappeared down the aisle, and I meandered over to the bread, finding what looked like a rye-wheat, the aroma telling me it was freshly baked. And last, for dessert, I picked up a slice of Black Forest cake.

I met Easton at the counter, where we set all the food and beer.

"Don't even think about it," he said as I began to take out my wallet.

"But this was my idea. Please let me pay."

"This entire trip, including the dinner, is on Hooked." He kissed the side of my forehead. "I'm paying." He handed his corporate card to the older woman and put his arm around my waist.

She silently ran his card through the machine once I selected the appropriate number of plastic bags we would need to buy, and I bagged our food, adding napkins and wooden forks and knives. "Beautiful night." Her accent was thick, her eyelids heavy as she scanned our faces.

"Is it going to rain?" Easton asked her.

She shook her head, her gray hair falling into her eyes. "A romantic mist."

"Perfect," I whispered.

I grabbed one of the bags, leaving the other two for Easton, and thanked her before we made our way outside. The remainder of the walk was down a narrow path, tightly squeezed between two buildings. Apartment windows ran across both sides, baskets of flowers hung from the ledges, and clothes were draped from lines.

Simplicity.

But such charm at the same time.

At the end of the walkway was a large body of water with tall planted trees surrounding the side we were approaching. Where the trees ended, a half wall began, standing about ten feet above the waterline, blocking the lake from the street. I placed the bagged food on the top of the wall and gripped the railing that ran across it, pulling myself up. I first landed on my knees, then my feet, reaching for Easton's bags once I found my balance.

He slid the thin plastic into my fingers. "We're eating here?"

I carefully placed the bags on one side of me while he sat on the other. "Trust me. You're going to love it."

With our legs dangling over the edge of the wall, many feet from the water, I handed him a pilsner and took one for myself. "Cheers."

"You're right," he said as we clinked cans. "I am going to love it."

My smile widened and I took a sip before reaching into the bags and removing all the food. "The last time I was here, I tried most of these. They were amazing." I gave him a fork, knife, and napkin.

He stabbed a piece of cabbage and brought it to his lips. "Do I need to know what this is before I eat it?"

"No."

He chewed, groaning. "You're right. Jesus, this is exceptional."

I stared at his mouth while he took in some potato salad, followed by sausage and the heavy strings of sauerkraut. Even though he was a silent chewer, there was something mesmerizing about watching this man eat, seeing him hold a fork, the way he licked his lips and wiped them with a napkin after each bite.

He made ordinary look sexy.

Enough so that my body vibrated. The tingling returned, moving lower, deeper in my navel.

"Maybe I should have bought more than a six-pack." He laughed.

I set the almost-empty beer down. "You're making me thirsty, that's all." I took the cake out of the bag. "This is for dessert."

"What is it?"

"Black Forest cake. It's one of the desserts they're known for."

"It has cherries, right?"

"Yes," I replied.

"I'll pass."

My brows raised. "Nope. Not happening. You love chocolate. You have to at least try it."

"But I don't love cherries. Fruit and chocolate just don't do it for me."

Before I could comment, my phone chimed. I took it out of my pocket, reading the message.

"Work?"

I nodded. "David wants to run something by me. One sec." I read the rest of his text and typed out a quick reply. "I adore him," I said once I hit send. "He's the most valuable asset on my team."

"David's great. He's been with us since day one."

I smiled. "He told me. He said you paid him in weed and beer before you were able to put him on salary."

Easton laughed. "And grocery store gift cards. I think we ended up throwing in a few of those, but yes, that's all he earned at first." His stare intensified as he said, "Do you miss it at all?"

"Faceframe?"

"Yes."

"No." I slid my cell back into my pocket and grabbed a fork. "I'm exactly where I'm supposed to be. I know I've only been at Hooked for a short time, but everyone has been so nice and welcoming. What you've built there is like a family and"—I shrugged, feeling the heavy touch of emotion—"I don't know, it's like family to me, and knowing I'm not alone, that I have you and them . . . well, that's an incredible feeling."

His hand went to my face, holding my cheek. "With you being at Faceframe for so long, I was worried you wouldn't feel that with us. It's extremely difficult to start something new and get to know the procedures and bond with coworkers. I knew everyone would welcome you. I'm just happy you feel the way you do."

I took the lid off the cake and stabbed a swirl of frosting, holding it out for him to eat. I pulled the fork out of his mouth and scooped some cake, this time with a hint of fruit, and it disappeared between his lips. "Aside from loving my job, there's you. It's hard to keep my thoughts of you and Hooked separate—so much overlaps, and it has since the moment I met you." I glanced toward the water. "But the happiness extends far beyond my employment. I feel it every second while I'm with you. Just know that."

His fingers slid into my hair, his palm staying on my cheek. "You know what I've noticed about the professional side of you?" He paused, but he wasn't looking for a response. "You have this quality that I've never seen in another leader. It's the way you encourage, motivate. It's almost like you put the listener in a trance and suddenly they're eating cherry cake and they don't even realize it until they swallow."

I laughed. "I'm a pusher."

"But you do it silently." His stare deepened. "And you're so down-to-earth, so humble, it comes across effortlessly. Like some of the times I've seen you with the coders and David. Rather than pull up a chair to their desk, you kneel next to them on the floor. Not squat—your knees are literally resting on the carpet. Or the meetings you conduct on the beanbags with your shoes off and your laptop on your lap. People want to work with you. They want to be around you." His thumb pushed my hair back. "They want to eat the cake they know they're not going to like."

I nuzzled my face into his hand. "But did you like it?"

"No." He smiled. "However, you're so convincing that if you put the fork up to my mouth, I'm sure I'd take another bite."

I leaned in and kissed him, immediately tasting the chocolate on his lips. "Forcing you to eat something you knew you wouldn't like. That's not very nice of me." As I squeezed my thighs together, I felt the soreness between them, and I pressed my lips against his again. "Sounds like I have some making up to do."

"I like the thought of that."

I already knew we were alone in the park, especially up here, on the half wall, a remote section with an audience of trees and birds, yet I still looked to my right and left and across the water. "Good, because I have another idea."

CHAPTER TWENTY-EIGHT

Easton

Drake had an idea, and I couldn't wait to see what it was.

It took only a few seconds for me to realize, when she moved the food and beer behind her on the half wall, holding the railing to help her onto her knees, that her focus was now on my dick.

She gazed up at me from my lap and I asked, "This is what you want?"

"Mm-hmm."

I needed zero convincing.

She loosened my belt, unbuttoned my jeans, lowered my zipper, and pulled out my hard-on.

"And you want to do this here?" I growled.

Hints of dusk moved over her face, a tamelessness in her eyes. "You spent the entire takeoff and first hour of the flight with your face between my legs. I can still feel your beard, and it's been, what, hours, followed by a nap and a long shower. It's my turn, Easton."

"Baby, you don't have to beg to suck my dick. It's all yours."

And with that, her eyes stayed on me but her mouth lowered, sucking my crown.

Air hissed from my lungs as she began to lick around my rim. "Yes, Drake, fucking yes." My fingers dived into her hair, guiding her, moving her where I wanted, which was down my shaft, ingesting as much of me as she could.

But she didn't accept my direction, despite how hard I held her.

Drake did whatever she desired.

And that was taking me in slowly, inch by inch, swirling her tongue around my dick while she cupped my balls. When she licked to my base, she rotated around it, making sure to cover both sides, before she continued to my sack.

Carefully, she sucked one of my balls into her mouth, giving it the gentlest flick with her tongue, and then moved on to the other, doing the same, leaving my sack to gradually lift to my tip.

There was no way I would fit all the way in her mouth.

She didn't even attempt it, and I wasn't going to make her gag if she wanted to try.

So, instead, she gripped my bottom half with her hand, her lips taking over my head, and she worked her way toward the middle.

Each time she lowered, she twisted.

Her tongue twirled one way, then the other.

"My fucking God," I roared. "You feel so good."

That mouth.

That tongue.

The way her fingers tightened around me, the pressure with which she circled.

How she sucked my tip, like it was the end of a straw, urging my cum to the surface.

I could barely handle it.

I was hitting the back of her throat, her mouth watering over me, her tongue as wet as mine was whenever I ate her out.

I bunched her hair into my fist and watched her bob.

Up and down.

"Fuck me, Drake. You are so good at this."

She didn't suck my cock like she had to.

She sucked like she wanted to.

Like she craved it.

Like she couldn't get enough of me.

Like she wanted me to have this orgasm as badly as I did.

Out of nowhere, there was a new sensation. With one hand pumping me, she used the other to tickle the skin around my sack, brushing her fingertips across it.

"Hell yes." I reached up and clasped the railing above the half wall. "Don't fucking stop."

She did the opposite.

She went faster.

Her suction increased, her lips lowering farther than she had before.

"Drake!"

The sound of her name brought another change.

A different level of speed that she hadn't reached before.

My eyes closed, my head tilted back in the air, and I took everything she gave me.

The pleasure.

The fucking passion.

The need that this was the only thing she wanted from me.

"You're going to make me come," I threatened.

I just wanted to give her a warning in case she didn't want my cum in her mouth.

But all those words did was make her go harder. Deeper. Her hand grinding over the spit that had fallen toward my base, lubricating me as she thrust up and down.

"Oh fuck!"

My hips began to rock toward her mouth, reaching, climbing to that peak.

She wasn't coaxing it out of me.

She was demanding.

And I was there.

That spot where the tingles left my sack and fired up my shaft, driving the blast through me.

I fisted her hair, roaring, "Yes," as the first shot came out of me, bucking forward and back, meeting her, as a second load hit her tongue, followed by a third.

I couldn't breathe.

My whole body was this sensitive mix of warmth and vibrations.

And she slowed down, ensuring she had every drop out of me before her lips left and her hand unleashed.

I held her face the moment she rose and stared into her eyes, touching her throat as she swallowed me, a sight that was so fucking sexy.

"Goddamn it, Drake. You are . . ." As my voice drifted away, I grazed my finger across her cheek and over her lips. "The most gorgeous woman I've ever seen." Her skin reddened and I continued, "I don't think you realize how special you are."

An almost coy smile tugged at her lips. "I've been wanting to do that."

"Oh yeah?"

"You just never give me the chance. You're always so invested in my needs."

"Obsessed with your needs. That's a better description."

Her lips turned into a full smile.

And I took that moment to really study her. "Your hair is dripping," I whispered, pushing it off her face.

Without touching mine, she replied, "Yours is too."

Not a single drop had fallen from the sky. The woman from the store had been right: it was just this incessant mist that had hovered around us since we'd stepped outside.

But now that Drake had mentioned my sopping hair, I suddenly noticed my clothes did feel damp and there were droplets running down the back of my neck, like I'd just stepped out of the shower.

"I like that you're unbothered by it," I told her. "That you didn't even want an umbrella."

She chuckled. "Really? Why?"

I shrugged. "Let's be honest, most women wouldn't sit here and get wet. They would have wanted me to get them an umbrella." My palm cupped her cheek. "But not you. You're different—when it comes to everything."

She was silent for a few seconds. "I want to feel it all, Easton. Even the things that fall from the sky."

I leaned into her face, holding it close to mine, and before I kissed her, I said, "And that makes you even more beautiful."

CHAPTER
TWENTY-NINE

Easton

"Hell of a job today," I said to Drake as we completed our final day of the conference, making our way out of the building.

She'd spent the entire two days representing our brand, discussing marketing opportunities with other tech giants, chatting about the upcoming international rollout. Watching her in action within this landscape was entirely different from seeing her at the office. Here, she wasn't training, mentoring, or problem-solving. A fire glowed across her face as she spoke so fluidly to other executives as they discussed best practices and shared pointers from teams that had experienced similar growth patterns.

I understood why Faceframe had sent her to conferences such as this one. She was a magnet. People couldn't pass her without exchanging words—they craved her attention, seeking out her advice in a way that told me they were as hypnotized as I was.

My girl was a fucking star.

And since the beginning of the event, I'd stood by her side, watching her shine.

"You weren't so bad yourself, Mr. Boston." She'd spoken over her shoulder, a pace ahead of me as we wove our way through the thick crowd.

Of course, being in this position gave me the opportunity to stare at her ass, and I watched it move within those tight black suit pants, a set of achingly gorgeous heart-shaped cheeks.

I was dying to grab them. To clutch them with both hands and lift her into the air and wrap her legs around me.

But I wouldn't, not until we were away from all these industry eyes.

Thankfully, that time was coming very soon, as we neared the exit of the building and went outside. We weren't more than two steps out the door when I heard, "Drake Madden? Is that you?"

She turned in a circle, scanning the faces of the people nearby. I knew she recognized the speaker when her eyes widened, her lips stretching into a smile, and she sang, "Jeremy, oh my God, hi."

He was a few inches shorter than me, and not nearly as broad or muscular. Still, my back stiffened, and my hands clenched as he closed in on her, her arms opening for a hug.

He held her for a few seconds longer than he needed to, her fingers landing on his forearms the moment she pulled back.

"It's so good to see you," she said. "What a great surprise this is." Her hands dropped and she faced me. "Easton, this is Jeremy. He worked on my team at Faceframe for years." Her eyes shifted to Jeremy. "Jeremy, this is Easton, one of the cofounders of Hooked, where you know I work now."

He extended his hand, and we shook.

His grip extremely unimpressive.

"Nice to meet you, Easton."

"And you," I replied.

Drake patted his shoulder the moment he faced her again. "How are things back home? How's the team? I miss everyone so much."

I wasn't surprised by the change in her voice and how much she cared for the people she used to work with; I just hadn't realized until now how much they actually meant to her.

"They're missing you," he replied. "We all are, but I know many of them have reached out since you left. You've been a lifesaver, I can tell you that. One issue after the next, and no one has been able to fill your role."

She beamed from the compliment. "Someone will come along soon, I'm sure of that. Regardless, I'm happy to help. I know what it's like to need answers and not be able to get them. I'm always here for you guys."

"You should see what's happening at work." He shifted his stance. "You know, the rollout and how it's all come together." He shoved a hand into his pocket, and the other went to his chin, holding it as he looked at her. "We've done some initial testing across a few markets. You'd be so proud with the results."

Her head shook. "I'm thrilled it went so well. We worked hard on those designs. I'd be crushed if it wasn't received the way I wanted."

"It's going to launch across all markets in the next couple of months. I'll ping you on Faceframe when it hits the US to make sure you see it."

She folded her hands together, holding them near her chest. "It's going to be wonderful. I'm so excited for the team."

He took a quick glance at me, like the motherfucker had forgotten I was standing here. "Does it feel good to be back in Boston? Closer to Saara"—his voice lowered—"and Mom?"

He knew about her family, something that felt slightly unsettling in my stomach. Saara was one thing, Drake talked about her constantly, but her mother was a topic she didn't bring up often.

"Yes! You have no idea how much I love being back on the East Coast." She glanced at me, a softness moving through her eyes. "And I'm positively in love with my new job."

Jeremy chuckled. "I'm sure your boss enjoys hearing that, don't you, Easton?" He didn't give me time to respond before he said, "It was great catching up with you, Drake. I'm sure I'll be talking to you at some point soon." He gave her another hug and shook my hand.

Drake watched him leave, finally saying to me, "Do you want to go back to the hotel and change our clothes or go for a walk and stumble upon something to eat?"

The idea of having fresh air sounded more appealing, but I still replied, "So, Jeremy, huh?"

She playfully slapped my chest. "Come on, I get the feeling we could both use a walk." We were at least a block from the conference center when she looped her arm through mine. "Jeremy came to work for Faceframe about a year after me. I've known him almost my whole career."

"He worked under you?"

"I was his boss, yes, but it was nothing like you and me. Not a single thing ever happened between us—"

"I didn't ask."

"You didn't have to. I see it all over your face." She looked straight ahead. "I never dated anyone from Faceframe, but I think I told you that before. Besides, Jeremy is very married and has the loveliest wife." She paused as we moved around a group of tourists. "My team worked closely together, the same way we do at Hooked. When that happens, you get to know them on a different level. They're family." She smiled, now giving me a side-eye. "Like David's been dating a woman on and off for years who he met on Hooked. And my new hire, Nicole, has three kids and has been with her wife since they were sixteen."

"And how Saara's your family and you're pleased to be near your mom's memory."

Her eyes narrowed. "I'm not sensing any jealousy, am I?"

I laughed. "No. But the dude finds you hot as hell." I unraveled our arms so I could finally grab her ass. "As he should, because you're hot as hell."

She swiped the air with her hand. "Nonsense—on the Jeremy part."

"Admittedly, I'm not upset to hear that he never laid a hand on you."

"Never." She stretched her arm across my lower back, holding one of my belt loops on the other side. "But it was good to see him. I miss that family we had. In the years I worked there, we all went through a lot together." She'd looked away, but her attention returned to me. "The biggest relief is to know I'm building the same thing at Hooked. Like I said the other night, I'm forming something there and it feels amazing."

"Roots."

She nodded. "That." We were approaching the crosswalk when she said, "What's on the agenda for tomorrow? I know your assistant sent an itinerary, but there weren't times or major details listed, just a few of the locations we'd be stopping at."

I reached for her free hand and brought it up to my mouth, kissing the back of it. "Since breakfast is your favorite meal of the day, I thought we'd start there."

We stopped at the end of the block, and she turned toward me. "What would make you think that?"

"Whenever we go out for brunch, you only ever order breakfast, never lunch, and if there's going to be a meal you miss, it's not the first one of the day." I licked my lips while I stared at her. "Plus, I've never seen anyone look at a plate of home fries and a cranberry mimosa as longingly as you do."

She laughed. "All right, all right. I certainly can't argue any of those points." Her hand fell to my chest as I released it, and she flattened it against my heart as she gazed up at me. "The details, Easton. The ones you notice, the ones you surprise me with. Each time"—she shook her head—"it makes me all tingly and breathless."

"I'm more observant than most men."

"And I love that about you."

I leaned down to kiss her. I didn't take her lips hastily; I didn't claim them. I just softly pressed my mouth to hers. "Breakfast is going to be a little different than you're probably expecting."

"Explain yourself, Mr. Boston."

I held her cheek. "A chef is coming to our room to make you something savory."

Our room.

Because before we'd left for Berlin, I had booked us a suite at the same hotel and paid for it personally, so I wouldn't set off any alarms when our head of finance got the corporate credit card bill.

Her brows rose. "Just for me?"

"Well, for us, and then we're being picked up to start our day of sightseeing. You know about the Jewish Museum, which we're going to first. I've hired a private guide, so you can ask all the questions you want, and we won't have to wait in any lines." I rubbed my thumb across her lips. "We'll then stop by Checkpoint Charlie, the Brandenburg Gate, the Wall Memorial—the required sites." I paused, letting that settle in. "But aside from the museum, my most anticipated part of tomorrow is going to be the underground tour."

"Underground?" Her head tilted. "I'm intrigued."

"It's a completely unexpected side of the city, where we'll be shown war bunkers and air-raid shelters, and escape tunnels that were used during the war. The museum will show us one side of the way things were, and the underground tour will show us the other." I fanned my fingers across her cheeks. "You're not the only one who enjoys having a little taste of history."

She wrapped her other arm around me, holding me as close as she could get me. "You're positively incredible, you know that?"

I knew there were people passing us on the sidewalk, moving around us as they went about their day, probably annoyed that we were in their way.

None of that mattered to me.

All I cared about was looking into this beautiful woman's eyes.

Kissing her.

And making sure she knew I felt the exact same way about her.

CHAPTER THIRTY

Drake

"Vodka," I said to the bartender as I leaned forward on my stool, placing my arms on the bar top, "on the rocks, please."

Saara clasped my shoulder. "*Ummm*, where's my best friend, and what have you done with her?"

I looked at Saara, and then at the bartender, grinning as I said, "And please make it a double."

"Okay, it's like that," Saara replied, and then added, "I'll take a double, too, I suppose." Still holding me, she turned on her barstool to face me. "You've been home from Germany for a month, and you've been seeing Easton for a little longer than that, and I feel like I don't even know you anymore."

"Because I'm drinking liquor?"

She twirled one of my locks around her finger. "That and because"—a smile grew across her face, filling her eyes—"you're in love." She cupped my cheeks. "Happiness is the best look on you. You're glowing, Drake. I've never seen you look more radiant." She squeezed my shoulder and face. "Do you know how happy that makes me? My heart is literally screaming for you right now."

I found my lip and chewed it. "Saara"—I took a deep breath—"I really, really like him."

"You . . . *like*? That's where we're going with this?"

"For now, yes."

"Just so you know, love is very much on the horizon. I'm not asking. I'm telling you."

Before I could respond, the bartender placed the drinks in front of us and wiped her hands on a rag. Each of her fingers was inked with a full-length tattoo, ending in chipped black polish. "If you decide the vodka isn't enough, you can always make it a dark and dirty night"—she turned, pointing at the top shelf of bottles behind her—"and anything on that row will do the job."

I let out a puff of air that was a semi-laugh. "Honestly, I don't even drink liquor, so I don't know what's gotten into me, but if I even glanced at that shelf for too long, I'd have to crawl home."

Her smile was so soft compared to an exterior that came across so hard. "You wouldn't be the first, I assure you." She ran a hand over her black, spiky hair before she pulled a bottle off a lower shelf and poured its contents into two shot glasses. "These are on the house."

I lifted it toward my face and took a whiff. "Tequila?"

"Only the best," she replied.

"How about I make a deal with you." I smiled. "We'll take these as long as you have one with us?"

She grabbed another glass and filled it. "Done." She raised her shot in the air. "I may have overheard your conversation. It's a side effect of being a bartender for over twenty years. We have dog ears. So, is it appropriate to toast to love?"

I laughed. "With a capital *L*."

"A capital *L*?" she asked.

"Long story." Saara groaned.

"To Love!" I shouted.

We all clinked glasses and I downed the booze, instantly fanning my hand in front of my mouth, hoping the movement would calm my burning throat.

"Let me know if you girls need anything else."

Once I could finally breathe, I thanked the bartender and turned my stool toward Saara, our knees brushing as we faced each other.

"Girl, tell me everything. I know I've seen you plenty since Germany, but if you want to start there, I wouldn't hate hearing it all again."

I shook my head. "I wouldn't torture you that badly. Besides, there isn't much to tell. Things have obviously been great with Easton."

"He's dreamy."

I thought about her statement, really letting that word set in. "He is, and we just fit well together. We're friends. We like the same things. It doesn't matter if we're at a restaurant or if he's cooking us dinner at his place or we're at a Sox game or in sweats glued to the couch—it all feels the same. It's just easy and seamless. Is that weird to say? I don't know, nothing has ever gone this smoothly for me when it comes to men."

She took a drink from her glass. "You guys are just über compatible. It's not weird at all. I kinda had a feeling it would be like this." When she put her glass down, she played with her necklace, moving the clasp from the front to the back. It was a piece of jewelry I'd just so happened to buy for her when Faceframe sent me to Switzerland last year. "Think of it this way: you got all of the hard stuff out of the way already, and this is round two. Plus, you're older now, you're deeper into your career, you're both in the same city and practically neighbors. Maybe the break needed to happen for you to get here."

I glanced toward the small crowd that had just walked in before I looked at Saara again. "It was more than a break. It was—"

"A castration." She laughed.

I winced at her description, and she pressed her knees into mine. "Don't stress over the details of the past. We've moved on. Things are fab now, remember?"

I nodded slowly. "You're right."

"And how are things going at work? You guys are together there every day. Is that affecting you at all?"

"Not really." I sighed, thinking of all the effort he put in to make sure work didn't get difficult between us. "He really gives me my space. I mean, sure, I see him, we pass each other constantly, sometimes we go out for lunch. But he doesn't hover, if you know what I mean."

"He gets what you need, and he gives it to you. That right there is the total package, my friend."

"I can't deny that."

"And the international rollout—is everything still on track?"

I lifted the vodka off the bar and took a sip. "Hence this," I said, wiggling the glass, shaking the ice before I set it down.

"Oh boy." Her brows lifted. "Do I need to whip someone's ass?"

"No, no, it's all good, it's just a lot. The new coders I recently hired are doing an incredible job, so I feel like I have a solid team. Don't get me wrong, there's a thousand and one hiccups a day, but we're working through them."

"Babe, that sounds stressful as fuck." She exhaled. "I know we deal with stress the same way: we hold it all in until we explode, and that explosion either comes with lots of screaming or endless tears or both. Tell me what you need and how I can help."

I set my hand on her wrist, wrapping my fingers around the inside, where she had her grandmother's initials tattooed, from a time in our lives when we were both grieving. "You're here. You're listening. That's everything I need from you." I squeezed before I let go. "But even with all the stress and hiccups, I still expect us to hit our rollout date."

"That's because you're a boss lady and one badass bitch."

I laughed.

"And then your lucky ass gets to go home to Easton, where he works out all your stress."

"Yup," I agreed. *"That."*

I felt a vibration in the back pocket of my jeans where I kept my phone, and I reached for it.

Easton: Grayson and I are going out for drinks. Tell me where you and Saara are hanging tonight so we don't crash your party.

"One sec," I said to Saara. "I just have to tell Easton where we are so he doesn't show up with Grayson."

"So what if he does? It's been a couple weeks since I've seen my semi-boyfriend. I wouldn't mind hanging with him."

"Are we talking about Easton or Grayson?"

When I'd gotten back from Germany, Saara had picked me up at the office for lunch, where she'd met all the guys. She'd also joined Easton and me for dinner a few times, so she could really be talking about any of them at this point.

"Grayson? No, no, *nooo*. I like dicks that can be measured in inches. That man has a constant snarl that I just don't jibe with. Besides, two type As in a relationship? Can you imagine? We'd go twelve rounds over something silly like who's making the bed. I just don't need that ugliness in my life." She flipped her hair off her shoulder, her face warming as she said, "I was talking about Easton. He's with my best friend, which means he's kinda married to me, too, and given your old username, he thought he was really dating me anyway, so that totally makes him my semi-boyfriend."

"That'll make him laugh when I tell him."

"Girl, I already told him when we all had dinner together. You're way behind."

"I love you." I puckered my lips and kissed the air. "But it's girls' night. The boys aren't invited."

"I support that answer."

I giggled. "I thought you would."

I glanced down at my phone and quickly typed a reply.

Me: Corner of Stuart and Clarendon Streets. The little hole in the wall, you know the place.

Easton: You love it there.

Me: It reminds me of college, and they have amazing vodka.

Easton: Vodka?

Me: Haha. Yessss.

Easton: Have fun tonight, baby. I'll see you at work tomorrow.

Me: XO

"Look at you," Saara said as I tucked my phone away. "You're glowing again." She held her glass to her lips. "I really hope that one day a man comes into my life and rocks my whole world like Easton has rocked yours."

"I promise it's going to happen." I wrapped my fingers around her upper arm, squeezing. "And I can't wait to watch once it does."

The bartender came back just as I was pulling my hand away and said, "A dude named Easton just called and picked up your whole tab. So whatever you order tonight is on him."

My heart began to throb in my chest. "He didn't?"

"Oh, he did," the bartender replied.

"Just when I thought the man couldn't get any dreamier, he goes and does that," Saara sang.

"This must be the man we love with a capital *L*?" the bartender asked.

"It is," Saara confirmed. "And we love him hard."

CHAPTER THIRTY-ONE

Easton

As I walked through the front door of our building and saw the elevator arrive, I rushed through the lobby and stuck my hand in the opening so the door wouldn't close on me. "Sorry to hold you up—" My voice cut off when I realized Drake was the only one inside.

Her gorgeous face stared back at me.

I made sure the button to our floor was pressed and moved toward the back wall, waiting for the door to close before I kissed her. "Hello, stranger." I pulled a chunk of doughnut from the bag I was holding and held it in front of her lips, watching her take it into her mouth.

"What, did you go for a walk?" I asked.

She finished chewing, licking off the flakes of glaze. "I went and got some avocado toast for lunch. I was so hungry, I ate it during the walk back. You just gave me the perfect dessert."

I glanced down her body. The sundress was loose on her curves and hung all the way to her feet, where her cute polished toes were wrapped in a pair of sandals. I focused just a little longer on her tits, the way the fabric hugged them, and hissed out a mouthful of air. "I bought four of these"—I held up a doughnut and chewed off a bite, returning the rest to the bag—"because it's been a hell of a day already."

"What's going on?"

I wrapped an arm around her waist and pulled her closer. "The usual hectic nightmares when you're trying to grow your business. Honestly, I'd rather kiss you than talk about it." I connected our mouths, inhaling the coconut that wafted off her face. "I missed you last night."

We didn't spend many evenings apart. Only if she had plans with Saara or I was going out with the guys.

Last night, she'd gone to the spa after work, then headed home to clean her apartment and get some things done that she'd been putting off, apparently.

"I missed you—"

Her voice cut off as a blaring sound came through the elevator, a grinding that caused the entire chamber to rattle. The floor was no longer steady, the light above flickering.

I grabbed the railing behind us and pulled Drake against me, holding her tightly as the noise got louder, the shaking increasing until the movement came to a screeching halt.

"Oh my God!" she gasped. "What the hell just happened?"

The light stopped strobing, and the noise dulled to a tick before it completely silenced.

I checked out the ceiling and the door, finally looking back at Drake.

Fear was so present in her eyes, practically pleading with me when she said, "This happens all the time, right?"

"Sure." I swallowed. "At least once a day."

I'd never heard that sound or felt that kind of tremor in this—or any—elevator, but the last thing I wanted was for her to panic.

"Easton . . ."

"Don't worry. Everything is going to be fine."

"Is it going to start up again?"

The button to our floor was still lit on the control panel, but we weren't moving. It seemed we were suspended somewhere between floors.

I shook my head. "I don't know. Let me call for help and find out." I stepped toward the control panel, where the box was located on the bottom, and reached inside for the phone.

"Do you think we're just floating somewhere between floors?" Drake asked as I pressed the button next to the phone and held the receiver to my ear. "Could we drop at any second?"

"No, we're safe."

An answer that I'd made up because I could tell her anxiety was rising.

"Can I help you?" a woman said from the phone.

"This is Easton Jones. I'm in the Boylston Tower, and we're stuck in the elevator."

"I'm so sorry about that," she replied. "I'll have a technician over there immediately. Is anyone hurt? Should I call 911?"

Drake was leaning against the wall, hugging her stomach, breathing out of her mouth, like her nose couldn't get the air in fast enough.

"No, we're both okay," I told her.

"It should take about fifteen minutes for the tech to arrive. If there are any issues or if I need to communicate with you, I'm going to call this phone."

"All right."

"Hang tight. Either myself or the technician will update you."

I thanked her and hung up.

I carefully moved toward Drake, not wanting the shift in balance to offset the elevator. "It won't take them long to get here and get it fixed. No need to worry, baby."

At some point, I must have dropped the bakery bag, and I lifted it off the floor, opening the top to take out the doughnut that I'd bitten into earlier.

I held it in front of her lips. "Sugar is a cure-all. Eat."

She shook her head. "I can't." She paused. "It feels like a coffin in here." She quickly peeked at the door. "I've never been claustrophobic in my life until now."

"I promise, nothing is going to happen."

"I'll just feel a lot better when we start moving again."

When things got stressful for her, her go-to was ice cream, and I kept plenty of pints in my freezer for when that happened. There was only one other thing that seemed to work when I needed to wring out the tension in her body.

I returned the doughnut to the bag and set it on the floor, then flattened my hands on the wall above her head.

I wasn't going to let her stand here and freak out.

I was going to do everything in my power to get her mind off it.

And I had that kind of power.

"Kiss me."

She took a deep breath. "Right . . . now?"

"Now," I growled.

She leaned up on her toes and kissed me. It took several seconds before her arms wrapped around my neck and I aligned our bodies, my dick immediately hardening, the tip rubbing against her.

"We have fifteen minutes before we're rescued," I told her. "I know exactly how we're going to spend every one of those seconds."

"Easton"—her eyes widened, her face moving away from mine— "in here? Now? While we're dangling in midair? Are you nuts?" She sucked in a breath. "And aren't we on camera?"

"I don't think this is a crazy idea at all." My hands dropped from the wall, and I lowered to the bottom of her dress, kneeling on the floor. "Besides, there are no cameras in here. They're only outside the elevators on each floor." I glanced underneath the hem, seeing a pair of lace panties. "We're safe-ish."

"Easton, I don't know—"

"Fifteen minutes, Drake. *Ticktock* . . . remember." I smiled before I ducked my face under the dress.

I placed my nose on the lace, right over her clit, and inhaled her.

That fucking smell.

I couldn't get enough.

Ever.

"Oh shit," she moaned, quivering.

I rubbed my nose up and down the thin material before I slipped the fabric to the side and licked from the lowest point of her all the way to the highest.

There would be no teasing in this elevator.

No waiting.

No punishing by drawing out her orgasm.

Drake needed one thing from me, and I was going to give it to her.

I pointed my tongue and focused on the top of her clit, swiping it back and forth while I used two fingers to spread the wetness down to her opening. I made sure to coat those same fingers as I prepped her, gradually inserting just enough that she knew where I was going, and then went as high as my knuckles.

Her hand found my head, the dress between us stopping her from pulling my hair—or even seeing me—but she still pushed against me. "My God, that feels good."

I knew what she liked: that two-finger combination, twisting while I moved into her, pulling straight out. After several plunges, I tilted my wrist so the ends of my fingers reached her G-spot.

"*Ohhh!*"

I knew that would speed up this process.

But that wasn't my intention.

I just wanted her to feel as good as possible.

And as she moaned, "Easton, *yesss*," I knew she was.

Her hips began to move, her legs tightening.

Sometimes, it took only licking, giving her enough pressure, moving my tongue horizontally across her. But there was another mix that had been making her wild recently: when I sucked her clit, holding the back of it with my teeth and rubbing the end with my tongue.

So I did.

And immediately she started to buck.

"Fuck! Yes!" she cried. "Oh shit!"

She was seconds away. I knew by the way she was hardening. How her body was rocking. How her palm ground over my head, her legs even shaking.

My fingers pushed deeper, turning, circling within her, my tongue moving faster as my teeth gently bared down on her clit.

Her wetness was covering me.

My mouth.

My hand.

I wanted to fucking bathe in it.

And I wanted to hear her muted screams, so I amped up the speed and power, and within a few more licks, she was shuddering.

"Easton!" She exhaled, tremoring. *"Ahhh!"*

Her back banged into the wall of the elevator, her breaths came out as moans, and she shook through her orgasm, each wave hitting my face as she swayed against me.

I licked until she stilled.

And I licked a bit more, making sure I got every drop of wetness.

I spread the lace across her, ensuring she was fully covered, and then I moved out from underneath her dress, getting back on my feet. My hands resumed their position on the wall above her head.

"How do you feel?"

She panted into my face, "Your tongue . . ."

"You love it."

"Yes"—she nodded—"I do." She was rubbing her hand over my zipper, cupping my erection. "And now it's your turn." She gnawed her lip, eyeing me.

As I leaned down and mashed our lips together, knowing she was tasting her own wetness, a thought that was so fucking hot, she lowered my zipper and took out my cock.

She clasped her fingers around my shaft and pulled her mouth away to whisper, "I want you."

I didn't know how much movement this elevator could handle, which meant I had to go slow. One way I could do that was by lifting her into my arms and holding her against the wall.

So that was what I did, aiming my dick beneath her dress, wrapping her legs around me, and just as I was about to slip her panties to the side, the phone in the elevator rang.

"You have to be fucking kidding me right now."

She wiggled a bit. "Put me down and answer it."

I reluctantly set her feet on the floor and picked up the receiver inside the box, saying, "Hello," as I held it to my ear.

"I just want to let you know that the technician has arrived, and he's discovered the problem. He should have you out of there in just a few minutes. Is everyone still doing fine? No emergencies that I need to be made aware of?"

The only emergency was that I wanted to fucking come.

"Things are all good," I told her. "Thank you." I hung up and said to Drake, "We'll be out of here in a few minutes—"

Before I'd even gotten the word out, the elevator was moving, the numbers on the control panel telling me we were rising to the top floor.

"You better do something with that." Drake pointed at my hard-on, smiling. "And don't worry, I plan to repay today's favor when I get to your condo tonight."

"And how do you plan to do that?" I tucked myself back into my jeans and zipped up.

She laughed. "Do you have a preference?"

I gave her a quick kiss before the elevator door swung open to the executive-level floor. "You can start with your mouth."

"It would be my pleasure."

The grin stayed on her face as we walked out, and she headed for her office.

I continued down the hallway. As I passed Holden's door, I heard, "Easton!"

I stopped after a few paces and backtracked, leaning against his doorframe while catching eyes with him and then Grayson, who was sitting in front of Holden's desk. "Yeah?"

"Where the hell have you been? We just checked your office and you weren't in there, and we called your cell several times and you didn't answer."

Holden's tone was setting off an alarm.

He sounded frazzled, anxious.

Angry.

Things I rarely saw from him.

He was always the more patient, calm voice of the three of us, and that had everything to do with Belle.

What would be causing this?

They couldn't possibly know what I'd just done to our director of app development and engineering in the elevator since there were no cameras.

The only other thing this could be about was that they suspected Drake and I were dating.

With Grayson being my neighbor, Drake and I had to be sly during a few unexpected situations—the first when Grayson had randomly stopped by my condo one evening to talk about work, and the other when Drake and I had almost crossed paths with him in the elevator after coming back from a night out.

I felt shitty that I was keeping my best friends in the dark. Doing that wasn't like me at all, but Drake and I just hadn't agreed to tell them yet.

But knowing Grayson as well as I did, if he thought or questioned whether Drake and I were together, he would have come to me—he wouldn't be part of a sit-down with Holden.

I adjusted my shoulder against the hard frame and said, "Drake and I were just in the elevator, and it broke down midfloor, and we were stuck in there for about fifteen minutes. There's no cell service in there—as you know—and the tech just came and rescued us. We just got out a few seconds ago."

"Are you all right?" Grayson asked.

I nodded.

"And is she?" Holden inquired.

I wiped what was left of her off my face, the coconut so pronounced. "Yeah, she's fine."

The two of them glanced at each other.

Holden said, "Come in and shut the door. We need to talk to you."

The moment I took a seat, Grayson barked, "We have a major fucking problem."

I leaned back in my chair and crossed my arms. "What's going on?"

"This is what's going on . . ." Holden handed me a manila folder.

I opened the top flap, staring at the first sheet of paper. Beneath it were at least ten or fifteen more. As I took in the images, processed the wording, a churning started to move through my stomach.

One that made my hands clench.

One that made my heart fucking pound.

I eventually looked up at them. "This can't be . . . I don't believe it."

"But it is," Holden replied. "And we're fucked."

CHAPTER THIRTY-TWO

Drake

After the last fifteen or so minutes that I'd spent in the elevator with Easton, I was practically out of breath as I got seated at my desk. A situation that, before those fifteen minutes, had induced a semi-panic attack eased only by his perfect, incredibly talented tongue.

My God, that man.

He'd read my body and known exactly how to get my mind out of the place it was headed, bringing me into a cloud of euphoria before the panic could really peak.

And just when I thought we were on the verge of having mind-blowing elevator sex, the call had come through. Not that I minded. I'd be spending tonight at his place anyway, where there would be many more opportunities to get physical. But after he'd knelt on the floor and slipped under my dress, lapping me with such vigor, I wanted to give back.

I wanted to make him moan as loudly as I had.

Easton was so good to me.

In fact, it was hard to believe someone like him even existed in this world. Someone who was so focused on my emotional and physical needs, who constantly wanted to spend so much time with me, who had so many endearing and unique qualities.

Saara was right.

I was falling in love.

And the only sound that could pull me out of those thoughts, popping the bubble of bliss that I was in, aside from Easton's voice, was the ringing of my office line. The caller ID showed the call came from the conference room, a source I found extremely strange.

I answered, "This is Drake."

"Drake, hi, it's Holden. Do you mind coming into the conference room? We'd like to speak with you."

We?

Since my monitor was on, I quickly checked my calendar, looking for a meeting the elevator mishap had caused me to miss.

There was nothing on the schedule.

"Of course," I replied. "I'll be right in."

I hung up the phone and grabbed a notepad and pen and made my way down the hallway. The door to the conference room was closed, a sight that caused me to pause the moment my hand clasped the knob. When I turned it and opened the door, I saw everyone was already inside.

All three partners.

The head of HR.

The head of finance.

And our in-house attorney.

The entire executive-level team I met with on a weekly basis.

Who had obviously spent the last few minutes—or more—meeting without me.

From what I had experienced so far at this company, meetings as formal as this didn't spring up out of nowhere. One of the partners would stop by my office, phone calls would be made, smiles were typically shared versus the aloofness that I saw around the table.

I suddenly had a bad feeling in my stomach.

"Thank you for joining us, Drake," Holden said. "Please take a seat anywhere that you feel comfortable."

As I made my way to an open spot, my hands felt odd and clammy, almost numb. My feet were moving as though I no longer controlled them. The breathlessness I'd felt earlier was back, but for an entirely different reason.

I caught Easton's eyes during my journey. I couldn't read his expression, nor did I understand what was behind his stare.

I had just been with him, and he hadn't mentioned anything about this meeting.

What the hell is going on?

Is this about us?

What just happened in the elevator?

But how would they know? He promised there were no cameras inside.

I adjusted my position after sitting, unable to find one that was comfortable. "What is this about?"

Holden crossed his hands, linking his fingers, setting them on a file that rested in front of him.

A similar-looking file sat in front of everyone.

Aside from me.

"Drake . . ." Holden started, inhaling a loud breath. "Easton, Grayson, and I realize we have competitors and there will be many more during our tenure. Sharing the market is inevitable in this business—and any business, for that matter. We can't trademark a dating app. What we have trademarked is our proprietary software and our psychological exam—things you're already well aware of." He paused, and my brain spun, trying to piece together what he was saying. "What we didn't anticipate and what we don't appreciate is a social media giant developing a dating model that is identical to ours."

I shifted from his face to Grayson's and then Easton's, waiting for the news to click.

But it didn't.

"Okay," I said softly. "Which giant are you referring to?"

Holden looked surprised by my question. "Faceframe."

"Faceframe?" I gasped, my hand going to my throat. "I'm sorry. I don't understand."

Grayson, who was sitting next to me, slid his folder across the small space between us. The moment it landed in front of me, I opened the top, viewing the papers inside.

On each sheet were several pictures of an interface, a design that allowed users to pick their reason for joining the dating app, their language less direct, but the path was—without question—achingly familiar to Hooked. Although Faceframe's world-renowned logo was in the top corner, this was an interface I'd never seen before.

I'd never worked on it.

I certainly hadn't helped design it.

I flipped to the last page, which was an email, the message only a few sentences long.

> Here are the designs Faceframe created once I sent them the information they needed to get started. Information you gave me direct access to. Thanks for that. Nothing like feeding bait to the enemy or, in this case, the company that's going to take you down. Faceframe Dating Place has now launched in several test markets, each one responding well over our predictions, as expected.
>
> Drake Madden
> Director of App Development
> Faceframe & Faceframe Dating Place

Why was my name signed at the bottom?

Why was this email constructed like it came directly from me?

My gaze slowly rose to the top of the email, and my eyes widened, my mouth opening as I read the address of the sender.

Drake@Faceframe.com

"Oh my God." I glanced up, looking at the faces around the table. "I didn't do this. I didn't send this email. I don't even know what Faceframe Dating Place is." I felt frantic, bits of information shooting through my brain, like I was writing HTML for multiple sources. "Once I left Faceframe, my email was turned off. This message sounds like I'm still employed there. I'm not. You all know that. And I wouldn't send them your designs or data—or anything, for that matter. I . . . don't . . . know . . . what's happening right now."

"Drake," Holden started, "there are only two things we know at this present moment. One, this email came into my inbox less than an hour ago and it was sent from your Faceframe email address."

"Allegedly," I quickly threw in.

"And two, the pictures that were sent in the email show an interface that's extremely similar to Hooked." He paused, as though giving me time to process even though both claims were completely ludicrous. "For someone to gain access to our designs and proprietary software, someone from this office would have had to send Faceframe the data, and according to this email, that person claims to be you."

I felt my head shake, my lips open the entire time. I couldn't believe what I was hearing. Seeing. That something this evil was attached to my name. "But I didn't do it. I'm telling you, I didn't send that email. I know nothing about this—not just the creation of the email or how my address was resurrected out of the blue, but I have no knowledge of the Dating Place. It didn't exist while I was employed there, or if it did, it was never shared with me."

"If your name wasn't listed as the sender of that email, we would be in full agreement," Holden said. His tone wasn't exonerating, but it wasn't accusatory either. "But you have to understand where we're coming from. The company in question is your previous employer. The designs are painfully similar to ours. As our director of app development and engineering, you have unlimited access to our systems and software, and that puts you in a precarious position. Not to mention you've signed an NDA with us."

"But I wouldn't do this. I'm not a spy or a thief. I wouldn't send you an email from my old Faceframe account and then sit at this table and defend myself. I would get on a plane and go right back to work for Faceframe if that was the case." As I glanced at Easton, my pulse was hammering away so fast, my tongue was vibrating. When I got no reaction from him, no response to anything I'd said, I looked at the attorney. "Isn't there a way to confirm I'm not employed there? That they haven't paid me a dime since my final paycheck?"

"Drake, whether you're employed there or not is only half the issue and a serious breach of your NDA," Grayson said. "The other half is that data was transferred from our company to theirs."

Hair fell into my eyes as my head moved continuously from side to side. "You don't believe me."

"We're not saying that at all, Drake. We believe—" Holden stopped to glance around the room. "Let me rephrase. I believe I can speak for everyone at this table when I say you're one of the best things that's ever happened to Hooked. At this moment, we're looking at the information that has been presented, and due to its nature, we must take action. This isn't an accusation. This is the start of a thorough investigation."

"Which will rule out any wrongdoing, or it'll show who in this office did in fact send Faceframe the data," Grayson added.

Their choice of words was no coincidence. Grayson and Holden had been prepped on what to say, the in-house attorney carefully providing the verbiage.

I knew how this worked.

But I didn't need to watch my verbiage.

Not when I was completely innocent.

"I know how this looks," I told them. "I know you got that email with my name at the top and my signature at the bottom and what you immediately assumed." I took a breath. "It's what anyone would assume. But I swear to all of you, I had absolutely nothing to do with this." I didn't know how to show them I was innocent. I didn't know how to prove that I wasn't this kind of person. "I'm still in contact with my old colleagues at Faceframe. They reach out to me on occasion with questions, and I'm the ex-boss who answers each and every one. I refuse to leave them hanging—I'm not a person who would do that. Just like I answer calls from my coders here when they phone at three in the morning. But never once during any of the conversations I had with Faceframe employees did they mention the Dating Place. I've been kept completely in the dark and . . ." My voice trailed off as I glanced down at the folder. "I realize now that was probably on purpose."

No one said anything.

Not even Easton.

His silence was maddening.

Didn't he have an opinion?

Didn't he know I would never do something like this?

Didn't he have anything to offer that would help my case?

I lifted the papers, running my fingers over the photos. "Are you positive these are real? That these images weren't Photoshopped? That someone from, say, another one of our competitors didn't send this in an attempt to rile you up?"

"David was able to find the test markets, and he confirmed the Dating Place is live, like the email stated," Grayson said. "And the interface looks exactly like the photos." He nodded toward the papers in my hand.

I set the pages down and closed the top of the folder. "I'm not a mole, a spy, or a thief—I'm an honest, dedicated employee who would do anything for Hooked, including working eighty hours a week, which I have been. I certainly wouldn't put in all those hours only to blow myself up this way." I was met with more silence, and I dug through my brain, scraping for more verbal evidence that would acquit me. "I'm one of the top coders in the country. If I really wanted to steal your designs, I would have just hacked in and gotten the information I needed. I most definitely wouldn't have put myself through this kind of humiliation and shame to get something I could have easily obtained while sitting at my desk at Faceframe." I scanned each face around the table. "Please tell me you believe me."

"Let me reiterate," the in-house attorney said, "you are not being accused of anything. As it currently stands, the only proof we have is this email. We don't have evidence that you acted as a mole or that you distributed or transferred any said material." As the attorney took a breath, I felt Easton's eyes on me. "The partners are going to assess the evidence that has been presented and open an internal investigation to determine if there's more evidence to be found. Based on those findings, they'll move forward with the next steps."

That meant they were going to comb through every piece of data on my computer to see if they could locate a transfer.

They knew that if I wanted to hide my tracks, it wouldn't be hard. I could make that transfer history completely disappear, where David or a forensic data analyst wouldn't be able to find it.

My skills were stronger than both combined.

Still, they couldn't accuse me unless they had proof.

I leaned my arms onto the table, my head falling forward as I searched, clawed, through my mind for the right words. And when I still had nothing, when I didn't even know where to begin, I glanced up. "I don't know what I can say at this point to clear my name. I know how terrible this looks. I know I'm being framed to appear like the worst employee in the world, but I hope that in the little time I've been here, I've shown how loyal I am to your company. How much I love working here and how much you all mean to me."

As I thought of the relationships I'd developed with the people around this table, my voice caught in my throat. Their opinions of me mattered, and it hurt to think those had now been tarnished.

I couldn't go down without a last-minute fight.

"Why would I do all this work here if my intent was to just destroy you?" I asked. "Why would I go to Germany to represent a brand I don't respect? Why would I be on the cusp of an international rollout if my intention was to never follow through? You've seen the work I've done with the rollout, and you know how long it's taken me so far. You've witnessed all the improvements I've made on the current app, the usability and retention I've increased—things I wouldn't even be bothering with if my motive was as nefarious as these accusations." I held up the folder and tried to bring more air into my lungs. It didn't help; I still couldn't breathe. "Analyze whatever you want, strip my work and home stations. I assure you, you'll find nothing. Your investigation is going to prove my innocence."

I waited for a response.

For someone, anyone, to acknowledge that something I'd said was true.

Or at least part of it was.

But they said nothing.

Until I finally heard in a soft, agonizing voice, "I speak for everyone when I say I hope that's the case."

Easton.

I couldn't define what he meant.

Or the battle that was becoming more prominent in his eyes.

Or the way each of his syllables banged my chest.

Holden's eyes were suddenly no different than Easton's.

Neither was Grayson's.

"Due to the evidence that's been presented and the level of access you have within Hooked, we have decided to suspend your employment until the investigation is closed," the attorney said.

They were . . . terminating me.

Even if it was temporary, they were still shutting me out.

Because some asshole, for some unknown reason, had framed me for something I didn't do.

Had I really thought that after I pled my case they were going to trust every word I said? That I would be able to continue working like none of this had happened?

Still, hearing that news, feeling the gravity of it all, caused everything inside me to tighten.

"I see," I whispered.

"I kindly ask you to remove all personal items from your office that you would like to have access to since you won't be able to return to the building until the investigation is closed," the attorney said. "Sometime today, I will be stopping by your apartment to pick up the workstation Hooked has set up in your home."

"Is that necessary?" Easton asked.

"I'm afraid it is," the attorney replied.

I nodded.

I was terrified my voice would crack if I spoke.

The tears were there, threatening my eyes. I was doing everything in my power to hold them off.

As I stood, I couldn't look at Easton.

It hurt too much.

That war—I didn't want to see another second of it.

Aside from Saara and Easton and the other people in this room, I was alone in this world. Losing their respect, trust, and support pained me more than all this.

I wanted Easton to believe me.

I wanted him to have my back.

I wanted him to look at Holden and Grayson and the rest of the team and shout from the top of his lungs that I would never do something like this.

But at the same time, I was wrecked that the man I cared about so deeply had been put in this situation where he had to question whether I was innocent.

That the look in his eyes was for me.

Was about me.

Was the middle ground between me and his best friends and the company he'd worked so hard to build. With nothing else I could say, I stood, wobbling as I pushed the chair back and walked around the table. The second I reached the hallway, I rushed to my office and shut myself in, pressing my back against the hard wooden door.

I had . . . no one.

I was completely alone, a feeling I hadn't experienced since Easton had come back into my life. I could no longer fight off the tears.

They came hard.

Fast.

Dripping over my lips and past my chin.

My stomach aching, my entire body shaking.

Why.

How.

I didn't understand.

I didn't—

"Drake, can I come in?"

Easton.

His voice was outside my door.

Could I even talk?

Did I want to see him?

"Please, Drake, open your door."

I twisted the handle, letting him inside, and went over to my desk, grabbing my bag, looking around to see what I wanted to throw inside it.

"We need to talk."

I heard the sound of my door closing. I heard his statement.

But I didn't look up.

I didn't acknowledge his presence.

I hovered my hand in the air, my fingers tapping invisible keys, taking an inventory of the things I'd brought and what I wanted to pack.

The succulent that sat next to my computer. The framed picture of Saara and me that was beside the plant. The sweater on the back of my chair. The coffee mug.

"Drake." His hands were on my shoulders, almost shaking me, forcing me to look up at him. "I didn't know when we were in the elevator that any of this was going on. I didn't know until we got out and they asked me to come into Holden's office and they showed me the same photographs and email that they just showed you. If I knew, if I had any kind of goddamn inkling, I would have told you."

I searched his eyes, really taking them in. "You would have warned me that I was going to be called into an executive meeting where I had to face the partners, the in-house counsel, and the other senior-level directors and look like a complete fool when I told them I didn't send that email? That someone framed me? You would have told me that the people I respect so much in this company think I would actually steal proprietary information? Easton"—I stopped to breathe, something I was positive I still wasn't doing—"never in my life has my character or integrity ever been called into question. Do you know how hard I have worked for my career?" My voice was rising, and I couldn't stop it. "Do you know what it's like to be a twenty-eight-year-old woman who is top in her field, a field that's lined with mostly men, and then to be accused of this?" My eyes were burning, my throat on fire. "Because from where I'm standing, you don't. You don't get it at all."

He held me even tighter, eventually moving his hands to my cheeks. "I would have prepared you. I would have put my own character and integrity on the line for you. Because even though Hooked is my dream and my dream child, you mean everything to me." He moved his face closer, locking our stares. "Do you understand the emotional stakes that are involved here? If Hooked fails, Drake, that's not personal.

That's years of hard work and financial risk and determination down the goddamn drain. But losing a company that was designed by the three of us, that gave us all a chance to work together, that brought me Love, and then brought you back to me after I thought I had lost you forever—that's personal." His thumbs strummed my cheeks. "Holden once said to me that the reason the app was created was for us to find each other—you and me, Drake. That's fate. That's what I believe. And I also believe nothing is going to take that away from me. I won't let it." He stayed in that position until he tilted his head back, looking at the ceiling before making eye contact again. "I know you didn't do this."

As his hands dropped to my shoulders, I wiped the droplets that were on the verge of falling into my mouth. "I understand how hard this is for you, but you have to understand how hard it is for me, Easton. Someone is making me look extremely guilty. Someone has either shared your designs or stolen them, and they're trying to blame it on me. I wouldn't still be here, I wouldn't care, I wouldn't have tears streaming down my face if I was that person."

"That's what I told the guys when we were in Holden's office."

"Did they believe you?"

My gut clenched as I waited for his response.

As I tried to envision what that conversation had looked like.

"I don't know, Drake. It was a hard thing to discuss. I couldn't exactly push your innocence onto two guys who don't know we're together. They would wonder why I was able to speak so confidently about your character and how I know so much—and I couldn't go there, at least not until you gave me the okay to have that talk with them."

"Fuck." I swallowed, trying to move the knot from my throat, but it wouldn't budge. "This is such a mess."

He gripped the sides of my face, holding me steady. "I know we agreed to keep things a secret between us, but I think it's time to tell them." He held me even tighter. "I want to go into Holden's office right now and defend your innocence and explain to them all about Love—about us. But I need you to tell me it's all right to do that."

"Us," I whispered. "Will there even be an us after this?" My lips quivered as I continued, "Easton, you and Saara are all I have. Besides the pseudo-family sitting around the table in the conference room. It devastates me that any of you would think I would do something like this. I wouldn't risk those relationships. I wouldn't risk my career. I wouldn't risk us."

He pulled me into his arms, pressing his body to mine before I could finish. "I believe you. I trust you. I don't think you would ever do something like this to me or our company."

My body sagged against him, and he took even more of my weight, breathing into my neck, cupping the back of my head until I had the energy to pull away.

"Are you sure?" I paused, staring into his eyes. "Easton, you're positive you have no doubt at all?"

His teeth found his lip, biting down for just a second before he said, "I'm going to be honest. There was a brief period when I questioned it. You've just been in contact with so many Faceframe colleagues lately, text messages and conversations, and I didn't know what any of them were about. And then there was that run-in with your colleague in Germany, and he mentioned the project you were working on—"

"A new messaging system for the Faceframe app. That was what we were designing when I gave my notice. A whole new interface for private communication. He wouldn't say that because of his NDA, but that's what we were talking about." I reached for my cell, which was on my desk. "Here. Look." I placed the phone in his hand and brought up the recent messages with my old team members. "These are the conversations I have with them." I watched him read each one, and then I opened another text box to show him a different exchange. They were all work-related inquiries, questions I offered to answer, issues I was helping to solve because I knew the adjustment would be challenging for them.

"Drake—"

"There are more, hold on."

He placed his hand on mine, lowering the phone. "You don't have to show me more. I believe you." He stared at me silently. "I'm going to go into Holden's office and talk to him and Grayson. Is there anything you don't want me to say?"

"I don't know." I shook my head, the movement causing more tears to fall. "No."

"Baby . . ."

His voice was so gentle, it sent me even further into an emotional spiral.

"I have to get out of here, Easton. I have to go home."

"I'm coming to your apartment tonight. After work. And we'll talk." His face moved closer to mine. "Or we don't have to talk at all. I just want to be with you."

Before I could respond, before I could even do anything, he was placing the softest kiss on my lips.

CHAPTER THIRTY-THREE

Easton

When I told Holden and Grayson I needed to talk to them and asked them to follow me to my office, I didn't have a plan. I took the seat behind my desk as they sat in front of me, and I stewed over the meeting that had just taken place in the conference room. I fucking ached for Drake and the emotion she'd expressed in her office. I tried to formulate how to best lead this conversation, given all the topics I needed to discuss with them.

Nothing I could say would change Drake's suspension.

I knew that.

Whether she was innocent or not, until the investigation was closed, she couldn't return to Hooked. Before the meeting with her, the three of us had agreed to hire a forensic data analyst, who would comb through both of Drake's workstations and determine if any data from her computers had been transferred.

That would take a few weeks at least.

But, in the end, I knew it would clear her name. It wouldn't solve who had sent the email, but at least it would prove she hadn't stolen our designs and software and acted as a mole for Faceframe.

Deep down, I knew she had nothing to do with this. Someone was responsible, and it wasn't her.

But how I approached that with the guys was a whole different story.

There were many layers to this.

And they all started with Love.

I pushed up my sleeves, despite the air-conditioning vent blasting above me, the sweat already bubbling on my face, and said, "I have something to tell you both. Something that's probably going to blow your minds."

"Does it have anything to do with what happened today?" Holden asked, his voice cautious, his expression somewhat concerned. "With Drake, I mean."

"It has to do with Drake," I confirmed.

The beginning was the only place to start. It was just a difficult point to get across because Holden wasn't going to approve of my actions, not after he'd warned Grayson and me about dating our employees.

Not that his approval mattered anymore; shit definitely couldn't get worse than it already was.

"The moment she came in for her interview, there was something about her that was intensely familiar," I told them. "I didn't know what it was, I just knew I'd somehow seen her or been around her, but what caused that feeling, I couldn't put my finger on." I rubbed my palms together, the heat from my face working its way to my hands. "That feeling grew over the next two weeks, and if I'm being honest—which is why I called you both in here—I did everything I could to be around her. I came up with excuses to go into her office, I was going for extra coffee when I knew she was in the kitchen, I would try to share elevators with her, I would hang around at the end of meetings just so I could talk to her more."

Holden's brows raised. "Because you were trying to pinpoint what it was that was so familiar about her?"

I looked at Grayson. Unlike Holden, I could tell he'd read between the lines.

"Well, yes, Holden, there's that, but I was also growing feelings for her at the same time. A type of connection that I'd only ever felt with Love."

"Love?" Holden's brows stayed raised. "Wait, wait, wait. You mean, she wasn't just someone you wanted to sleep with—which upsets the hell out of me, but we'll get to that in a second. You wanted *more* with Drake?"

"Yes."

Holden crossed his legs, his foot shaking while he silently gazed at me. "You know I'm all about you finding Love or love, but as a cofounder of this company, I'm going to have a hard time supporting that you wanted more with her." His stare intensified. "Easton, please don't tell me you're sleeping with our director of app development and engineering."

"You mean Drake," I corrected.

"Her title matters," Holden countered. "She's a director at our company—or was—and she's—"

"She's Love." My stare shifted from him to Grayson. "Drake is SaarasLove."

"She's . . . *what?*" Holden exhaled.

Grayson's hand landed on the edge of my desk. "Shut the fuck up." He lifted his finger, stopping me from commenting, and went on. "Drake Madden is Love. Is that what you're telling us? That the woman you fell for all those years ago is her?"

"The woman who broke his heart," Holden added.

"They're one and the same," I told them.

I went over to the bar in my office, pouring myself several fingers' worth of scotch.

I didn't even know what time it was.

I didn't fucking care.

Nor did I offer any to my friends when I returned to my desk and took a long drink. "Now you know why she was so familiar to me. Why her lips, eyes, her body, even her goddamn scent were all things that resonated every time I looked at her, every fucking time I got a whiff."

"You've slept with a lot of women, Easton," Grayson said. "I don't know how you remembered, especially given that her face was wrapped in lace that night."

I shook my head. "She was different. I said that from day one." My eyes narrowed. "You both know she's the girl who had the potential of changing me."

Holden nodded.

So did Grayson.

"And now she really has." I drained several sips.

"When did it start?" Holden asked. "When did you find out that it was her?"

"The night we all went to the bar to celebrate month end, I walked her home, and I kissed her." Jesus, that felt like years ago at this point. "That's when she figured it out and she went into the system and found my name under BostonLifer." I explained how she wanted me to hear it from Love, so she set up a temporary membership and reached out to me through the app. "You remember when I told you Love was back and she wanted to meet up?" I nodded at Grayson. "I just never told you that meeting took place."

"Dude." Grayson sighed. "That's some shit right there."

I rubbed my hand over my scruff. "You should have seen my face when she came up to me at the bar and told me who she was."

"I can't imagine," Holden replied.

"I still can't wrap my head around the fact that Love is Drake," Grayson said.

"Or that Easton is dating one of our directors, putting the entire rollout at risk," Holden said. "As your best friend, I'm high-fiving the hell out of you. As one of your partners, this scenario scares the shit out of me."

"I get it." My chair felt too tight, too closed in, so I picked up my drink and walked over to the windows. "That's why, since the discovery, we decided to take things slow. To not tell you guys until we had a better idea of where things stood between us. To, in a way, put the company first." I glanced out the glass beside me, searching for Fenway Park in the distance. "But we've been seeing each other ever since that night, and things have been amazing."

"The woman who got away is now back," Holden said softly.

When I connected my stare with Holden's, I said, "My heart was fucking breaking for her when you told me the news in your office today. It shattered again in the conference room. And when I went to her office right before she left, I told her, as long as it was okay, I was going to talk to you guys and tell you everything."

"To plead her case," Holden said.

"Listen, I know it's not going to change anything. But Drake is more than just our director. She's a woman who I believe would do anything for our company. I can speak about her character. I can speak about her morals and ethics because she's the woman I love."

"Goddamn it," Grayson groaned. "This is a lot."

"A lot because Holden warned us not to date anyone at the company. And a lot because Love and Drake are the same woman. And a lot because Drake is getting wrongly accused—"

"We have no choice, Easton," Holden began. "These are the steps we have to take to protect Hooked. You know that. Hell, I'm positive even Drake knows that." He adjusted himself in his seat. "We'd be fools if we didn't do our due diligence. This isn't about something minor that we can easily see past. We're talking about a major competitor that's already international that could take more than half of our business. An email with her name on it and a whopping accusation that I can't even stomach."

My back straightened against the glass. "Half of our business?" I exhaled, the tension still unbearable in my chest. "It can't be half. Besides, they don't have the anonymity that we do. Your personal profile on Faceframe will become your dating profile, and users don't want potential dates to have that much access to their information—"

"That's a moot point," Holden said. "We're not arguing over the percent we could potentially lose. We're arguing over their design and how they gained our data."

"It wasn't her." I ground my teeth together. "Someone restored her old email address and sent that email to make her take the fall."

"Buddy, you know I'd fight like hell for her, and I want nothing more than to clear her name. But I need to see it with my own eyes. I need to be assured, and we won't have that proof until the forensic data analyst wraps up their findings," Holden said.

"That'll prove whether she sent them the data, but it won't prove if she really sent the email or not," Grayson added.

"There has to be another way," I said, pounding my fist on the glass.

"I can tell you one thing," Holden shot back. "If she's innocent, I'll do whatever it takes to get her back here."

I shook my head. "This is so fucked."

All I wanted to do was show them that Drake wasn't guilty of this.

I wanted to take down Faceframe.

And I wanted to walk down the hallway and see Drake sitting behind her desk.

I drained the rest of my scotch and walked back to the bar to pour myself more.

Just as I reached for the bottle, an idea came to me.

"Fuck . . ." I growled across my office.

"You're onto something, aren't you?" Holden said.

"Oh hell yeah he is," Grayson said. "I know that expression on his face."

I brought the bottle back to my desk, twisting off the cap, not even bothering with my glass. "I have an idea." I wiped my lips. "Call the pilot right now. We need the plane."

CHAPTER THIRTY-FOUR

Drake

"Ice cream, cookies, doughnuts, chocolate cake, salt and vinegar chips in case we need to offset the sweets, and I brought over some fries that I stuck in the freezer that are just waiting to be put in the air fryer," Saara said.

She was standing next to my coffee table, looking at the sugar-inspired charcuterie board that she'd been working on for the last several minutes.

While I was slumped on the couch, drinking.

More like guzzling every drop of wine in my glass.

"What am I forgetting?" she asked. "Oh, maybe we need some tart fruit to counterbalance the salty chips. I brought strawberries and raspberries too."

I held up my glass. "More wine."

"*Ahhh*, that." She hurried off to the kitchen and returned with two more bottles. "For this round, do you want white or red—"

"Just pour. I don't care."

I heard a twist and then the sloshing of liquid, the glass getting heavier in my hand.

But I wasn't watching her fill it.

I wasn't looking at anything.

I'd zoned out, like I'd been doing since I got home from work a handful of hours ago. A ceaseless pattern repeating in my head where I first racked through every thought, trying to figure out how I hadn't heard about Faceframe's Dating Place, and then remembered the heaviness of the day—the faces that had stared back at me in the conference room, the words that had been spoken. The conversation I'd had with Easton in my office before I left. If my name was never cleared, could we continue as a couple? Would Grayson and Holden ever accept me being a part of Easton's life? Would the tech industry—an industry where Easton had such a remarkable reputation—respect him if his girlfriend was pegged as a corporate spy who sought to destroy his company?

But it didn't end there.

It got worse.

Because there was also the personal weight of it all. The one request Mom had before she died was for me to graduate from MIT, but I still wanted to make her proud. I wanted her to look down and see what I had accomplished. And if I had the reputation of being a spy, no other tech company would ever want to work with me.

I would be finished.

Breathe.

Sip.

Repeat.

"Drink up," Saara said.

With my hand still raised, I brought the wine to my lips, swallowing until my throat burned.

How did I not know? Who designed the content to be so similar to Hooked? How quickly can the forensic data analyst prove that I had nothing to do with it?

"How do you like this red?" she asked.

Breathe. "It's fine."

"Is it too dry?"

Dry?

Sip.

I finally looked at her as she hovered over me, both bottles in her hands, her brows raised high. "Saara, I honestly didn't even know it was red."

"Babe . . ." Her voice was soft, gentle. So was the sound when she set the bottles on the table and the feel of her sitting next to me, and the arm that wrapped around my shoulders. "We're going to get through this. I promise."

If I shook my head, which was what I wanted to do, the tears would fall. If I stayed still, like I was doing now, I could keep them at bay, halfway between my lids and tear ducts—where they'd been frozen since she'd handed me my first glass of wine.

"I don't know, Saara . . ."

"Hey . . . look at me."

I hadn't realized I wasn't.

I turned my face, feeling a drip round my eyelid, meeting an expression that caused even more tears to fall.

Fuck.

Fuck, fuck, fuck.

She was hurting, hurting for me, and that killed me.

Saara and I shared happiness and pain.

I just didn't want there to be pain.

I didn't want today to happen.

Breathe.

Sip.

Repeat.

"Listen to me," she started. "The forensic dude is going to prove your innocence. The second they get their hands on your computers, it's going to be more than obvious that you didn't transfer anything to FaceDicks."

Normally, that would have made me laugh.

But I couldn't even imagine that sound coming through my lips.

"Easton is trying to put a rush on it, but it could take weeks," I said. "In the meantime, I need to figure out how that email was sent, which I can do, once I get my head on straight and sober up a little. But still, even if I figure that part out, I have to sit here, unemployed like a total shit. Embarrassed. Disgusted. Pissed off. Confused. Cranky. And impatient as fuck until they prove I didn't send the data. Ugh."

"There's no need to feel embarrassed. You've done nothing wrong." She reached toward the table, grabbed something, and handed it to me. "Disgusted, pissed off, and all the rest, I can totally get on board with."

Though I wasn't hungry, I didn't even look to see what it was before I took a bite.

I chewed without tasting.

I didn't know if it was a cookie or cake.

And I didn't care.

"Let's look at all the positives, shall we?" She found my phone, which was tucked under my thigh, and pulled up my messages. "Look at all these texts you've gotten. Here's one from the head of HR, who reached out to check on you. Another from the head of finance." She continued to scroll. "And here's a bunch from all of your team." She nuzzled up even closer to me. "Is that a smile I see?"

"Definitely not."

She set my phone in my lap. "I'm on a mission to make that smile appear, regardless of what I have to do."

I immediately tossed my phone a few cushions down.

I didn't want to see it anymore.

"I know what will do the trick," she said. "We can talk about the fact that Easton and Grayson are flying somewhere right now with all the intention of clearing your name."

Breathe.

Sip.

Repeat.

"I can't even process that," I admitted.

"Why, babe? He loves you. That's why he's out there, acting all Jedi-like, heading off to who knows where to lightsaber someone's ass."

I stopped trying to hold back the tears, and the moment I dropped the little effort I'd been putting in, my chin quivered, the water making my vision blurry. I set the wine down and covered my face, leaning into Saara's shoulder while she wrapped her other arm around me.

"He's got you."

And that was the part that made me cry even harder.

Easton had called me from the car not too long after I'd left the office. He told me he and Grayson had just left their condo building, where they'd stopped to pack a few things, and they were on their way to their private jet. Holden had only stayed back because of Belle. Their mission was to clear my name, but how they planned to do that and where they were going, I didn't know. He didn't have time to share those details. He just phoned to tell me that he wasn't going to make it over after work, that he'd been in touch with Saara and she was going to come in his place, and that he'd be back in a few days.

Since Easton and Saara were now FaceDick friends, it made it easy for them to communicate without me.

"I can't believe he's doing this for me," I whispered.

"Why? He knows you're not at fault, and he obviously thinks he can fix it. I get the feeling Easton would do absolutely anything for you, and I feel like today proved that."

Oh God.

That thought, that realization, caused even more emotion.

I tried to breathe, and when I couldn't, I leaned back, wiping my face with my sleeve.

"*Ummm*, why is there a half-eaten cookie in my hair?" Saara asked.

I looked at her just as she pulled it out of her locks. "Sorry. I forgot you even gave it to me. I must have set it down—on you."

She laughed as she placed it on the table and picked up a pint of ice cream. "Oreo and peanut butter cup, our fave." She dipped a spoon into the creamy mixture and dug out a heaping mound that she handed to me. "Another thing we haven't talked about yet is how your relationship with Easton has now been aired. The guys know, so you don't have to sneak around anymore and check to see if Grayson is in the elevator at Easton's building and hide out in the kitchen at the office to make out."

"Which we didn't do."

She pulled the empty spoon out of my hand and covered it with more from the pint before giving it back to me. "You didn't?"

"That happened once."

"Only . . . *once?*"

"Maybe twice." I chewed off a huge chunk of Oreo before washing it down with a gulp of wine. "And I guess it's a relief that they know, and Easton and I have definitely established a flow at the office that works for us, but . . ."

"But what?"

"What if they can't prove my innocence and everything explodes, and I never return to the office?" When I tried to inhale, my lungs ached. I stabbed the spoon into the ice cream, my stomach reaching the breaking point from all these sweets. "What if my time at Hooked is over?"

She lifted the bottle off the coffee table and poured some wine into my glass. "You need more. Maybe it'll knock some sense into you, because what you're saying is far too wild to be true."

I set my hand on hers. "Saara, it's not."

She returned the bottle and faced me. "You're not going to work tomorrow and maybe for a few days—"

"More like a few weeks. It's going to suck. And while I'm up at the crack of dawn every morning, pacing my apartment, watching the sun rise, all I'm going to think about is how I should be at work. How I should be getting prepped to motivate my team so we can accomplish the day's tasks that will get us one step closer to the rollout."

"And that's going to happen. I bet my life on it." When I tried to interrupt, she continued, "You won't even have to explain to your team what went down since the guys were nice enough to tell everyone you had to go on medical leave." I attempted again and she lifted her hand, stopping me to say, "And while I know medical leave isn't something to lie about, the last thing any of us wants is to have rumors and gossip floating around the office when not a single word of it would be true."

I leaned forward, freeing my hands of the glass, holding my palms over my head. "This is too much."

"Drake—"

"I can't." I got up and walked to the kitchen. There wasn't anything I wanted there, so I headed for the bedroom, turning at the doorway to move back across the living room. "I feel like I'm being caged. Like I can't breathe. Like I'm losing it. Maybe I need to get out of here. Maybe I need to go for a walk and clear my head."

She glanced down at her watch. "You can't leave just yet."

"Why?" I halted in front of the couch.

"It's supposed to be a surprise."

"Don't do that to me. The thought of another surprise makes my skin crawl."

"Bad choice of words—I take those back." She took a drink of her own wine. "In thirty minutes, some massage therapists are coming over. One for each of us. Easton thought it would help you relax and make you feel better." She got up and went to my pantry, opening the door. When she returned to the living room, she had a giant basket in her hands. "He also had this delivered while you were in the bath." She set the basket on the couch and began to unwrap the clear plastic wrapped around it. "Look at all this stuff."

I went over to it, seeing the bottles of bubble bath and candles and aromatherapy and sweets and—I had to look away.

Breathe.

Except I couldn't.

I lifted my wine off the table and downed what was left.

The moment I finished swallowing, I headed for the dish where I kept my keys, tucked them into my hand, and turned to face her. "I'll be back."

"Where are you going?"

I shook my head. "I don't know. I just need to get out."

"Then I'm coming with you."

The knot was pushing so hard against my throat, I felt like it was making my heart stop.

"No. I need just a second to be alone. I need air and space from these walls and silence and—"

"Babe, I get it." She gave me the most understanding nod. "I really do. Go out and take all the time you need. I'll be here when you get back."

I tried my hardest, I gave it everything I had to make the smile slowly creep across my face.

She acknowledged the expression with a grin and said, "Take your phone so I can reach out." She lifted it off the couch and handed it to me.

I tucked it into my back pocket and rushed out the door and down the hallway, into the elevator, and then out the lobby door of my building.

I had no destination in my mind.

My feet just wandered.

My eyes taking in the unique characteristics of Boston.

My mind trying to empty from everything plaguing it.

My lungs filling with air that I hadn't been able to suck in while I was at my apartment.

I didn't know how long I walked. How far I'd gone. What time it even was.

But at one point, I realized I was no longer moving. I was sitting on a bench in front of a small pond where ducks and swans were floating across the top.

The Public Garden.

My favorite place in the city.

Easton's too.

Oh God.

I pulled my phone out of my back pocket, ignoring all the notifications on the screen. I found the last message he'd sent, and I began to type.

Me: I appreciate you. More than words can say.

Easton: Hi, baby. How's your walk going?

Easton: Don't be angry with Saara for telling me. I told her to keep me updated, she's only doing her job.

Me: I'm at the Public Garden.

Easton: As you should be. The swans and ducks all good?

Me: Lol. All good.

Me: Where are you?

Easton: 33,000 feet up in the air.

Me: Are you going to tell me where you're going?

Easton: I'll tell you where I've gone when I'm on my way back.

Me: Fair enough.

Easton: I'm not going to ask if you're okay. I know you're not. But I'm going to tell you that everything is going to be okay and I'm going to do everything in my power to make sure of that.

Me: I don't deserve you.

Easton: You would do the same thing for me.

Eason: Try to enjoy the park. I'll call you later.

CHAPTER THIRTY-FIVE

Easton

My hands fucking shook as Grayson, David, and I left the hotel we'd stayed in last night and got into the SUV waiting for us outside the lobby. David had never been on a business trip with us before, but once the idea came to me and several messages were exchanged, it became apparent that he was a significant part of my plan. And as the events began to unfold yesterday—first at the office and then on the plane and shortly after we landed in San Francisco—it turned out that the plan wasn't just genius, it was one of the best I'd ever come up with.

It was exactly what needed to happen to clear Drake's name.

Originally, using David had merely been a way in. An unprotected pathway, as though I were hacking into the truth. Never did I think it was going to be this easy to get the information I needed.

Of course, there was still lots of work to do, but at least this trip to the West Coast hadn't been a waste. Within the next hour, I would have a much better understanding of how Faceframe had a design that looked almost identical to Hooked's.

The SUV dropped us off at a café several minutes before the scheduled meetup. David and Grayson grabbed themselves a coffee while I waited for them at a table. I didn't need any more caffeine in my system. I was already wired enough, even though I'd been up all night.

Knowing how badly Drake was hurting had prevented me from even closing my eyes.

So I'd spent time researching.

Investigating.

Carving out the remaining steps of my plan.

San Francisco was only our first stop in California. We still had one more to go before we flew home.

When David and Grayson joined me at the table, they silently drank their coffees, waiting.

The time ticking.

The anxiousness inside my body coming to an all-time peak.

We'd spent all morning in my suite, going over today's possibilities, how the upcoming conversation needed to be shaped. What type of additional proof we had to gather to make our case.

That was why I felt prepared when the door opened and the motherfucker walked in. He took off his sunglasses, his long, shaggy hair falling into his eyes as he scanned the café's interior. He first connected stares with David.

Then Grayson.

And finally me.

As the door closed, the bell above it chimed on a bit of a delay. But it was that sound, that high-pitched ring, that set off every alarm inside me.

I expected him to walk over. To sit. To look at us as though we meant nothing to him.

That was what had happened.

I just didn't expect him to laugh while doing it.

"What do you want?"

251

Those were the first words that Brennon spoke.

The guy who, at one point, had been our close friend. Had partied with us in Boston. Had been one of the founding coders of Hooked.

Had left because we couldn't afford to pay him what he'd asked for.

"I think you know what we want," I replied.

He ignored me and looked at David, the laugh now turning more sinister. "I thought you were coming here for an interview. That you were finally ready to join the team that you should have been a part of a long time ago." He hissed out some air, scratching the side of his thick beard. "I should have known you didn't have the balls to leave Hooked. Just like you didn't have the nerve to ask them for more money."

"He didn't have to ask. We gave it to him anyway," I countered.

"And they would have given it to you too," David said to Brennon, "if you'd just waited until the company grew a bit more and could handle that kind of salary bump."

"God, you're fucking gullible," Brennon barked. "You'll literally believe anything they tell you, won't you? Meanwhile, we designed that whole fucking app. We barely slept for six months. We worked day and night, doing everything they asked. For what? A shitty fucking salary? A mention in the developer description?" He rolled his eyes. "Such bullshit."

"If you'd stuck around, you would know that your loyalty would have earned you a lot more," David said, pushing up the tiny frames of his glasses. "More money, more benefits, and more perks than you'd ever dreamed of. But you had one thing on your mind, and you were too impatient to wait for it."

This wasn't part of the conversation we'd prepped for.

This was David sticking up for us all on his own.

Brennon leaned back in his chair, crossing his arms, extending his legs out in front of him. "You're boring me to death, and you obviously lied to get me to meet you." He glanced at me, then Grayson. "Why are you really here?"

I held up my phone, showing him screenshots of the conversation he'd had yesterday when David had reached out to him in my office, inquiring about a position at Faceframe, a way to just get the conversation rolling with Brennon. That simple question had led Brennon to immediately start discussing the Dating Place, and we'd learned that he had much more pull than we anticipated. David then laid it on even thicker, really complaining about Hooked and that he was tired of working there—all lies to get Brennon talking—and Brennon asked him to come in for an interview to join the launch team.

Because it turned out, Brennon was the director of Dating Place management and development and had designed the app himself.

"Drake Madden," I said. "That's why we're here."

Brennon stared at me, emotionless. "What about her?"

"I know you're setting Drake up, and I'm going to find the evidence, no matter what it takes."

Brennon's unruly brows furrowed. "You're fucking kidding me, right?"

His response could have been taken many ways. I needed clarification.

"Kidding about what? My statement, my—"

"I don't owe you anything, including a response to your hilarious accusation," Brennon shot back. "I've fulfilled every obligation I had to you a long time ago, even your ridiculous noncompete that expired last year. Fuck you and your assumptions."

"Yes or no?" I roared. "It's that easy."

He got up from his chair and stood in front of us. "You know that the Dating Place is going to own the market share of dating apps. That it's going to destroy Hooked and whittle you away until there's nothing left. That you two and your little Holden are going to lose everything David and I built."

I sat up in my seat, thankful I hadn't grabbed a coffee, or I'd be throwing it across the fucking room.

"You may have built the infrastructure, but you can't take a single ounce of credit for anything we've accomplished," Grayson said. "That credit goes to the three of us and Holden." He nodded at Brennon. "You're getting a little cocky, even for someone with a head as big as yours."

"Grayson, you're fucking pathetic, you know that? You were always jealous that Easton came up with the idea first. Always pissed off that Holden got the better-looking women because he's the nice guy that you're not."

I was on the verge of verbally destroying him when Grayson moved his coffee aside and set his arms on the table. "What scares you the most, Brennon? The fact that we have proof that the Dating Place designs are yours? That even though you met the end of your noncompete, we can and will file suit? Or that your design will never be as successful as ours because, in this day and age, people want anonymity? They want to avoid getting into bed with motherfuckers like you, and the Dating Place can never offer that."

"You're going to sue me?" His laugh turned even louder. "I dare you to try."

"Try?" I laughed back. "That's what you think we're going to do? We've hired Declan Shaw, the top litigator in the state of California, and the second we leave this café, we're flying to LA to meet with him. If there's an attorney in this state who can shred you, it's him."

His hands balled into fists at his sides. "On what grounds?"

None of us replied.

We didn't have to.

Even if his noncompete had expired, he knew damn well he couldn't use our entire concept, our proprietary software, an infrastructure he'd designed and helped build, and apply it to a competitor in an identical market.

But I wasn't going to argue that point.

I'd let Declan do that in court.

But I also wasn't going to leave this table until I had a firm confirmation of Drake's innocence.

I knew the data hadn't been stolen or transferred from our system to theirs. Brennon didn't need to steal anything, nor did he need a mole. He'd created our system; all he did was duplicate it for Faceframe.

"Was Drake affiliated with the Dating Place or not?" I repeated.

The frustration was clear on his face.

So was the nervousness that he was attempting to hide—and doing a shitty job at it.

He shifted his weight. "She had nothing to do with the concept. She wouldn't even know about it. Her old team and my team—there's zero crossover."

I anticipated that response, but it still wasn't good enough. "You're saying you received nothing from her while she's been employed at Hooked—no data, no information, absolutely nothing?"

"Going to work for you was the worst move she ever made—"

"Brennon, did you receive anything from her or not?" I growled, cutting off his bullshit. "Answer the fucking question."

"No. Not a single line of code."

Just what I thought.

"Then why did the email come from her address?" Grayson asked.

Brennon smiled, a look that made my stomach churn. "That was a nice touch, wasn't it?" He seemed to stare off into space as he continued, "I was going to send the email from my own account, but I thought restoring hers would be much more fun. Why not send you on a little scavenger hunt, thinking your director is fucking you, ripping your own hair out in the process." He eyed me up. "Ah, the satisfaction. I can't tell you how good it feels."

"You're a weak motherfucker, you know that," I bellowed.

"I'm a genius." His lips were almost hidden from all the hair, but I could still see the smile that rose through it. "I planned out every single step of this. How the Dating Place app was going to look. How it was going to target your clients. How I was going to deliver the information to you—you've got to admit, using Drake was brilliant." He laughed. "That's how determined I am to ruin you. I did a good job, didn't I?"

I looked at David and then at Grayson. "I think we have everything we need, fellas."

We got up from our chairs, the two of them fisting their coffees, and as we passed Brennon, I heard, "That's it? You're just going to threaten suit and then fucking leave? What about—"

I glanced over my shoulder and said, "It's not a threat. It's a promise," and then I continued out the door and got into the SUV.

The driver took us straight to the airport, where we boarded our private plane, and less than two hours later we were landing in LA.

The entire way to the law firm, I couldn't stop thinking about Drake.

How she was the woman I was supposed to be with.

How there wasn't anything in this world I wouldn't do for her.

Some men were fortunate enough to find a partner. Some found their best friend. I'd found both, a talented, stunning woman who was everything I wanted.

Everything I needed in my life.

And I hadn't bonded with her just once.

But twice.

If my past had taught me anything, it was that no matter what, you didn't let go.

You fought.

And that was just what I was going to do when we walked through the doors of The Dalton Group, a sign for which was displayed at the top of the high-rise in downtown Los Angeles.

We were brought into a conference room where two men already sat, and they stood the moment we walked in.

"Declan Shaw," the first gentleman said, sticking out his hand for me to shake.

From his grip alone, I knew this man was like a raging, snarling pit bull. I saw it in his eyes. His stature. The way his presence dominated the room even though he'd said no more than a few words.

"Easton Jones," I replied.

"Easton, this is my colleague, Camden Dalton."

The Dalton Group, I thought.

"Partner?" I asked Camden while David and Grayson introduced themselves to Declan. "Related to the family somehow?"

I'd done my research last night. I knew there were three brothers who ran this practice, their parents semi-retired, their firm the largest and most victorious in California.

"Nephew to the original owners, cousin to the trio of brothers who now run the practice," Camden replied, shaking my hand. "And one day partner."

We took a seat around the conference room table.

"I've taken a look at the information you and your assistant sent over," Declan said from the head. "And I want to run something by you."

I clasped my hands together while a woman, Declan's assistant, I assumed, delivered a bottle of water to each of us. "All right," I responded.

"Faceframe is well aware of its competition. They know Brennon was previously employed at a company that offers the same type of product and service. So why would the social media site approve a design that was stolen from a competitor and allow the concept to go live in certain markets, where it's currently being tested?"

"That's a good question," Grayson said. "I'd like that answer as well."

Declan smiled. There wasn't a single feature on his face that warmed from the expression. "I don't think Brennon is the only person at fault here, although I fully plan to roast his ass in court."

"Are you saying . . ." My voice faded out as Declan nodded.

He knew what I was about to voice.

He adjusted his cuff links and set his arms back on the table. "Yes, Easton. I think we sue the social media giant and take both mother-fuckers down."

◆ ◆ ◆

Me: I know it's late, but I just got back to the hotel and wanted to say good night. Hopefully, this text doesn't wake you and you see it in the morning.

Drake: I'm up.

Me: I had a feeling you would be.

Drake: How did things go today?

Me: I'm going to tell you everything tomorrow. Will you meet me and the executive team at 6:00pm at the office?

Drake: At the office? Are you sure that's okay?

Me: It's more than okay. It's where you should be—and where you should have been today. Once the forensic research gets wrapped up tomorrow, I'll have a lot to tell you.

Drake: Tomorrow? I thought it would take much longer?

Me: No, that's all the time we need.

Me: I miss you, baby.

Drake: I really miss you.

◆ ◆ ◆

The entire executive team was already sitting around the conference table when Drake walked in. I could see the hesitation on her face when I asked her to take a seat. I could almost feel the anxiety in her body, similar to when we'd gotten stranded in the elevator. Even though I'd told her last night that this was where she should be, that she shouldn't have missed even a day of work, I still saw how nervous she was. Especially when she moved through the room, her hands clenched at her sides and then fidgeting in her lap the moment she sat, causing her shoulders to shake. Her stare bounced from one face to the next until it landed on me.

"Thank you for coming in," I said to her. "I'd like to first explain what happened, where Grayson, David, and I went, and the information we gathered while we were there."

"Before we get to that," Holden said, "I think it's important to let her know that the investigation we conducted is now closed. After thoroughly analyzing your workstations, zero evidence was found that you sent or transferred anything outside this office."

"I'm relieved it's closed," Drake said. "I guess I'm just a little confused. Easton told me you were going to put a rush on the forensic data analyst, but I never thought they would be able to work this fast."

Holden smiled at Drake. "We didn't end up hiring one. After the events unfolded—the ones Easton will tell you about—we decided to do the investigation in-house. In fact, David completed it before you got here."

"David?" She shifted her gaze to her team leader. "Oh." Her hand went to her chest. "I'm sorry, I assumed everyone aside from the executive team was told I went on medical leave. But now that I hear he traveled with Easton and Grayson, that makes a little more sense."

"Drake, both workstations were perfect." David pushed his long bangs away from his glasses. "I found nothing—and I knew I wouldn't."

Drake nodded and reached into her bag, taking out a piece of paper. "I thought I'd bring this, for what it's worth." She pushed the paper toward Holden, who sat closest to her.

He opened it up and said, "This is proof that the email Drake supposedly sent from her address at Faceframe was traced back to an IP address in Palo Alto."

"Where I clearly wasn't," Drake replied, "since you all know I was stranded in an elevator with Easton."

She'd hacked into Faceframe's database to get that information, something she hadn't needed to do. But I understood why she'd gone that far. Drake wasn't the kind of woman who was going to let everyone else do the work while her name was being tarnished.

"No longer needed, but a hell of a finding," I told her. I unscrewed the cap of my water bottle and took a long drink. "Let's talk about David for a second and paint a clearer picture, so you understand everything that transpired. He's the reason we were able to prove that you had zero involvement with the Dating Place."

David, sitting next to me, tapped his fingers across my arm. "You came up with the idea. Don't give me all the credit."

I waved off my longtime employee, appreciating his humbleness, but he needed to know that most of this was because of him. "On my suggestion, David reconnected with his old partner, Brennon, one of our founding developers. We've discussed him before, Drake, and you know he went to work for Faceframe." I paused, receiving no reaction from her. "My intention was to use Brennon to get an in, for David to fake his unhappiness to him and score an interview so he could get in the door and obtain as much information as possible on Faceframe's new division. I certainly didn't expect to uncover that Brennon was the director of Dating Place, but that's what happened."

She pulled her sweater closed, wrapping her arms around her stomach. "I knew of him. He was a developer. I had no idea he'd been promoted or that this division had been created."

"He told us as much," Grayson said. "And not only did he confirm your innocence, he confirmed he was responsible for the design of the Dating Place."

I could tell she was processing this news, so I added, "Here lies the problem. He helped establish Hooked—the design, the proprietary software, the entire infrastructure. He then went to Faceframe and copied our designs. He shared our software with intent to hurt our company, and now that concept has gone live in certain markets."

She shook her head. "He can't do that."

"We know," I told her. "After we met with Brennon, we flew to LA and had a meeting with Declan Shaw, the top litigator in the state of California, and with his associate, Camden Dalton. We're going after Brennon and Faceframe."

Silence filled the room.

"I'm sorry Brennon did this," Drake said softly. "I didn't know him well. Only in passing. But I hate that he went against Hooked, the company that started his career. That would be like me going against Faceframe—something I wouldn't dream of doing." She stared at Holden, Grayson, and finally me as she said, "I wouldn't go after Hooked either."

"You shouldn't be the one apologizing." Holden rubbed his hands together. "You've been hurt by this, severely affected—we know that. We aren't happy about it."

"Drake . . ." I shook my head as I gazed at the woman I loved. "You have to know that if I was in your shoes, as a partner, I would have been treated the same way. Our in-house counsel has standard operating procedures. All she was doing—all we were doing—was following them to protect Hooked. This wasn't personal, trust me when I say that."

"I know," she replied.

"We didn't want to do this, Drake," Holden added. "We didn't want to have that meeting. We didn't want to even consider that you had something to do with the Dating Place or that you were acting as a mole or that you had sent that email. But for the sake of Hooked, we had to do our due diligence. Although none of us were able to voice this, we didn't think for a second that you were involved in any way."

"Shit no," Grayson said. "If you wanted access to our system, you would have hacked in—we all know that. You wouldn't have wasted your time and taken a job here."

Holden chuckled. "What he said, but that still doesn't change our process and the steps we had to take." He twisted the bottle of water between his hands. "In this building, Hooked comes first."

"I get it," she voiced. "And I appreciate the explanation. I knew my innocence would be proven, I just didn't know how long it was going to take." She eventually met my eyes. "I certainly didn't expect the three of you to get on a plane and get answers as fast as you did."

Grayson said, "We want you back, Drake."

I watched his words resonate across her face, the emotion filling her eyes. The way she released her sweater, flattening her hand on her chest.

My hands tightened in my lap as I dreamed about holding her waist. "We wish you never had to leave, but we want you to be here now."

"Absolutely," Holden agreed. "You can easily explain to your team that the medical leave was halted earlier than expected or you were misdiagnosed—whatever you decide to tell them, we support. If you'd like to take a week or two before you return, you're more than entitled to that time off. Or if you'd like to start back up tomorrow"—he grinned—"that would make us very happy."

She wouldn't allow the tears to drip, but they were there, pooling, softening the lines in her face.

"Whatever you decide," I chimed in, "we just hope you do come back."

She took a moment to respond, "I want that."

"How quickly?" Grayson asked her. "My friends here are all about time, but I'm you in the interim and I have no idea what I'm doing." He ran his hand over the top of his head. "Let's just lay it out there and say I'm no Drake Madden and the idea of leading your team on an international rollout is nothing short of fucked. So I'm going to ask you: Is tomorrow too soon?"

She smiled, even laughed a little, patting her fingers under her eyes. "If I didn't know better, I'd think you're groveling."

"Grayson, grovel?" I teased. "I've never seen such a thing in my life." I smiled at my girl, winking at her. "Whatever you decide, we support. We just ask that you give Grayson a little heads-up regarding the timeline of your plans before he shits himself."

CHAPTER THIRTY-SIX

Drake

"Fuck me," Easton growled as I stood at his front door, his stare lapping the length of me as though I were naked. "Get over here."

He opened his arms. I fell into them, and he pressed his lips against the top of my head while he wrapped his body around mine.

It didn't matter how often I came over—even though it had become nightly, he still greeted me as though it were the first time he was touching me.

As though he couldn't get enough.

There was something about the tone of his voice, the way he instantly reached for me, how his lips found some part of me and stayed there, breathing me in, that I couldn't get enough of.

I wasn't just wanted.

Desired.

I was loved.

And it was this spot, this safe embrace, that I never wanted to leave.

A place where I completely lost myself.

Where time no longer mattered.

Where I felt weightless, his arm bearing every pound while I leaned my body onto his. I tucked my face into his chest, feeling the hardness of his pecs until he lifted my chin, aiming my gaze at him.

"Kiss me."

So I did.

It wasn't just my breath that Easton took with his mouth.

It was my trust.

Because I knew, because it had been proven, that he wouldn't let me fall unless it was toward him, and then his arms would be there to catch me.

Like they had been several weeks ago, when he'd flown to San Francisco to meet with Brennon, doing everything in his power to show my innocence.

Like they did the following morning, when I returned to work, my desire to be at Hooked outweighing how upset the entire Dating Place scandal had made me.

Like they were now after the longest day at work.

"Fuck, I missed you," he said when our mouths parted.

"You just saw me a few hours ago."

Since next week was phase one of the international rollout, I'd stayed later than I intended.

"Seems like much more than just a few hours." He brushed his nose against mine. "Besides, I didn't get to do this in the office." He kissed me again. Slower this time, as though he were sipping me like a drink, savoring. "Or this." His hand lowered to my ass, squeezing my cheek.

Even though our relationship was out in the open, we were extremely professional when we were there. A topic we had discussed immediately upon my return to work. Physical boundaries had been set, and I wouldn't break them for a quickie.

Some things were worth losing, but my team and their respect weren't.

"You better come inside before I eat you in this doorway." He turned, giving me enough space to slide into his condo.

I'd already smelled dinner the moment he opened the door, but the closer I got to the kitchen, the stronger the aroma became.

I set my overnight bag on one of the barstools, and that was when I heard *"Draaake!"*

Heavy, clunky footsteps came barreling out of the living room. Belle's head barely exceeded Easton's high counter, her pigtails bopping just above the edge of the stone, her ringlets finding flight as she sprinted toward me.

"Belle," I sang back, kneeling on the kitchen floor so I could give her a hug. "What are you doing here?"

As she circled her small arms around my neck, I immediately got a whiff of chocolate chip cookies. A dessert, I was positive, Easton had fed her.

Although Belle's nanny often brought her by the office, those stops were quick. The most time I spent with her was during occasions like this, when Holden needed to speak to Easton and they were here when I arrived.

"Daddy and Uncle Gray and E had to talk. We stayed extra long to see you!"

"Is that so?" I gazed past her shoulders, catching eyes with Holden and Grayson in the living room. They stood from the couch and made their way into the kitchen. "Well, I'm glad they did because that means I get to see you." I pulled away but stayed low, Belle's hands instantly moving to my hair, which she began to play with.

"Uncle E says he made something extra spicy for dinner and I can't have any 'cause it'll hurt my tum."

I straightened her purple glasses, which were crooked from our hug. "Then I think you should tell Uncle E that he needs to cook you something special. Like some mac and cheese. Wouldn't that be—"

"Uncle E is tied up for dinner," Easton said to the both of us.

He gave me wide eyes, a look that told me what he had in mind didn't mesh with the presence of a five-year-old.

"What's *tied up*?" Belle asked.

"It means Easton is busy, baby," Holden replied from where he and Grayson leaned over the counter, watching us.

Belle laughed. "I thought he meant he's tied like when Miss Small walks her little doggy and we see her in the elevator, and she lets me hold the leash."

"That is *tied*, baby, but a different kind of *tied*," Holden told her.

"Or not," Grayson said. "Leash play, I wouldn't put that past him." He nodded toward Easton.

"Hey there," I called out to Grayson. "Little ears are tuned in." I stood but stayed close to Belle, looking down at her to say, "Since Uncle E isn't making you dinner, I think you should ask Uncle Gray to take you somewhere extra fancy to eat and spend lots of money on you."

"Sushi!" Belle yelled.

Grayson walked around the counter, making us a trio. "Is that what you want?"

"It's what she always wants," Holden added.

When Belle agreed, the tails of her hair fell into her face. "With 'mame."

"And edamame?" Grayson clarified. "I don't know if I can handle that—it sounds like an impossibly difficult order to fill."

The only time I ever saw Grayson soft, without his edge, was around Belle. It was adorable to see him caving to her mere smile.

"I think you should tell Uncle Gray that he needs to step up his game," I said to Belle, curling one of her locks around my finger. "Nothing is too difficult for our girl."

She put a hand on her hip, tilting her body with sass. "Step it up, Uncle Gray!"

Everyone in the kitchen laughed, even Easton as he came up behind me, handing me a glass of wine, his palm going to my stomach once I took the drink from him.

"We're going to get going," Holden said. "I just wanted to stay long enough so my daughter would stop begging to see you"—he winked at Belle—"and to tell you I took a peek at the designs before I left the office today."

My chest clutched and I took a sip of the wine. "You did?"

My assumption was that tomorrow, when I presented the concepts to the executive team, that would be the first time anyone would see them.

"Drake, they're incredible," Holden said. "I was blown away."

Grayson lifted Belle into his arms, turning toward Easton and me. "I might have looked too."

"And?" Easton said to him, tightening his grip around my waist.

"They're sick."

Not only had the both of them appreciated my prompt return to the office, but they made sure I knew how much that meant to them. How I was admired for the devotion I had to their company. And even though that short period had been extremely rough, I'd never felt more loved by an executive team.

A burst of excitement replaced the tightness in my chest. "Thank you."

"It's good to have you back, Drake." Grayson put his hand on top of Belle's head. "Are you ready to ditch Dad and get some sushi?"

"*Yesss!*"

"Then let's blow this joint," he said to her.

The arm that wasn't wrapped around Grayson's neck, she held out to me. "Bye, Drake."

I hugged her and said, "I'll see you soon, okay?"

"You better."

I laughed at her response and watched her embrace Easton, a sight that made me smile every time, before the three of them made their way out.

Once we were alone, I turned toward him. "That was a welcome surprise."

He kissed me, holding my cheeks until he pulled his mouth away. "I thought you'd be happy to see Belle."

"Always." As my stomach grumbled from the scent of dinner, I glanced at the stove, where several pots rested on the gas range. "Did you cook tonight or was it your chef?"

"All me."

Half of our dinners were prepared by his private chef; the other half Easton made himself. The latter was my favorite, the time he spent mixing flavors, overlapping cuisines, impressing me each time.

"I love that," I whispered.

"I tried something different tonight."

I smiled, taking in more of the aroma. "Oh yeah?"

"When I brought you to lunch last week, you ordered a salad with grilled shrimp. It got me thinking about seafood." He led me over to the stove, opening the cover to the large, flat oval dish. "I just took this out of the oven before you got here. It needs time to sit and gel and cool off from its current molten-lava state."

I laughed at his description. "It looks divine." The base appeared to be thick rice with sausage and seasoning and a large collection of seafood on top. "What's it called?"

"Paella." He took a spoon from one of the drawers, dipping it into the mixture. He blew on the rice and sausage before holding it up to my lips. "Taste."

Now that it was closer, I saw the bits of onion and the small round peas in the rice. "Easton, my goodness," I moaned, covering my mouth the moment it hit my tongue. "This is heavenly."

"The first time I had this was when I was in Barcelona. I've never attempted to make it, but something about the shrimp you were eating sparked an interest and inspired me."

I dipped the spoon in and took another bite. "I could eat this every day."

He smiled, holding his mouth near my ear when he whispered, "I'm happy you like it."

"You know, the rule is, you have to be exceptional at making one thing. Your signature dish. The app, main course—whatever—is what you serve if you're ever pressured into a situation where you have to bring something or have someone over." I licked the back of the spoon, thinking I really needed to figure out what that dish was for me. "But you're good at everything. I'm on uneven territory here."

He pulled his mouth away from my neck and laughed. "I've had your tacos. They're pretty badass."

I gently slapped his chest. "Seriously? Come on. You can't even say that. It's meat and vegetables with store-bought guacamole. I can't fuck that up even if I tried."

"Then what's your specialty?"

I shook my head. "I don't have one."

He released my waist to put on an oven mitt and reach into the stove, pulling out a lump of tinfoil, which, when he opened it, turned out to hold bread. "Then I have an idea." When he removed the mitt from his hand, he grazed my chin with the lightest touch. "Why don't we take a private cooking class together?"

I broke off a corner of the bread and popped it into my mouth. "Here? At your condo?"

"Anywhere."

I thought about it for a moment, tried to really picture what that would look like. "I think I'd enjoy that."

"You think?" He smiled, cocking his head to the side.

"I mean, my skills aren't anywhere close to yours, so I'd need some heavy-handed instruction, but yes, that would be a lot of fun."

"I'm going to put something together. I'll make sure you love it."

I gave him a kiss. "I can't wait."

He took the wine from my hand and brought it over to the table. During his next trip, he delivered the bread and a glass of red for himself. And before we sat down, he added several scoops of paella into two bowls, and we occupied two chairs across from one another.

I didn't wait. I immediately dug in, pulling off the tail of a shrimp as I bit into the meaty body, groaning as all the flavors hit my tongue.

"Why aren't you eating?" I asked, realizing I'd finished several bites' worth at this point and he hadn't even touched his food.

His eyes narrowed. "Watching you devour my cooking is so fucking erotic."

I laughed. "I'm eating like an animal."

"And it's hot." He picked up his wine. "I'd much rather have you for dinner than anything that's on this table."

His admission was thick, like the steam coming off the paella.

His words struck up a feeling.

One that, even months after our first kiss, hadn't dimmed in the slightest.

If anything, the way he made me feel was stronger than it had ever been.

"I'm pretty sure you can have both." I ran my teeth over my bottom lip. "You don't have to choose me over the food."

He took a drink, brushing his thumb over his mouth. "I'm just not sure I want to wait."

I glanced down at my plate. "And let this masterpiece turn cold?" I speared a scallop and stuck the whole thing into my mouth. "Not a chance," I mumbled through my fingers.

He laughed. "In that case, I have another idea." He got up from his chair, and at first, I thought he was going to come over to mine and pick me up and take me into his bedroom. Something he'd done before. But he walked through the living room and what sounded like his office, returning a few seconds later with an envelope that he slid across the table to me. "Open it."

I was in the middle of cutting a piece of lobster tail and set down my knife and fork, slipping my finger under the flap of the envelope. "What is this?" I waited for him to answer. When he didn't, I continued opening the top, then pulled out a series of photographs that showed a mountain range that was positively breathtaking. The rock was deep in color, burgundy, eggplant, even a burnt pumpkin. And in the middle of those mountains was a strip of land that looked to be covered in dirt.

I gazed up at him again, and since he hadn't answered my first question, I added, "Where is this?"

"Moab, Utah."

"I've never been." I glanced at the photos again. "It looks positively stunning."

He reached across the table, putting his hand on my arm. "You'll be seeing it in person in a few weeks."

My heart began to flutter, the same sensation moving into my stomach. "I will?"

"That's where we're going. Just you and me. And in that section of dirt in between the range of mountains is where we'll be camping."

"Camping?" My eyes widened, a bit of panic now filtering into the spots that were tingling. "You're kidding . . ."

He chuckled. "Not even a little. You're going to love it." He squeezed my skin. "And don't worry, there's even a bathroom."

I sighed. "You just made me the happiest woman alive."

"And I haven't even told you about the bathtub yet . . ."

CHAPTER THIRTY-SEVEN

Easton

If I was going to take Drake on a trip, our first that wasn't work related, I wanted to make sure she never forgot it. That it was a location she could absorb on a level that went beyond restaurant reservations and tours and cultural experiences I normally planned. I wanted her to connect to the landscape, to feel the air. To listen to the stories the mountains whispered.

Utah was a place where I'd spent a lot of time. Not just skiing in the winter, but camping in the spring, summer, and fall. Never promoted as much as Colorado or Nevada or Montana, more of a hidden secret that always surprised people when they arrived, it was a state that was often overlooked.

I didn't know why.

These grounds were some of the most beautiful in the world, and as someone well traveled, I had every authority to say that.

That was why I wanted to share this with Drake.

I wanted her to know what it felt like to be in the middle of nowhere. To have to rely on nature and her own senses for entertainment. To be in a place where there was a very good chance her cell phone wasn't going to work.

As we got into the SUV waiting for us on the tarmac at Canyonlands Regional Airport, where our private plane had just landed right outside of Moab, I said, "You better text Saara now and tell her you've arrived, since she most likely won't be hearing from you for a few days."

She looked at me from across the front seat, slight panic in her eyes. "Really? It's like that?"

I laughed.

She had no idea what she was in for, despite how many times I'd attempted to explain the remote aspect of these trips.

"It's very much like that, baby. You saw the photos. There isn't exactly a cell phone tower next to our tent."

"Wait, wait, *waaait*. I thought we were going to have a bathroom? And didn't you mention something about a tub?"

My chuckle ended in a smile. "You're going to have both. I promise." I nodded toward the phone that sat in her lap. "But in about fifteen minutes, that thing is probably going to stop working. Before you freak out and semi-lose it, let your bestie know you're alive and the only bear that's going to be eating you will be me."

"Oh boy." She lifted the phone and held it to her ear. "I think a phone call is required for this. She may think I've been abducted and the abductor texted her those messages, because when I tell her I'm going camping with no service, she won't believe me." She paused. "Saara, wait until you hear this . . ."

As I began the drive toward the site I'd rented, I reached across the front seat and placed my hand on her thigh. I was listening to her describe the plans to Saara, but those involved only the camping part of our trip. What I hadn't told her, what I wanted to keep a surprise, was that after we left Moab, we were headed to Park City, an experience that wasn't going to be anything like our time in the tent. I'd visited Park City several years ago, and the hotel we would be staying in was a suggestion from Declan

Shaw. Since he was neck deep in our legal matters, during one of our many chats, I'd told him I was going to be traveling, and he had recommended to extend our trip and book the hotel owned by the fiancée of Jenner Dalton, one of the partners of The Dalton Group. He said it was one of the nicest hotels he'd ever been to, and Camden agreed.

The moment I heard that, I was sold.

Once we checked into Park City, one of the many things I'd planned was a private cooking class hosted by the town's top-rated chef. We were also going to see the entire area from a helicopter, getting a full tour from the sky. We were going to end our afternoons with massages and our evenings with fire and mountains and my hands on every single part of her body.

"Saara?" Drake said anxiously. "Are you there? Have we lost connection . . ." She looked at her screen. "Shit. You weren't kidding. I have no service . . . and she's gone."

I gently took the phone out of her hand and placed it in the compartment between our seats, closing the lid so it was secured inside. "You won't be needing that for a while." I clasped her hand. "Look around, Drake. Tell me what you see." I was beginning to slow as we were nearing the area, and I rolled down the windows so she could get hints of the air, the scent turning cleaner as we got deeper into the mountains.

I took a quick glance in her direction and watched her take a deep breath, her eyes closing, her free hand moving out the open window, her fingers spreading wide as the breeze passed over her skin.

Her eyes opened, and after a few seconds, she said, "Serenity."

"What else?"

"Beauty."

"Yes, lots of that." I turned at a gravel road, the tires kicking up dust and rocks behind us, causing a brown cloud to form in my rearview mirror. "Do you feel anything?"

"I didn't believe you when you said we'd be fully disconnected. I didn't think you lied. I just, you know, didn't fully process the idea of it. But now that I'm out here and I see this view"—she turned her face toward the open window, the wind blowing her hair everywhere, a smile growing over her lips—"I feel a lot calmer."

I brought her hand up to my lips and kissed the back of it. "You once told me you weren't afraid of anything. Do you still feel that way? Or are you intimidated by what we're about to do? Where we're staying? What things are going to look like over the next couple of days?"

She glanced at me, scanning my eyes.

"I don't want you to feel anything but amazement while we're out here," I continued. "But, at the same time, I realize this is my kind of vacation. I'm hoping you'll experience it the way I want you to . . . I just don't know if that'll be the case." I nipped one of her knuckles and soothed it with a kiss. "To make that adjustment easier on you, I want to deal with any concerns you have before you see our accommodations."

She laughed. "Are you reading me the back of a Moab camping warning label?"

"That's exactly what I'm doing." I winked at her.

"And you're saying I may hate you after this?"

Now it was my turn to laugh. "Hate is a strong feeling. Let's go with . . . camping will continue to be my thing, and all other non-camping adventures will be our thing."

While her hand was still near my lips, she wiggled it out of my grip and cupped my cheek. "I'm going into this very open minded. I want to love it."

"Good." I kissed her fingers as they got close to my mouth. "Because I want you to take this all in, and I don't want you to be closed off to the idea of what it can do for you."

I stopped the SUV just as she said, "I wish I knew what you meant."

"You will very soon." I unhooked my seat belt. "Let's get out. I have a lot to show you."

We climbed out of the front seat, and I met her at the passenger side of the SUV, locking my fingers with hers as I led her toward the tent. From the outside, it didn't look like anything special: a large double-wide, equally extended canvas that peaked at the entrance, held up by thick, sturdy logs. But once you walked inside, you saw that there was nothing average about this tent.

Like an old-school circus tent, the canvas rose in the middle, dipping to hang across the tops of the logs, creating layers of shapes as it lifted toward the ceiling. The floor inside was hardwood, raised several inches off the dirt, so it felt like you were stepping on a platform. Above the king-size bed that sat on a wooden frame, outfitted in lush bedding, was a clear section of covering, thin enough that we'd be able to see the stars when we went to sleep. A small love seat and table and chair sat in the corner, and on the other side was a barn door that, once opened, revealed a full bathroom, outfitted with a large soaking tub.

I gave Drake the entire tour of the interior, and when we finished, she stood near the bed, glancing around the space, her eyes eventually finding mine.

"This isn't what I expected. At all." A smile was now on her face. "Nor is this camping. Easton, this is straight-up glamping, and I can absolutely handle that. It's like a hotel in the middle of nowhere—there just isn't anyone to make our bed or change out our towels."

"But there's plenty." I pointed at the large cabinet by the barn door that held all the towels we'd need. "I requested extra."

"Of course you did."

"And there's this . . ." I walked over to the cooler near the entrance and opened the lid, finding the bottle of champagne I'd asked for along with the two glasses chilling inside. "Which I think I should open now."

"I agree." She moved closer, wrapping her arms around my waist, looking up at me. "I'm dying to know how this tent has running water and an option to flush the toilet versus just a terrifying hole and the ability to fill a massive tub that I plan to use every day while we're here—but I don't think I want to know that answer."

"Let's not even address it," I said, setting down the bottle so I could rest my arms on her shoulders. "But I can tell you, they're not all like this. Maybe for our next trip, I should show you the other side of camping."

"Baby steps," she whispered, laughing. "How about I grab our stuff and unpack, and you get us those drinks?"

"You're not lifting a finger."

"I'm lifting more than a finger and don't try to stop me." Her eyes turned stern. "I mean it. Let's divide and conquer."

I kissed her. "All right, deal."

While she disappeared from the tent, heading toward the SUV parked less than fifteen yards away, I worked on opening the bottle, untwisting the metal, and popping out the cork. As I was pouring some into the glasses, she was rolling our suitcases inside. I filled both flutes and brought them outside, where I located the set of Adirondack chairs that I'd specifically requested. They were behind the tent, a tiny table in between them. I moved all three pieces a bit farther past the tent to give us a better view, and placed the champagne on the table.

When I returned inside, she had both suitcases unzipped, our personal items laid out in the bathroom, our hiking boots lined up, and our packing cubes full of clothes and undergarments resting in the cabinet next to the bed.

Pleased with her progress, she turned around and faced me. "I think I'm done."

I held out my hand, waiting for her to grab it, and then I brought her outside, back behind the tent, showing her the setup that she hadn't seen until now.

"Okay. This is adorable."

I laughed. "Sit. Get cozy."

Once we were in the chairs, we held our glasses and clinked them together.

"To glamping," she said, smiling.

"To making you scream under the stars."

She took a drink. "Your toast was much better than mine."

"It wasn't just a toast, Drake. It's a promise."

"I don't doubt that at all." She glanced away from me and looked toward the range that surrounded us. "It doesn't even look real."

She was right.

Our view was so beautiful, it could have been the backdrop to a movie set.

The colors of the rock. The different textures of nature that drew my eyes in. The way the tops of the mountains were already covered in snow.

How every breath I took whittled away at the stress of work and fucking lawsuits.

Her hand rested on the armrest, and I set my fingers over hers and squeezed.

"Can I admit something to you?" she asked. "It's kind of a biggie . . ."

I nodded. "You can tell me anything."

She straightened her head and closed her eyes. "I now know what you were talking about before when you asked me not to be closed off to the idea of what this can do for me." She was quiet for several seconds, then opened her eyelids and turned her head toward me. "I feel it."

"I knew you would."

Her chest rose and fell. "It's everything I needed—just like you're everything I need."

I brought her hand up to my face, smelling her skin, kissing it. "I love you."

As she gazed at me, emotion moved into her stare. It thickened the longer she went without blinking. "Easton . . ." Her teeth moved to her lip, dragging the ends across the bottom, back and forth, taunting me. "I love you too."

CHAPTER THIRTY-EIGHT

Drake

When we'd gotten into the car and started driving to the campsite, Easton's warning had made me extremely nervous. Although I'd tried not to let on—I didn't want him to think I was regretting my decision—I was certainly wondering if agreeing to this trip had been a bad idea.

He was just so excited about taking me camping and showing me Utah that I didn't want to break his heart.

Still, I wasn't sure if this type of traveling was really my thing. If I could become one with nature to where I was literally sleeping in it.

But once we parked and I thoroughly checked out the tent and we occupied the little seating area outside, where we drank champagne and took in the scenery, blanketed under a stunning canopy of mountains, I couldn't imagine being anywhere else.

This spot, this view, this ambiance—it was as perfect as he was.

And so was the dinner we prepared over the fire, using meat and vegetables that had been stored in coolers, even boiling rice to make it a stir-fry. When our stomachs were full, we cleaned up, making sure there weren't any scraps left behind since the last thing we wanted was to attract wildlife, and we decided to end the evening by warming up in the bath.

There was no electricity in the tent, so after sunset, we had to rely on lanterns, spreading them methodically throughout the interior, giving the whole space a dim glow. While I poured us more champagne, Easton worked on filling the tub, and by the time I joined him in the bathroom, there were already bubbles floating across the top of the water.

I dipped my hand into the soft foam, flinging a few suds at him. "You thought of everything, didn't you?"

"You take bubble baths at my house. Why not take one here too?"

He unzipped his fleece, removed the T-shirt he wore underneath, along with his pants and boxer briefs, and stood before me completely naked.

Since I'd set both glasses by the sink, I wrapped my arms around his warm, hard shoulders. "Thank you for this."

He smiled, rubbing his scruff over my cheek. "I think you're having a good time. In fact, I think you're having a much better time than you anticipated."

I laughed. "Isn't that the truth."

"Tomorrow is only going to get better." He brushed his fingers over the cheek he'd just roughed up. "We're going to do some hiking in Arches and you're going to see things you've never experienced."

I sucked my bottom lip into my mouth before I said, "And what about tonight?"

He'd been holding my ass, but moved his hands to the front of me, lowering the zipper of my fleece and dropping it from my body. He undid the buttons of my flannel button-down and added that to the pile building on the floor. My bra was unhooked, my leggings lowered, my feet slipping out of my boots and socks until I was as naked as him.

And as he said, "After you," and pointed at the water, I twisted my hair into a messy bun and stepped into the large tub.

"This feels incredible," I moaned, resting my back against the deep wall, bending my knees so he would have enough space to get in.

He sat opposite, his legs stretching far past me, our bodies criss-crossed but sandwiched together.

He turned the water off when it reached a high enough point and settled his back onto the wall, glancing up. "It's the same view as the one above our bed."

I hadn't noticed until now, but the covering was so thin and translucent in this section, I could see the dark sky and the bright stars.

I cupped my hands over his knees. "What's more magical than this?"

When my gaze lowered, I realized he was staring at me.

"Get over here."

Based on his tone, the deepness of his demand, I knew exactly what he wanted and what that order was going to lead to.

A smile stretched across my face. "The water is going to go every-where, we're going to make a mess—"

"Now."

There was something about that solo word, the way it dripped with urgency, that was beyond sexy.

I moved gingerly, so I wouldn't wave the water too much, and I got onto my knees and made my way up his legs, straddling them the moment I reached his lap. I gripped the hard edge of the tub right behind his head and aligned our lips. "Better?"

"Not yet."

As he kissed me, his mouth was ravenous, his tongue slithering in, circling mine, while his hands wandered down my back and over my ass and around my sides until they eventually landed on my breasts.

The water made everything slick except for his movements.

They weren't brief or gentle, especially when he flicked my nipples. When he tugged them.

When he held them between his fingers and grazed the edge, a harsh back-and-forth motion that had me pulling my mouth away from his and moaning, "More." He disconnected our lips again and began to kiss my cheek and gradually slide down to my neck. There was a spot there—right above my collarbone, at the lowest part of my throat—that made me bend back every time he reached it.

Tonight was no exception.

I rocked my hips forward, the desire pooling inside me, and I met his hard-on, filling the silence in the room with my heavy breathing.

"You taste so good." He licked a path to my nipples, replacing his hand with his mouth, sucking one, nibbling. Biting. "Always so hard and ready for me."

He wasn't even talking about my clit or the wetness waiting for him below.

He was just referring to the way my nipples responded to him.

But it didn't stop at just my chest. Easton caused my whole body to react. Even if it was just the delicate touch of his fingertips or the slightest graze of his tongue.

I felt it.

I responded.

And it was those sensations that made me crave more.

That made me beg, "I need you."

The greediness had taken over and I was adjusting his tip toward my entrance, needing the friction, the fullness.

"Yes, someone does want it, doesn't she." He called me out as I rubbed my clit over his crown, exhaling against the top of his head as he gave my chest more attention.

"Please."

I gasped when his fingers landed on my clit. "I can feel how badly you want me, but why don't you tell me, Drake."

Even after all the ways my body had shown him, he wanted more.

He wanted my voice.

My pleading.

My head tilted back, arching my chest even farther into him as he traced around the top of my opening, dipping low enough that he could feel what was waiting for him.

"So fucking wet," he growled.

"That's because I'm dying for you." I released the tub and grasped his shoulders, piercing his skin with my nails. "I can't wait, Easton. I need you now."

"I think you can wait a little bit longer." He ground his tongue over my nipple, pulling back to say, "You need to let that build ramp up a bit more, and when I think you're ready, I'll give you my dick."

"You're cruel."

He looked up and sucked my lip into his mouth, finally releasing it. "You won't be saying that when you're screaming in a few minutes."

But I didn't know how I was going to wait in the meantime.

How anything could be stronger than what I was feeling right now.

But if he was going to torture me, then I was going to do the same to him.

I clasped my hand around his shaft, using the bubbles as lubrication when I lowered to his base, twisting my hand to rise to his tip. Even though he was in water, I swore I could feel the thick bead of pre-cum as it leaked out of him. I pressed my thumb against it, spreading it around before I dipped to the bottom of him again, creating a pattern of swiveling, rising, and dropping.

"And I'm the one who's being mean," he roared, looking up from my nipple. "You're making me fucking ache for you."

"That's the point."

"Do you know what's going to happen when I give you my dick?"

"I'm going to scream." I sighed.

He stuck his tongue out, flattening it wide, and lapped my entire breast. "Yes," he hissed, "you are. And do you know how good it's going to feel?"

I held his cock against me, my palm gliding down one side while my pussy rubbed against the other, my thumb focused on the top. "But this wait is agonizing. Easton . . . it hurts not to have you."

"Where does it hurt, baby?" He took my free hand. "Show me each place."

I led him between my breasts to my clit, and I took the pad of one of his fingers and I held it against the highest point. "Here."

He didn't just stop at one finger. He added a second, swiping me back and forth.

"Just like that," I breathed, rocking with him, hoping the movement would add more friction.

He spoke against my lips. "Where else?"

I took his same hand and brought him to my entrance, forcing one of his fingers inside me. The moment it broke through, where my walls could clench him, I began to grind myself over him.

"Yes, you do want to be fucked." I lowered, aiming him toward my G-spot. "And you want to come."

He allowed me to have only a few more dips before he pulled out. "Are there any more spots?"

There was one.

A place he had once teased about a week ago.

A place that had never even been touched prior to him.

I moved his hand toward the back, rimming that forbidden entrance. "Here."

"What do you want in here, Drake? My finger . . . or more?"

More, in that virgin space, was something I really needed to think about.

He was just so large, so powerful, I wasn't sure I could handle it.

So for now, I said, "Your finger." I gripped his wrist even tighter. "But go slow. I need to get used to it."

His gaze lowered to my lips. "One day, I'm going to slide my dick in there. You know that, don't you?"

"Yes."

"And when I do, you're going to enjoy every second of it." He moved closer, nearing the pucker. "But for tonight, I'm just going to play with it. I'm going to show you what it's going to feel like when I fill this hole with my dick. How hard you're going to get off while my finger is inside you."

"*Yesss.*" I drew in a breath as he pushed through, staying still to allow me to get used to it. "Wow." I swallowed, absorbing the unfamiliar feeling. A fullness that I couldn't process yet, that felt so different from anything I'd experienced. "This is . . ."

"Not what you expected."

I shook my head, my eyes closing as my mouth hovered above his. "No, it's not. But I like it." I tucked my face into his neck as he went in more. "*Ahhh.*"

"You want all of it."

It wasn't a question.

And I swore that, even though he was in as far as what seemed to be only his knuckle, I was pulsing. Coaxing him to go in deeper.

"*Yesss.*"

"Then here's what I'm going to do. I'm going to fill your pussy and your ass at the same time."

God.

That word was almost as hot as when he'd said *now*, only because he was referring to my body part and what he was going to do to it.

"Finally," I panted.

"Take it, Drake." He waited for me to move. "Take what you want."

I lifted my body from his lap and positioned his tip, rotating it all around me to add in that brief layer of teasing, and eventually, when I began to sink down, his finger inserted more until both were fully buried inside me.

"Damn it," I groaned.

I was thankful that a few weeks ago we'd decided to no longer use condoms, that there was nothing separating us from experiencing this.

This overwhelming feeling.

But one that was so extremely satisfying.

"You're so fucking tight."

I didn't know which part of me he was talking about. It didn't matter. He sounded as pleasured and as turned on as I was, and when he gripped my cheek and kissed me, his eyes feral when we parted, I knew his body was as lit as mine.

But what was happening beneath the water wasn't as active as what was going on above it.

In fact, neither of us budged.

I just stayed still, taking it all in, getting acclimated to these senses before I rocked forward and back. When I did, when I drew my hips up and down, his finger went in the same pattern.

"Easton . . ." I didn't have words. I searched, but they were gone. Too much was in motion. Too much was at play. I just had breaths and moans and squeezes—his shoulders, neck, anything within range of grasping.

"You feel fucking amazing." His hand was holding my hip, guiding me, leading me.

The problem was, I was already so near that place, and I wasn't sure I could stop from toppling over the edge.

I definitely didn't want to.

"You're going to come."

He always knew, but I didn't know how.

I tightened my grip, crossing my arms around his neck. "I can't . . ." I brought in more air. "I can't even think. I'm just . . ."

"Lost."

"*Yesss.*"

And I never wanted to come back.

This felt far too good.

"Just keep fucking me," he ordered.

Instead of constantly ascending and falling, I spun my waist, the movement causing his dick to hit different parts within me, and I leaned forward, brushing my clit against his trimmed hairs.

The combination was lethal.

I didn't have the words, but I certainly had the sounds, and I didn't hold those in, my voice rising, my pitch increasing as I began to soar. *"Ohhh!"*

This time was so different.

There wasn't just that tingling, bursting feeling that lived in the front and traveled high. There was also this intensity in the back. An erotic churning that was moving through my body, meeting the eruption in my clit, mixing and completely taking over.

"Fuck" was what came shouting out of me. "Easton!"

When I slowed, no longer able to own the control, the passion too much, he took over.

His speed was powerful. His thrusts were hard and deep.

"I can feel it," he hissed. "You're tightening around me, getting extra wet."

As I gripped him, holding on while he hammered into me, he brought my orgasm through my body and to this raging peak, where I clung, where I waited to fall.

But it didn't happen immediately.

I just hung there.

Suspended.

Screaming, "Fuck yes," as loud as I could.

And when it finally closed in, I shook. Every part of me. The most mind-blowing bolts of electricity that shot straight up and directly down my body.

Over and over.

"Easton!" I stabbed my nails into whatever skin I was holding. "Amazing!"

And those bolts didn't let up until I was shuddering, shaking over him, closing in to the point where I could only whisper, "What the hell was that." I wheezed. "What did you just do to me."

He still moved, still thrust, working out the final tails until he sensed that I'd finished. "You liked that . . ."

"Liked?" I laughed. It was the most ridiculous description for this moment. "Whatever that was, I loved."

"You're going to get more of it. Not now, but soon." And with that promise, he gently pulled his finger out and held me against his body, my walls still hugging his dick. "Are you ready to come again?"

I loosened my arms, released his skin from my nails. "You say that every time and I always question you, and you always prove me wrong."

"Because I know your body, Drake." Staying inside me, he lifted me and turned me around, positioning me in the same place I was before, when I'd first gotten into the tub, but this time he was on top of me. "And I know what it takes to make you feel your best."

"What's that?"

He partly answered me with his lips, hastily devouring mine, and then with the way he stroked, a fierce, hypnotic rhythm that gave me the other half of his answer.

But he still mashed our lips together, pulling back to say, "This."

When it came to my body, Easton Jones owned every bit of my pleasure.

He could bring me anywhere, even to that place where I was ready to come again only moments after I just had.

"Oh yes," I urged, my head pressing against the hard ceramic. "That feels incredible." I spread my legs as wide as they could go, taking all of him in.

While he held the back of the tub, using it to drive himself forward, his hand wandered down my body. He paused at my breasts, giving me a quick burst of pain in each nipple, twisting them just enough that I cried out, and then he continued to my clit. "I don't know how, but you just got wetter."

I knew how, because he'd just picked up speed. Not just in his hand while he rubbed that tender spot, but in the way he plunged into me, turning, letting me pulse for just a second, before he pulled back and did it all over again.

"Yes!" I encouraged. "Fuck me!"

My hands returned to his shoulders, his lunging causing the water to slosh over my face and across the edge of the tub, but the sound of it hitting the floor wasn't even close to as loud as I was.

"Harder," I pleaded. "Please."

I didn't want him to think he could break me. I wanted just the opposite—I wanted him to attempt to try, for his movements to turn even rougher, stronger.

For him to completely dominate me.

And my wish came true as he leaned up onto his knees, wrapping my legs around his waist. He ignored the fact that we were in a tub, that bubbly water was leaking out. That he very well could crack the base and we could crash to the floor.

When Easton was inside me, when he was focused on giving me as many orgasms as possible, nothing else mattered to him.

"I want you to come again."

A sentence that made me the luckiest woman alive.

And something I wanted.

But there was something I wanted even more and said, "Let's come together."

Just as the words left my mouth, he slowed almost to a stop. "That's what you want?"

"Yes."

As he sank into me, it brought an entirely new feeling. He was enticing me, challenging me to get there. An achingly slow but mighty build that was more sensual than anything he'd done tonight. His hand stayed on my clit, but it wasn't that quick swipe that I'd gotten used to. It was a gyration with medium pressure, a tempo similar to a crawl. His momentum was just as unhurried, but he buried himself each time, rooting me, making me search for that feeling. When the sparks began to fire up, his pace allowed them to simmer. The small, even steps grew to an explosive spike.

"Easton . . ." My voice was a whisper. That was as loud as I could go. Everything else—my screams, my breath, my thoughts—was being taken over by him. "I'm there."

"And not a single thing in this whole fucking world feels better than what you're doing to my dick right now."

I reached under my ass and found his sack, holding it in my palm, rubbing my thumb across it.

"Except when you add in that," he groaned.

My legs were turning numb. My shoulders, which had been grinding into the relentlessly hard material, I could no longer feel. I was in a different space. Everything adrift.

Aside from what was happening between my legs.

"You're pulling the cum out of me," he moaned. "Drake . . . *fuuuck*."

I didn't know what I was doing.

I just knew that I was on the verge of something outstanding, and all I could do was hold on and experience it.

"Don't stop," I told him. "Don't"—I dragged in more air—"stop."

He rocked forward just a few more times with a passive pace, but a force that was blunt and sharp, and it took only those pumps to get me there.

To have me screaming.

To have my back arch and my legs open from around him and for the shudders to pass across my entire body. And what made it even more pronounced was that I was watching him go through the same thing at the very same time.

"Drake!"

We adhered to each other. Fingers, legs, arms—anything we could use. And we tremored as the orgasms rolled right through us.

"Easton!" I yelled back.

Clinging.

Loving.

The roar of tickles shot across my body, keeping me captive for several breaths until I could wail, "Yes." I finally exhaled— *"Ohhh"*—when I started to come down.

Easton was holding our bodies together, moving even slower as he grunted through his last several plunges. "Fucking perfect." And when he came to a halt, he continued, "What you do to me"—his head shook before he kissed me, softly, slowly—"there's nothing like it." His lips pressed down on my neck and around the top of my chest and finally met mine again. "Are you ready to get out of here and get into bed?"

My energy was gone.

The only thing I had left was my desire to sleep.

"That's everything I want," I told him.

He gently slid out of me and dropped my legs from around him and got out of the tub. Once his feet hit the floor, he gave me his hand, helping me step out. He then grabbed two towels, one that he wrapped around me, the other for himself.

Now that we weren't in the warm water, I realized how cold the air was inside the tent. There was no heater, no fire, the canvas too thin to stop the cool from entering.

I needed layers.

I needed the drips to dry from my skin.

I wiped off as best as I could and rushed over to the cabinet where I'd stored our clothes. Just as I was reaching for a sweatshirt, he came up behind me.

His mouth went to my neck, his hand to my stomach. "You're sleeping naked tonight."

"Easton . . . it's freezing."

"I'll keep you warm."

I turned around to face him.

"I want to be able to feel you in the middle of the night, Drake. To have your skin at my access whenever I want it." As I searched his eyes, he added, "I won't let you shiver. I promise."

A request I absolutely couldn't deny.

He unhooked the towel from around me and flung it toward the bathtub and led me to our bed.

We climbed in and my face went to his chest. His arms circled around me, the heavy blanket weighing on top of us. The heat from his skin instantly started to warm me.

I took out my messy bun and he began to play with my hair, running his fingers through it. A calmness entered my body, a weight sitting on top of my eyes, making them want to close.

Silence ticked between us.

Until I tilted my head up to look at him, the nearby lantern giving off just enough light that his features were revealed. "This was the best day."

"It was."

"And the best night ever." I pushed higher and connected our lips.

When he pulled away, he said, "Our days and nights are only going to get better."

"Impossible."

"Do you trust me?"

I smiled. "Always."

"Then believe me when I say that."

The room turned quiet again.

And then I heard, "I love you, Drake."

The first time he'd spoken those words was earlier that day, when we'd been sitting in the Adirondack chairs outside, viewing the mountains. A feeling had come over me when I'd processed what he'd said, when that admission had settled in my chest, when the same words worked their way through my throat, and I'd finally voiced them.

The same thing happened again.

But this time, deeper.

Stronger.

His affection having even more potency.

Because the first time was a surprise, but the second time was a confirmation.

"You're right," I whispered. "It just got so much better."

EPILOGUE

Easton

Drake asked me to meet her at a coffee shop not far from the office in the heart of the Back Bay. I was running a few minutes late. Since Holden had taken Belle to Disney to celebrate the international rollout and Grayson was in Saint-Tropez doing the same, there was a lot to hold down.

Especially because the last month had been the most successful in Hooked's history.

So to find a lull and be able to escape the office was even more challenging than normal. But the truth was, I needed the downtime. I was positive Drake knew that, and that was why she'd asked me to meet her.

That woman's ability to read me was almost uncanny.

It was as though she sensed my energy and knew just what I was most desperate for.

Today was a break from the room filled with the sounds of my ringing phone; the constant popping in from my assistant, who needed something almost every few minutes; and the ping of emails coming in faster than I could respond.

I needed quiet.

I needed my girl.

And I was about to get her as I rounded the corner, catching sight of her almost immediately. Despite the chilly weather, she was outside, her coat wrapped tightly around her. A cloud of breath smoked from her lips every time she exhaled. An espresso was in front of her, her hands wrapped around it.

There was something about this scenery that brought me back. Not to a moment I had experienced before, but to one I'd heard about.

Years and years ago.

When Love had dominated my life and Drake wasn't even a thought yet.

She saw me as soon as I got a little closer, approaching the strip of commercial space where the café was nestled. The sidewalk was heavily occupied, but that didn't stop us from locking eyes. It seemed Drake could find me no matter where I was. I could be dressed as everyone else, a color that matched the crowd, but once her senses took over, it was as though a spotlight were shining on top of my head.

She saw me.

Felt me.

And a smile came over those gorgeous lips.

As I neared, she brought the small cup up to her mouth and took a drink, and I slowed by her table but didn't stop. I held her gaze the entire way, past her seat, until I'd gone too far and couldn't see her anymore.

That was when I heard, "Easton!"

A warmth filled me, and it didn't come from the café as I opened the door.

As I recalled the story in my head, she'd let the first man pass without stopping him.

It seemed she wasn't going to make the same mistake, even if I was only going inside to get a coffee.

I glanced sideways across my shoulder, meeting a grinning face. "Yes?"

"Hiii."

I chuckled. "Hi, baby."

"I would have grabbed you a coffee, but I wasn't sure if you'd be in the mood for a dark roast or an espresso. I was leaning toward espresso. Am I right?"

"You're right." I nodded toward the door I was still holding. "I'll be right back."

She crossed her legs, positioning her body toward me. "For the record, had you not grabbed the door handle to go inside, like you're doing now, I would have chased you down."

Now I was positive she recognized the moment.

I winked at her. "I know you would have." And then I went inside the coffee shop and ordered two espressos, hers with oat milk, and I carried them outside once they were ready. "A refill," I said, placing the new drink in front of her.

Once I sat down, her lips found mine. "Thank you."

"Of course."

I pushed my back against the simple metal seat and took a deep breath, bringing the coffee up to my mouth and taking a long sip. "Damn it, I needed this."

She set her hand on my thigh. She didn't say anything. She just left her fingers there, allowing me to feel her touch, to take in the sounds of the city while I cleared my head.

I didn't know how much time had passed, but at some point she reached into her pocket and took out her phone. She chuckled as she read whatever was on the screen and said, "Looks like Brennon is getting desperate."

I glanced at her just as she set her cell on the table. "Why do you say that?"

"He reached out to one of my old Faceframe colleagues and asked if she knew of any job openings in the tech space. She texted me to tell me."

"He's burned every bridge."

She nodded. "No one will hire him after what he's done."

For such a huge industry, the circle was small. Word spread. And as soon as we filed suit against Brennon and Faceframe, he was fired, his reputation so tarnished he hadn't been able to find employment anywhere in Silicon Valley. He was getting to the point where he was reaching out to everyone he knew to see if they could help him find something. They certainly weren't going to put their names on the line to help a traitor and a thief.

That thought should have made me happy. Brennon was nothing but a motherfucker who had tried to take down everything Holden, Grayson, David, and I had built. But part of me felt bad for him. That he felt so underappreciated that he wanted to hurt us. That he stooped to a level as low as he had.

That instead of creating something on his own, he'd stolen our designs and software.

It said a lot about his morals and character. And now those decisions were going to affect his future, one that looked extremely bleak from where I was sitting.

I'd already let Brennon take up too much real estate in my head.

He wasn't getting any additional square footage, nor was that topic getting another second of attention. Instead, I addressed something that would cheer me up and that would return the breathtaking smile to Drake's face. I asked, "Has Saara gotten back from her work trip?"

"Tomorrow. We're going to meet for drinks after work."

"*Ahhh.* A night of debauchery."

She squeezed my leg. "Not true. We can go out for a glass of wine and catch up and act like civilized, responsible women."

"I'm sure you can, but you don't." I laughed, thinking of the last time they had gone out and Drake had practically crawled into my apartment, her hangover lasting a full day. "You girls hit it hard and make every meetup as memorable as possible." I set my hand on top of hers. "It's all right, I love that about you—and your ability to now drink as much vodka as I can."

She glanced toward the street as though remembering the last few times they'd had a girls' night. "Okay, so you might have a point there."

"You know, you owe her a trip to Utah."

She shook her head, reconnecting our stares. "I keep forgetting to book it, but she's been giving me not-so-subtle reminders that she wants a tent with a bathtub in the middle of Moab with zero cell service." She scrunched up her face. "You've created a camping monster."

"In you? Or her?"

"Both."

I laughed again. "Have my assistant book the trip and take the plane."

Her eyes widened. "The guys wouldn't care?"

"Drake, you just launched the biggest rollout in Hooked's history, and it went off without a goddamn hitch. Our membership rate has skyrocketed. Our income has soared. No, I'm positive they wouldn't care."

"I have kicked ass the past month, haven't I?"

I reached across the small space between us, placing my hand on the back of her head. "Just a tiny bit." I squeezed. "But that started when you came to work for us, not just in the last month, Drake."

She nodded, her way of appreciating my compliment. "Saara will be thrilled."

"And you?"

She made it visible that she was taking a deep breath. "I'm going to miss you."

I gave her a brief kiss. "You haven't even left yet."

"Just the thought makes me feel that way."

I rubbed my nose against hers, breathing in the coconut scent that wafted off her skin, the sweetness on her lips from the coffee. "What would I do without you?"

"You'll never have to know."

We stayed like that, locked together, until a sound came through her phone. She gave me a small peck and reached for her cell. The only thing that would make her move that fast was if she assumed it was a text from one of her team members—she refused to ever keep them waiting. But as she read the message, her laugh told me it was something entirely different.

"Oh God," she said, "now this is interesting." She tilted the screen in my direction so I could see what she was talking about.

I took the cell from her, resting it on my palm, reading the notification. It was from some gossip site. I didn't subscribe to those kinds of messages, but for some ungodly reason, Drake found them entertaining.

The notification had the headline Boston's Biggest Bachelor Hooked SIX.

I sighed. "This is about Grayson, isn't it?"

Her expression was like a wince. "I think so."

I clicked on the alert, and it brought me to an article that showed a photo of the hundred-plus-foot megayacht Grayson had rented for the week and was currently floating around in within the waters of Saint-Tropez. He was shirtless on top of the boat, in a pair of swim trunks, and six women sunbathed near him.

What the photo didn't show was that there were other men on the yacht with Grayson. A few of his friends had gone along, but the women, probably at least three, were definitely hooking up with my best friend.

He gave zero fucks.

And he wouldn't care about this notification that had gone out across the world either.

He was out there celebrating, having fun, unplugging from the last few months, which, between the lawsuit and the launch, had been some of the toughest we'd ever gone through as a company.

"I guess it's a good thing we didn't go with him," Drake said. "Can you imagine the gossip if I was on that sundeck in a bikini and you just happened to be inside the boat and the headlines were *Boston's Biggest Bachelor Hooked Best Friend's Girlfriend?*"

I reached for her hand and kissed her ring finger, reminding her she wasn't going to be my girlfriend for much longer. And the second her lease was up, she would be moving into my condo, a decision we'd already agreed on. "I knew there was a reason we turned down that trip."

Even with the other partners gone, there was no way we could have joined Grayson in France. There was far too much shit to be done at the office. Two weeks post-rollout and things hadn't even come close to calming down.

I pulled her chair closer, so our legs were touching, and my arm returned to her shoulders. We stayed quiet for several moments, and that was when something hit me.

Something that was supposed to happen and didn't.

"I forgot a very important step," I told her.

I leaned into her cheek. Still breathing her in but waiting for her to respond.

"What's that?"

"Drake, my Love, I didn't whisper something into your ear . . ."

She realized what I meant, what part of our story I was referring to.

Love had told me about the man passing her table at the coffee shop, but I'd replied to that conversation and told her what I would have done if it were me who had walked by.

"Mr. Boston . . ." A flush crossed her cheeks. "I'm afraid to know what those words would be."

My lips hovered above her ear, and I said, "Don't be."

There were several things that would make her smile.

But I whispered the words that would also make her wet. "I'm going to make you scream so loud tonight."

ACKNOWLEDGMENTS

Nina Grinstead, there are just no words to describe us, this process, the journey, the experiences we've gone through together, so I'm just going to say I love you, and so many of my dreams are coming true because of you. Team B forever.

Nicole Resciniti, your unwavering belief in me is something I cherish. Thank you for everything and for giving me the encouragement I needed to finish this book. You were such a light during an extremely dark time.

Maria Gomez, from the moment we met in Dallas to our meeting in the middle of a hurricane (ha ha) to the beautiful moments of now, I treasure you. I will never be able to express how much this all means, how much you mean. I don't think I've still fully processed the magnitude of this, but it's all possible because of you. Hugging you so, so hard.

Lindsey Faber, your patience and guidance and pep talks and compliments—they mean more to me than you'll ever know. It's been the biggest honor to work with you on this book, to tap into that incredibly creative brain of yours, and to see how far this story has come, all because of you. Thank you for everything. ♥

Nikki Terrill, my soul sister. Every tear, vent, dinner, virtual hug, life chaos, workout—you've been there through it all. I could never do this without you, and I would never want to. Love you hard.

Sarah Symonds, I wouldn't want to do this without you. Ever. Thank you for being my rock and for holding my hand through every draft. You mean everything to me. Love you.

Monica Murphy, I know everyone comes into our lives for a reason, but the number of reasons you're in my life is endless. You've been there through every step of this journey, from the very beginning to the moment I turned the book in. You've guided me, inspired me. You've talked me off ledges I was clinging to with both hands. Thank you. I love you. Times a million.

Devney Perry, when I think back to the hardest times, you were there. When I think back to the moments where I wasn't sure, you assured me. When I think back to the days when I couldn't find my way out of the fog, you gave me a path and you held the flashlight and you helped me crawl my way out. I'll never be able to thank you for everything you've done. I appreciate you and love you so hard.

Brittney Sahin, you've been my partner throughout this entire process. My rock. The words you've shared with me, the encouragement, love—I'll never be able to thank you. Meeting you at BB is one of the best things that's ever happened to me. Heart you hard.

Rachel Baldwin, getting to meet you and sharing each of these moments with you has been incredible. From our chats to our love of undereye gold masks (LOL), I couldn't adore you more. Thank you for everything, and I especially thank you for all the love and support.

Kimmi Street, my sister from another mister. There's no way to describe us; there's just something special when it comes to our unbreakable bond. Nothing and no one will ever change that. I love you more than love.

Extra-special love goes to Chanpreet Singh, Ratula Roy, Valentine Grinstead, Valentine PR, Kim Cermak, Christine Miller, Rachel Brookes, Kelley Beckham, my babes—Jan and Pang, Tracey Waggaman, and Jennifer Porpora. I'm so grateful for all of you and I love you so much.

My Midnighters, my ARC team, my Bookstagram Team, you are such a supportive, loving, motivating group. Thanks for being such an inspiration, for holding my hand when I need it, and for always begging for more words. I love you all.

Mom and Dad, I love you.

Brian, I am me because of you, and you are the best part of me. There is nothing I love more than our love.

MARNI'S MIDNIGHTERS

Getting to know my readers is one of my favorite parts about being an author. In Marni's Midnighters, my private Facebook group, I post covers before they're revealed to the public and excerpts of the projects I'm currently working on, and team members qualify for exclusive giveaways. To join Marni's Midnighters, click HERE.

Newsletter

Would you like a free book? To qualify for exclusive giveaways, be notified of new releases, and sales? Then click HERE to sign up for my newsletter. I promise not to spam you.

SNEAK PEEK OF *The Lawyer*

Are you interested in the story of Declan Shaw and Camden Dalton, the lawyers who represent Hooked? Check out the entire Dalton Family Series, starting with book one, *The Lawyer*. Here's a sneak peek.

CHAPTER ONE

Dominick

Los Angeles is fucking lit tonight. That was the only thought in my head as I stood twenty-seven stories up on the roof deck of the city's newest and hottest high-rise hotel, overlooking our famous skyline. Jenner, my middle brother, was the attorney who had represented the closing, and everyone who was anyone had come out this evening to celebrate the grand opening.

Not only was this a huge win for Jenner, but for The Dalton Group as well—the law firm my parents had started over twenty years ago, where my brothers and I were now partners. We represented some of the largest-earning corporations and individuals in the world. In my case, concentrating solely on entertainment law, I was surrounded by many of my clients, this event like a mini version of the goddamn Oscars.

"Jenner has come a long way," Brett Young, my best friend, said. He was next to me on the balcony, nodding toward my brother, who was schmoozing with the CEO of a massive online retailer. "I remember when we were in law school, that motherfucker still had zits all over his forehead. Now, instead of carrying textbooks, he's got multimillion-dollar contracts in his hands, closing transactions like this one every day, from here to fucking Dubai."

Brett pointed at Ford, my youngest brother. "And the baby in the family? Man, I definitely didn't anticipate him being the first one in our group to father a child." He smirked. "Certainly not before me or you." His eyes caught mine. "I think you wake up every morning, hoping like hell that some woman doesn't come banging on your door, asking for a paternity test."

I laughed in agreement. "Isn't that the fucking truth?"

Before Brett had met James Ryne, one of the highest-paid actresses in Hollywood, he had lived the same lifestyle as me. Bachelor brothers was what we used to call ourselves. But now, they were engaged, and he was more whipped than a sub.

He clinked his glass against mine, and we downed what liquor was left. Immediately, a waitress appeared to hand us refills.

He held his scotch over the side of the railing, balancing the liquor in the air.

I did the same, sighing as I gazed at all the twinkling lights below. "It's been a hell of a run for us so far, and we're only getting started."

When Brett and his buddies had opened The Agency—a firm of agents representing actors, athletes, and musicians—I had just passed the bar, and we would refer clients to one another. Now, all these years later, we sat in many of the same meetings, negotiating deals for the top earners in the business.

"You've got that right, my friend. Wait until I tell you about this new actress I just scouted and how much money she's going to earn us . . ." His voice faded as he grabbed his phone and read the screen. "Fuck."

"What's wrong?"

Still staring at his cell, he said, "You know our client Naomi, who I cast for that reality TV show that's filming in two weeks? Her manager just texted and said she's in the hospital with two herniated discs in her neck and another three in her back." He slowly glanced up at me. "Ski accident in Vail this morning."

"Jesus, is she all right?"

"She's going in for surgery tomorrow. She'll be bedridden for the next nine to twelve weeks, which means she'll miss all of filming."

"That shit is painful. I hope she pulls through." I took a drink. "I also know what that means for you—you have to find someone to replace her."

He typed a reply, calling over a waitress the moment he put his phone away. "Another round for both of us and two tequila shots." As she walked toward the bar, he said to me, "Getting drunk is the only solution to this."

"Tell me exactly what you're looking for. Maybe I can help."

"If you remember, the show is about well-off, young girls, living the LA life. Private jets, VIP club treatment, walk-in closets that have as many Birkins as my fiancée. The studio will provide all of that. I just need the right face."

I quickly glanced around the roof, taking an inventory of the different looks and talent up here. "What kind of face?"

He twirled the glass in his hand, the scotch swirling like a tornado. "Early twenties, gorgeous. She needs to have perfect tits and a body to fucking die for. Personality-wise, I need someone who can put the cast members in their place—not a villain, but someone with spark."

Not finding what I was looking for, I mentally ran through my roster of actresses who focused only on reality television. Daisy Roy was the most talented one I had. Even though she was a villain off camera, she was the girl next door on-screen. She was good-looking, but she didn't possess the heat he was after.

I shook my head. "I can't think of anyone."

"I was afraid of that."

The waitress returned, setting the four glasses on the balcony's wide brick edge.

We went straight for the tequila, downing the shots before we moved on to the scotch.

313

Brett held the fresh drink against his chest, tugging at the strands of his hair. "We start filming in two weeks. I need someone—yesterday."

I grabbed his shoulder, shaking it to loosen him up. "Don't stress, brother. When I get to the office tomorrow, I'll dig through my clients and see who I can find."

The words had barely left my mouth when I turned toward the thick crowd and linked eyes with the most beautiful girl. Goddamn it, she was more stunning than any woman I had ever seen. Long, dark hair with pouty, thick lips and a light-blue stare that was so intense that I could see the color from all the way over here.

But the connection didn't stop with her looks.

I could almost feel her in my hands, as though her body were lying beneath mine, slowly caressing her smooth, naked skin, warming the areas that my mouth was soon going to devour.

Fuck me.

"Do you know who that is?" I asked Brett.

"Who?"

I broke our connection to look at my best friend. "I can't point—she's watching—but the girl at three o'clock in a tight emerald-colored dress with endless fucking curves. There's a tall blonde next to her, who doesn't compete at all."

"I've never seen either of them before, but you're right; the brunette is hot as hell."

With my eyes on her again, I brought the glass up to my mouth, not feeling the burn as I swallowed.

Because there was only one fire in my body.

One that sparked an aching need to be inside her.

"Whoever she is"—I licked the wet booze off my lips—"I'm tasting her before this night is over."

"Is that right?"

A smile grew across my face as I started at her heels and worked my way higher. "Hell yes." When I reached the top of her head, I glanced at Brett. "You do remember what it's like to have a one-night stand, don't you?"

He laughed. "It's been an eternity, but I'll leave those nights to you, bro. James is more than enough for me."

"I won't hold that against you," I bantered.

The space between us got busier, filling with people, causing my view of her to disappear. My brothers happened to be part of that congestion and were making their way over to us.

I clasped Jenner's arm the moment he was within range, pulling him in for a hug. "You've outdone yourself, my man. A hell of a hotel your team has built here, and this party is off the charts. Whoever put together the guest list deserves a fucking raise. Some of the women here tonight—*mmm-mmm*."

As I looked over his shoulder, there was sexiness everywhere. Outfits that revealed bare, toned backs, lean arms, legs for fucking centuries.

And then there was the girl in the green dress, the queen of them all.

Through the smallest opening, a crack between two men, her eyes met mine again.

"Speaking of women . . ." Jenner said, pulling back to reach inside his sport coat. He placed something in my hand and then Ford's, skipping right over Brett. "No reason to bring one home when I got you a room downstairs."

A key card was now tucked under my fingers, the room number written on its paper sleeve.

I put it in my pocket, punching Jenner's shoulder with just a little strength. "Always looking out for us single men."

"I've got your back," he replied, including Ford. "Always."

The four of us raised our glasses, carefully tapping them together, before we went our separate ways, kicking off several hours of small talk with the industry professionals in attendance tonight. I gave out my card to a few up-and-coming musicians, their popularity rising enough to where they were ready for representation, and to some influencers whose following was gaining them endorsements, contracts they couldn't negotiate on their own.

Many more drinks later, I was coming out of the restroom when I spotted her.

The girl in the emerald dress.

She was standing at the mouth of the hallway that led to the ladies' and men's rooms, her back against the wall, her arm wrapped across her narrow waist as she spoke on her phone.

I assumed she'd come in here to get away from the noise, to have some privacy since there was none to be had on the rooftop.

Her focus elsewhere gave me the opportunity to appreciate the view, and I took my time to observe every goddamn inch of her.

Hair I wanted to twist around my wrist and pull.

Lips I wanted sucking on my crown.

Legs I wanted to spread wide.

An ass I wanted pulsing around my cock.

Perfection came in many forms. Hers was unique and breathtaking.

I walked until I was in front of her, and her eyes instantly locked with mine, widening the longer she looked at me.

"It's you . . . the guy from across the bar."

Her whispered admission made me grin.

"I have to go," she said into the phone. "I'll get it all done, I promise."

She slipped her cell inside her purse, and I reached for her hand the second it was free.

"Dominick."

Her gentle fingers fell into my grip. Ones that would soon be wrapped around the base of my dick while she sucked my crown down her throat. "I'm Kendall."

"I want to tell you something, Kendall."

Her cheeks reddened, and her breathing sped up, her chest rising faster with each inhale.

"Since the moment I saw you, there's only been one thought in my head."

She pushed herself farther against the wall, her knee bending so she could place her heel there as well. "And that is?"

"That I would do anything to taste you."

Her lips stayed parted, like my tip was already between them, her voice getting lost in her breathing.

"Do you know what happens when I want something?" The top of her head came to the center of my chest, and I placed my palm on the wall just above her. There was plenty of room for her to leave, but it was a tight-enough cage that positioned her right where I wanted her. "I do everything in my power to make it mine." I leaned in close, my lips hovering inches away from hers. Her eyes told me she was preparing for me to kiss her, but after a few exhales, I moved my mouth to her ear. "You're all I can think about."

"I"—the syllable sounded like a gasp—"don't know what to say."

My finger ran across her cheek and down her collarbone, goose bumps meeting me. "Say I can have you." I pointed toward an escape route. "Or walk away. You have ten seconds to decide."

While my hand circled the back of her neck, the key in my pocket was like a thirty-pound weight, conjuring up all the surfaces in that room that I could potentially fuck her on.

"Nine," I breathed the number against her mouth. "Eight, seven." I counted in my head until I reached, "Five."

She shifted her weight, her foot dropping to the ground, her gaze changing every time I voiced a lower number.

"Four, three."

Her chest stilled, telling me she was holding air in her lungs. "Two."

"Dominick . . ." My name came out like a moan.

"One."

ABOUT THE AUTHOR

Photo © 2021 Moments by Jade Photography

Marni Mann is the *USA Today* bestselling author of numerous series, including the Dalton Family, the Agency, Moments in Boston, and Spade Hotel. Marni knew she was going to be a writer since middle school. While other girls her age were daydreaming about teenage pop stars, Marni was fantasizing about penning her first novel. She crafts unique stories that weave together her love of darkness, mystery, passion, and human emotions. A New Englander at heart, she now lives with her husband in Sarasota, Florida. When she's not nose deep in her laptop and working on her next novel, she's sipping wine, traveling, boating along the Gulf of Mexico, or devouring fabulous books. For more information visit www.marnimann.com.